SLAY

SLAY

BRITTNEY MORRIS

SIMON PULSE
NEW YORK LONDON TORONTO SYDNEY NEW DELHI

SIMON PULSE

An imprint of Simon & Schuster Children's Publishing Division

1230 Avenue of the Americas, New York, New York 10020

First Simon Pulse paperback edition June 2020

Text copyright © 2019 by Brittney Morris

Cover photographs of girl copyright © 2019 by Kiuikson/Getty Images and Tara Moore/Getty Images

Cover photographs of glitches by The7Dew/iStock and noLimit46/iStock

Interior emoji illustrations by RaulAlmu/iStock

Interior fist illustrations by Kirill Veretennikov/iStock

Also available in a Simon Pulse hardcover edition.

All rights reserved, including the right of reproduction in whole or in part in any form.

SIMON PULSE and colophon are registered trademarks of Simon & Schuster, Inc.

For information about special discounts for bulk purchases, please contact Simon & Schuster Special Sales at 1-866-506-1949 or business@simonandschuster.com.

The Simon & Schuster Speakers Bureau can bring authors to your live event.

For more information or to book an event contact the Simon & Schuster Speakers Bureau at 1-866-248-3049 or visit our website at www.simonspeakers.com.

Cover designed by Laura Eckes

Interior designed by Mike Rosamilia

The text of this book was set in Iowan Old Style.

Manufactured in the United States of America

10 9 8 7 6 5 4

The Library of Congress has cataloged the hardcover edition as follows:

Names: Morris, Brittney, author.

Title: Slay / by Brittney Morris.

Description: First Simon Pulse hardcover edition. | New York : Simon Pulse, 2019. | Summary: An honors student at Jefferson Academy, seventeen-year-old Kiera enjoys developing and playing SLAY, a secret, multiplayer online role-playing game celebrating Black culture, until the two worlds collide.

Identifiers: LCCN 2018052663 | ISBN 9781534445420 (hardcover)

Subjects: | CYAC: Video games—Fiction. | Fantasy games—Fiction. | Role playing—Fiction. | African Americans—Fiction. | Dating (Social customs)—Fiction. | High schools—Fiction. | Schools—Fiction.

Classification: LCC PZ7.1.M6727 Sl 2019 | DDC [Fic]—dc23

LC record available at https://lccn.loc.gov/2018052663

ISBN 9781534445437 (pbk)

ISBN 9781534445444 (eBook)

To everyone who has ever had to minimize who you are
to be palatable to those who aren't like you

1.   PLAYING THE GAME

By day, I'm an honors student at Jefferson Academy. At night, I turn into the Nubian goddess most people know as Emerald.

The second the bell rings, I'm out of my desk seat and bolting through the classroom door. There's a battle tonight between PrestoBox, a master wizard from the Tundra, and Zama, a Voodoo queen from the same region. I absolutely can't miss it. Once safely in the hallway, I pull out my phone and open WhatsApp to find a new text from the game mod, Cicada.

Cicada: You watching the tundra semifinals tonight?

I smile, glancing up for a second to watch where I'm going as throngs of students pour from classrooms and navigate around me.

Me: Wouldn't miss it.

"Hey, Kix!" comes Harper's voice, startling me from my thoughts. I look up to see her and my sister, Steph, walking toward me in their matching pink T-shirts with the Greek letters for Beta Beta Psi, a collective of the eight most outspoken, unapologetic, woke feminists at Jefferson Academy. Leave it to my parents to transfer us to a high school that prepares its students for college so thoroughly, they claim to have the most robust high school Greek life program in the country.

"Hey, Harp. Hey, Steph," I say, trying not to sound disappointed that I won't get out of here for another ten minutes. I slip my phone into my back pocket and put on my best *happy to see you* face.

"Hey, Kiera," Steph says with a grin, brushing her bangs out of the way of her lime-green glasses. Steph has a new pair of cheap plastic glasses for each day of the week, and her hair is always pressed straight and cut neatly at her shoulders. She insists keeping her hair straight saves time in the morning, but until she can prove it, I'll keep my five-minute wake-up-and-shake-out-my-twist-out routine.

"I'm heading home early today to get started on our Beta Beta posters for the game next week," she says. "Each one is going to have an inspirational word at the top in huge bubble letters—like 'endurance' and 'perseverance.' We're going to have the players sign them and put them up in the halls around school afterward. Plus, Mom said she'll take me out later tonight to get more permit hours. Wanna walk with me?"

I thought endurance and perseverance were kind of the same thing, but if I start in on that conversation, I really won't get out of this hallway before the duel starts. Harper chimes in before I can answer.

"Actually, Steph," says Harper, "I wanted to talk to Kix for a second. Need to ask her advice about something."

That's what she calls me. Kix. Like the cereal. Or like the shoes. I can't tell and never bothered to ask. Steph and I look at each other. We both know what's coming. Harper is about to ask me an impossible question, because she knows Steph isn't going to give her a straight answer.

"Well, now I'm curious," says Steph. "What is it?"

Harper glances over her shoulder as if she's watching for someone, and she folds her arms across her chest and shrugs.

"It feels kind of weird to even be asking this question, but I'm asking because I genuinely don't know the answer."

I sigh and nod at her to just ask the question already. She always prefaces these with a disclaimer if it's going to be one of those questions with two wrong answers. She didn't used to be like this. When we were kids, Harper used to come over our house for *Mario Kart*, *Legacy of Planets*, and snacks. We used to talk about Usher and *Fresh Prince*, and boys in our class, and babysit her little brother, Wyatt. But now Steph is president of Beta Beta, and Harper is VP, and as royalty of the most feminist high school sorority in the country, Harper acts like she has to talk about polarizing stuff all the time.

"Okay, fine," says Harper when it becomes apparent Steph isn't going anywhere. "I was thinking about changing my hair. Something fun and new, but, like, with bohemian vibes. There's one style I really want to get, but I need to ask you about it first."

Steph and I exchange looks again. When it comes to hair discussions, Steph and I have been on the Black girl hair journey together, and we have more in common than she and Harper ever will in the hair department. But I look back up at Harper, with her short blond pixie that hasn't held a curl since middle school prom, when her mother had to use half a can of hair spray. She's the only person I know who can rock a pixie like that, and since she stands about a foot taller than me with a long, willowy frame, it fits her. But I let her finish her question.

"I need to, like, ask you, though, and don't be afraid to say no," she begins. "Am I allowed to get dreadlocks?"

Oh, what a question. Is she *allowed* to get dreadlocks? She's asking permission to wear a hairstyle that's been debated by people of many races for years and years as to whether it's appropriating Black culture. How am I supposed to tell her yes without giving the disclaimer that I can't speak for all Black people, and that she could ask any of us this question and get a different answer every time?

"That'd make a great question for the *Weekly*!" chimes in Wyatt, stepping between Steph and me, leaning his arm on her shoulder and grinning at me. Nobody would guess by their looks that Harper and Wyatt are brother and sister. And by Wyatt's freckles, bright blue eyes, messy dishwater-blond hair, lanky frame, and lack of height, nobody would guess he's sixteen, and not twelve.

"I, uh . . . ," I begin, looking to Steph. She's always better with these kinds of situations than I am.

"Seriously, Kiera, can I interview you about this?" Wyatt asks with that big, toothy grin. Even though he's only a junior, he's chief editor for the *Jefferson Weekly*, and he runs the political topics column like a criminal investigator, hyperanalyzing his interviewees' answers, looking for cracks in their views so he can write them up with those clickbaity titles he always uses. I can see it now: "Black People Don't Mind White People Wearing This ONE Hairstyle."

Between Wyatt as chief editor for the school newspaper even though he's only a junior, and Steph, also a junior, as president of Beta Beta Psi, I feel like my college applications could have been so much more resplendent than they were when I submitted them. If only I could include my favorite after-school activity in my list of accomplishments.

"You can interview me!" offers Steph, and I can't help but smile a bit. There's no way Wyatt's going to go for that. Steph is an expert debater who gives airtight answers to any question you ask her.

"We all know what you think about white people doing things, Steph," says Wyatt. "You tell us all the goddamn time."

Steph punches his arm so hard, he flinches and holds it close to him.

"Really?" he asks.

"I mean, if you're going to assume I'm going to be an angry Black woman about this, I wouldn't want to disappoint you."

"Steph," I say, shaking my head. She's talking too loud in this hallway, and people are looking at us now. The last thing the only two Black girls at Jefferson Academy need is to be seen as the *loud* ones. I just want to go home. Without having to answer Harper's question. I just want to log in, transform into Emerald, and talk to Cicada for the rest of the night.

"I'll have to think about that, Harper," I say, hoping she'll wait awhile and maybe forget about it.

"Okay," she says, obviously disappointed, folding her arms over her chest. "Oh, we're still on for math at eight tonight, right?"

Oh shit. It's Thursday. I had to move Harper's and my tutoring lesson to Thursday this week since Wyatt is playing in the Civil War baseball game next week and Steph and Harper need time tomorrow when they're both available to write their opening speech as president and VP of Beta Beta. But I do need the money. Cicada and I want to add more RAM to our servers because we're about to launch more game cards soon. That's sixty bucks down the drain if I cancel this week.

"Uh," I begin. When I say I absolutely can't miss the Tundra Semifinals today, I mean it. I need to be there. The game gets bugs sometimes. Weird stuff starts happening when people try to hack in coins or trade new weapons.

Lately, characters have been glitching out when they use a new crossbow that was released last week—falling through the map or losing upgrades—and when that happens, everyone blows up my DMs. Why?

Because I'm the game developer.

Nobody knows. Not even my family. Not even my boyfriend, Malcolm.

"Pretty sure my queen is busy tonight," comes a familiar voice from behind me. Two strong arms encircle my waist and kisses are being planted gently up the back of my neck, and I can smell Malcolm's Ralph Lauren cologne behind me.

"Hey," I say happily, looking up to see the progress he's making with his goatee, smiling when I see he had his dreads freshly twisted this weekend, his Killmonger hairdo. I cuddle up under his arm. Normally, I would call him Boo, but I feel weird using that word in front of everyone here.

"Aaaand, that's my cue to go!" announces Steph, turning on her heel and heading swiftly for the front door.

I have to physically concentrate on not rolling my eyes. Steph and Malcolm hate each other for the pettiest reasons. Malcolm thinks Black women don't need sororities because they're already sisters, and the word "sorority" is a fancy word for clique. Steph thinks men have no business telling women what to do. That leaves me in the chasm in the middle, agreeing with both of them.

Harper and Wyatt exchange glances. They always get

quiet around Malcolm, the kid who got expelled from Belmont High on the south side.

"Right," says Wyatt, glancing over his shoulder, probably to make sure Steph is far enough away not to hear him. "Soooo, just let me know about the interview, okay?"

I look up at Malcolm, whose thick eyebrows have sunken slightly.

"What kinda interview?" he asks.

"Wyatt wants to interview me for the *Jefferson Weekly*," I say quickly, hoping Wyatt catches my hints. "It's about Black hair. I think Wyatt's trying to give diverse opinions some visibility in the paper."

Malcolm motions to Wyatt with his chin and says, "'Bout time we had more diverse opinions in the *Weekly*. Okay, Wyatt, I see you."

Which means, in Malcolm-speak, "well done."

I nod and smile at Wyatt and glance at Harper, who's looking between me and Malcolm like she knows there's nothing she can contribute to this conversation, and that we'll have to discuss the whole dreadlocks thing later, when we're not in front of Malcolm, whose verdict on the subject she already knows.

"Tutoring some other time, Harper, okay? I'm sorry, but I really am busy tonight. We'll meet next week."

I'll let Harper and Wyatt think I want a night alone with Malcolm. I'll let Malcolm think I have homework.

"Thanks," I say to him once Harper and Wyatt have turned and walked halfway down the hall. But before I can even begin explaining to him why he can't come over tonight, he's looking at me with disappointment in his dark, glistening eyes, studying mine.

"What's up?" I ask.

"You were doing it again," he says, pulling his arm from around me and opening his locker. He slings his backpack off his shoulder, pulls out a couple of textbooks and his vape pen from the bottom shelf, and stuffs them inside his bag.

"Doing what?"

"The voice."

I roll my eyes.

"That's the only voice I have."

"That's the only voice you have when you're around those two," he says, pointing down the hall at them. Then he pauses, and his expression softens. "I love you. You know that."

He leans in and kisses my forehead before pressing his forehead against mine.

"I want you to be yourself around me, *and* around them. I want my Black goddess all the time, but you out here sounding like you work in a call center."

I wish I could invite Malcolm into my world after school, into my game, where every word I speak reflects the Black goddess he sees in me, the one he got to see at Belmont, the one who rocked braids and almost made the Belmont High drill team. The walls may have been defaced with vandalism, and the lockers may have been falling apart, but at least we got to be ourselves.

I smile up at him now. He has a scar in the middle of his bottom lip from the fight that got him expelled from Belmont—the fight that might have gotten me hurt if he hadn't intervened.

I step up on my tiptoes and kiss that scar. Malcolm and I left Belmont together after freshman year, and Steph joined us. I left so many of our Black friends there, and I appreciate Malcolm doing his best to make sure I don't leave my Blackness there with them. If he knew about *SLAY*, if he'd just give the game a chance, he might realize just how proud I am of us. But I can see the whole conversation now. He'd ask me why I've poured so much effort into a video game when I could be focusing on college prep and getting a good job, so I don't join what he is constantly reminding me of: the mass of Black people who waste their lives on video games, junk food, drugs, unemployment, baby daddy drama, and child support. According to him, video games are distractions promoted by white society to slowly erode the focus and ambition of Black men. He wouldn't understand.

"I'm sorry," I admit. If I was doing the telephone voice, I didn't mean to.

He grins and rubs his nose against mine.

"Now, about me coming over tonight."

I know in my head that I can't actually have him over to my house tonight, but the way he says it . . .

I bite my lip and smile. Malcolm is fine as hell, and he knows I know it. We're lucky—his parents don't care what he does or where he goes, and my parents don't mind giving us privacy at the house, since they'd rather we be there than at "some drunken party," as Mom puts it.

Not sure what kinds of drunken parties she thinks are going down here at Jefferson. If people are throwing them, Malcolm and I are never invited.

"I have homework," I say. It's not a complete lie. I do have homework. There's a math test next week on polynomials that's going to kick my ass if I don't get it together and start studying.

"Can I help?"

He knows damn well if he came over, we wouldn't be studying anything but each other.

"It's American history," I lie. His least favorite subject. It's the only way to keep him away from the house while I immerse myself in the game. As far as Malcolm is concerned, American history is white history, and therefore antiBlack.

"You actually study for that shit?"

"I study so my final transcript doesn't disappoint Spelman. Even if they admit me, if my final grades are too low and they change their mind, Atlanta won't be a thing for us."

That's it, Kiera, I think, *guilt-trip him.*

"Fine, whatever." He shrugs. "I've got some decolonizing to do anyway. S'called *The 48 Laws of Power*. Robert Greene. You heard of it?"

By "decolonizing," he means reading. Knowing Malcolm, the book is written by a Black man about Black men getting their education, starting their own businesses, becoming the heads of households, and raising gorgeous little Black children with their gorgeous Black queens. Malcolm's happily ever after. He'll stay up all night reading books like that. I can't complain about it, though—there's something sexy about a strong, stoic boy who reads a lot. But he *only* reads books by Black men, Black women who edify Black men, and white men who reinforce his non-race-related philosophies, leaving me to keep my Cline and Le Guin to myself.

I laugh at the irony of all those conversation-ending texts I get saying he's going to go "decolonize," leaving me to play *SLAY* uninterrupted.

"Well, maybe I should read it to you sometime," he says, leaning in close and whispering in my ear. "Maybe right before I put you to sleep."

I roll my eyes, but his game is working. My whole body is screaming to let him come over tonight. The duel starts in fifteen minutes, which means it might be over by the time he reaches my house. That should give us a couple of hours together before Mom gets home. Just because my parents are lax about us having sex in the house doesn't mean we want them hearing us.

But just before I can give in, Malcolm is backing away from me.

"But I'll leave you to your homework," he says, hands up comically with that big, goofy smile of his. "Just let me know when I can come over. I want to worship my queen."

And he winks and turns away, shrinking farther and farther down the hall among the rest of the students clustered in groups to gossip before whatever after-school clubs they might have. I sigh, wishing so badly that I could invite him into the game with me. His attitude and curiosity would make him an expert dueler. I don't know if I'll ever convince him that SLAY is different. To him, video games may be a distraction from becoming great, but I meant for it to do the exact opposite: to showcase how awesome we are as Black people, how multifaceted, resilient, and colorful we are. And I've tried hypothetical questions with him, like *What if someone made a game that was just for Black people?* but he doesn't even entertain the idea. "They make things 'just for us' all the time—we've got Black movies and Black History Month. They give us our own shit to distract us from the fact that we don't have control over *their* shit. Separate is not equal. That doesn't even come *close* to leveling the field."

He'll never get it. It's whatever. I've just decided to stop bringing it up.

At least, at last, I'm finally free to go home. I clip my backpack across my chest and race down the Jefferson front steps, past the students clustering in their cliques, past the kids waiting for their parents to pick them up.

My house is just down the street from the school, so I walk home most days. It gets annoying sometimes, living so close. Game days make traffic on our street a nightmare.

But I can't complain about the neighborhood. Bellevue, Washington, is one of the cleanest cities I've ever seen, in real life or on TV. Perfectly manicured trees line every public sidewalk, like they do at Disneyland, and I haven't seen a pothole since we moved here from SoDo—that's "south downtown"—three years ago, when Dad got promoted. Lucky for me, it happened shortly after Malcolm got expelled, and I got to follow him out here to Jefferson, which I love and hate. I love that I can charge these kids sixty dollars a session to tutor them in math. It's a nice addition to my résumé, and it gives me extra cash to spend on RAM, server maintenance, and in-game artwork. But I hate, and I mean *hate*, being "the voice of Blackness" here. At Belmont, where 50 percent of the students are Black, and 70 percent are people of color, Malcolm and I got to be normal. Nobody was asking to touch my twist-out, nobody was asking him about his locs, and nobody was asking us for permission to appropriate Black culture as if we're the authority for our entire race.

I take in the fresh air. It's only Thursday, and if I'm going to get through the rest of this week, the rest of this semester, and graduate, I'm going to have to stay calm and focus on my homework. I'll be out of here, and hopefully into Spelman, soon enough.

I reach our little gray house at the end of the cul-de-sac that caps Newberg Lane. It's smaller than most of the houses on this street, but it still doesn't feel like home. Not like our home in SoDo anyway. This new house has two obnoxious white pillars on either side of the front door, and a wreath, and a peephole.

I notice a new decoration on the porch—a stuffed rabbit

doll made of pink tube socks, sticks, and various brightly colored plastic eggs. That wasn't here when I left for school this morning. Mom is clearly home early, and in a decorating mood, which means she's going to ask me for help. Good thing I *didn't* invite Malcolm over.

I mentally prepare myself for the encounter, since I have to get through it quick. Then I pull my keys out of my backpack's water bottle compartment, unlock the front door, and swing it open.

"Mom?" I ask.

"We're in the dining room!" I hear Steph from the other side of the house, since she had a five-minute head start on me. A much quieter voice mumbles something, and I assume it's Mom reminding Steph not to yell in the house, even though no one's home but the three of us.

I carefully untie my shoes and carry them with me into the kitchen, where I keep my shoe toothbrush in the pen drawer, so nobody will confuse it for a mouth toothbrush. I don't know why I'm so particular about keeping my white shoes white. They're just Keds. Not like they're a pair of two-hundred-dollar Yeezys a lot of other Jefferson kids have. But it still irks me when they get dirty.

I find Mom and Steph sitting at the dining table, which always has eight place mats and a seasonal centerpiece, just in case Mom ever wants to throw a spontaneous dinner party. Although with her new schedule at the dental clinic, I doubt she'll ever really have time. She and Steph are hard at work poking pink and yellow plastic gerbera stems into a horn-shaped white basket in the center of the table and eating popcorn.

"Hey!" exclaims Steph. She looks up at me through new red glasses—apparently, she's already bored of the green ones she was wearing earlier. These ones are as big around as baseballs, with the lenses punched out. Mine are boring black frames, with prescription lenses. Simple.

"Hey." Mom smiles up at me.

"You're home early," I say.

"I finished with my last patient and they told me they were okay for the rest of the day, probably because of that billboard we put up last year reminding people to brush twice a day. I *told* y'all it was a good idea," says Mom, tossing a few kernels of popcorn into her mouth.

"Haven't you also been telling people to avoid hard candy, caramel, and *popcorn*?" Steph asks, reaching for another handful and widening her eyes and smiling playfully across the table.

"I know optometrists who stare at their cell phones all day, and I know doctors who eat peach cobbler," says Mom with a grin, sliding the bowl closer to herself and grabbing a huge handful. She shrugs and looks up at me.

"Sit down with us and have some, Kiera. We're decorating, if you want to join us." Mom pulls out the empty chair between them at the head of the table.

"No thanks," I say as politely as I can. "I have homework. Steph, I thought you were coming home early to work on posters."

Steph wrinkles her nose playfully at me and glances at Mom.

"I can't have a snack first?" she asks, and shoves another handful of popcorn into her mouth.

She's staring at me with one eye narrowed, which means she's analyzing me. It's like she can see exactly what I'm thinking. Since I'm the worst at maintaining a poker face, I reach for the bowl of popcorn and toss a few kernels into my mouth. They're buttery and salty, and I think Mom used some of that cheese powder her assistant, Karen, got us for Christmas last year. But Steph isn't letting me off that easy. She's still staring at me.

"Why do you ask?" she pries.

"No reason," I say, just as my phone buzzes with a text.

"You expecting someone? Maybe a *certain* someone? A certain Hotep whose name I won't mention?"

She calls Malcolm a Hotep, which, in her mind, is a brotha who claims he's for Black power, when he's really for Black *male* power, homophobia, misogyny, and other regressive ideologies. I say as long as Malcolm is encouraging our people to do better, and me to do better, I can't complain, even if he says a few off-color things every so often. He may not "get" feminism all the way yet, but he's a work in progress.

I deflect her question. "Jealousy ain't cute, Steph."

"Don't say *ain't* in my house," says Mom with raised brows.

I made "Ain't" a card in the game, since Ebonics is part of what differentiates the American Black experience from American "other" experiences. It's ours. And I'll use the word "ain't" however I please as soon as I log in.

But my mom's raised eyebrows ain't playing. "Boo-Boo the Fool" is another card in the game. It's a Battle card, since "Do I look like Boo-Boo the Fool?" is a rhetorical question that essentially translates to "I wasn't born yesterday." It's a challenge to say something else and see what happens, and so are raised eyebrows, which is why the card features an artistic rendition of my mom's. But as long as my mom still feels the need to "correct" Ebonics, like when we say words like "ain't," she'll never see the card, or the game. She'd just be disappointed.

It's not that I don't get why she does it. She doesn't want us to walk into a job interview one day with "Ay, bruh, I ain't got much 'sperience, but I'ma do what I gotta do to get the job done, you feel me, cuz?" but Steph and I know how to alternate. It's like speaking two different languages. One when I'm home, FaceTiming Malcolm, and one when I'm at Jefferson, blending in. I can do both flawlessly. But some nagging fear in the back of my mom's mind thinks that if she doesn't snuff out every "finna" and "talmbout" and "I'on," Steph and I will be forever unemployable, and every dime she's spent at Jefferson will go down the drain.

"Yes, Mom," I say, pulling my phone out and stealing a glance at the screen. A new text from Malcolm.

Malcolm: See you tomorrow. Until then, listen to this and miss me.

He attached a new song by the Weeknd—that one that was nice and slow that I suggested we make love to. Why does he insist on teasing me like this when he knows he can't come over tonight? I let out a frustrated sigh and look back up at Mom and Steph.

Steph is looking at me with a smirk now, and I'm sure she knows it's Malcolm. She changes the subject, and I'm grateful, but the new topic she chooses is one I've heard a thousand times.

"Did you notice my new glasses?"

I nod. "Red looks nice on you."

"Thanks!" she beams, rolling up both sleeves of her tight pink sweater.

Mom leans in closer to Steph, examining her glasses extra close, so close that Steph actually leans backward a bit.

"Is that . . . Scotch tape?" asks Mom.

"They're from Goodwill," explains Steph with a shrug as she picks up a big green leaf and nestles it in the basket. "But they broke in my purse on the way home. Had to fix 'em somehow."

"You couldn't find another pair of red glasses?" asks Mom.

"Not ones that look like the ones from Rihanna's music video. I may go to Jefferson, but I'm not about to spend Jefferson money on glasses."

I smile at that. Steph and I have our frugality in common, although mine is mostly based on the fact that I use every last dime I can find to maintain the game.

"But *Scotch tape*, Steph? Really," says Mom. "You could find a nice new pair on Amazon that doesn't look so . . ."

Steph leans back against her chair and folds her arms over her chest, challenging Mom to finish the sentence.

"Tacky," says Mom. I know she's avoiding the word "ghetto," after Steph's lecture to the family last week about how "ghetto" is just a derogatory code word for innovative. "I just don't want those kids at Jefferson ostracizing you and your sister."

Too late for that.

"I get it, Mom," replies Steph. "But I genuinely don't care. If I wear red tape-covered glasses, quote lyrics from *The Chronic* regularly, and speak in AAVE, and *that's* enough to get me ostracized, it's going to happen no matter what I do."

Okay, I have to ask. "What's AAVE?"

"Oh, *please* don't get her started," sighs Mom, looking up at me like I just asked Steph to recite the Gettysburg Address for us.

"No, Mom, this is important. Kiera needs to hear this. It stands for African American Vernacular English, and—"

"Actually," I say, glancing back at my phone. It's already 3:08. I have seven minutes to log in. "Sorry I asked. I need to get to studying. Biology exam tomorrow."

I turn to leave through the kitchen just as Steph launches into, "Okay, we'll talk later, though, right? This is important!" at a thousand decibels, after which comes a swift *shhhhhhh* from Mom to remind her not to yell in the house.

When I get to my room, I lock the door and run to my computer chair. When I log in, there are 641 new DMs in my *SLAY* inbox. That's the name of the game—*SLAY*. It's not an acronym, although that's always the first question of anyone who joins, and people have been offering suggestions for acronyms ever since its launch. It's a double entendre, meaning both "to greatly impress" and "to annihilate." I thought the name was more than appropriate for a turn-based VR card game where players go head-to-head in card duels using elements of Black culture. Steph would love it if she ever knew about it. Or if she knew I was the developer. But for all the confidence I have in my sister, one thing she absolutely can't do is keep a secret. And on top of that, her constant jabs at Malcolm make me wonder if she'd *get* the game. There are players from all over the world, all walks of life, many who grew up poor like Malcolm, regularly "decolonize" like Malcolm, and surround themselves with specific kinds of Black influences, like Malcolm. I don't know if I can share *SLAY* with her, because I don't know if she'll accept it—*all* of it. Not without overthinking it. So I won't. Probably not ever.

I scan the messages for anything important, like major game glitches. I don't want people to miss the semifinals because of technical problems. Most of them are asking what time the duel begins, even though I put a section clearly marked *Duel Calendar* in the navigation panel on the left side of the screen, the panel that you have to look at whenever you're configuring your character.

I roll my eyes at the willful ignorance and glance at the clock. Five minutes till duel. I'll read the rest of the messages later. I unlock the bottom drawer of my desk and pull out my headphones, and the gray VR socks, gloves, and goggles my family doesn't know I bought.

My heart pounds as I slip them on. I can't wait until I go off to Spelman so I can play with a noise-canceling headset. For now, I have to listen for my mom yelling through the door that it's dinnertime, so I can say *five more minutes* and deflect suspicion.

I log in and my pulse races as I watch my logo appear in brilliant green all caps against a black background. *SLAY*, it says on the screen inside my goggles.

I get up and stand in the middle of my room so I don't knock anything over. All I keep in my room are my bunk bed with the sofa on the bottom, my bookcase, my dresser, my pouf, my desk in the corner by the door. When it comes to VR, the less furniture around me, the safer. *Come on, come on*, I urge as the map fills the screen. It's nighttime in this region—the Tundra—so the navy skybox is up, almost black, peppered with shimmering stars. I look up and around at them all, and suddenly I miss all those summer nights Malcolm and I used to lie in my backyard in SoDo and watch what little of the night sky the city smog would leave us. Nights when we got to shut out the rest of the world and just be ourselves, swapping music, talking about which Black genius's opinions he was reading that day. I captured several of his favorites in *SLAY*—Maya Angelou, James Baldwin, and Langston Hughes.

I left my character, Emerald, here in the Tundra so it would be easier to get to the duel. The snowy mountains contrast nicely against the sky, spiking upward in a basin all around me. I raise my hand to slide the virtual keyboard from the right side of the screen, type *Fairbanks Arena* using the holographic keys, point my left hand to the north, and pull my trigger finger, allowing me to teleport at light speed. New players might think I named the arena after Fairbanks, Alaska, but the information panel would tell them I actually named it after Mabel Fairbanks, one of the first Black professional figure skaters.

Mountains zoom past me. I smile, impressed at how good they look up close. I was having a fantastic day when I created the Tundra. The textures are flawless—smooth and realistic. The snow looks fluffy up close. Every mountain looks hand-painted, thanks to donated art from a few indie artists who *SLAY*. I built the arena itself entirely of diamonds, because I could, and because a diamond arena in an icy region is hella dope. It's one of the biggest, too. It can hold three million people, since I hope one day the game gets that big.

For now, chat reads over a hundred thousand logged-in people out of the five hundred thousand people with *SLAY* accounts, which is still a lot for a single duel, even if it's the semifinal round of a tournament, but I guess it's prime time for people my age to be online, at least here on the West Coast. I'm close enough to see the people forming a line into the arena now. I slow my pace and I'm flying smoothly over all the attendees. Most players choose to be either royalty or characters with special powers or weapons. I descend to the ground and join them, walking in place in my room to make Emerald move.

A few people recognize me and step aside.

"It's Queen Emerald!" says the text over the head of an especially tall woman in a bloodred strapless gown with a fifty-foot train flowing behind her. Her wrists have golden bracelets up to her elbows, and her neck has similar ones. Her hair is twisted up into an enormous bulb on top of her head, with a huge golden crown encircling it, a giant ruby as wide as her torso set right in the middle.

At first I tried to make the dresses realistic and material, but it was causing problems when people would step on the trains, veils, and robes, and keep characters from walking smoothly. So she's wearing a dress that's immaterial, meaning the fabric will go right through other players and objects without obstruction, a weird concept—based on collision physics—to think about when you're talking to her face-to-face.

A woman in bone armor notices me and takes a fighting stance. Her unnaturally large boobs and red headband around her enormous Afro make her look like a *Mortal Kombat* character.

Text appears above her head. "I hope you got my message, Emerald. We meet at dawn."

Everyone says, "We meet at dawn." It's how we say, "I challenge you to a duel at a later time." In fact, it's become an identifier in the real world. About a year ago, kids in the grocery store started coming up to me and asking, "Did you thaw the meat?" or "Did you get the meat?" or "Do you eat meat?" and after some perusing in chat, I realized it's a coded question. They ask pretty much any question involving meat, to which I'm supposed to reply, "We meet at dawn" if I want them to know I *SLAY*.

When Reddit first launched, it was so secretive that Redditors in real life used to ask the highly conspicuous question "When does the narwhal bacon?" but I like our version better. It's more covert. "Did you thaw the meat?" is a totally normal question to ask. "When does the narwhal bacon?" will make people ask, "WTF are you Internet kids up to?" which is exactly what I *don't* want to happen. I know there are *SLAY*ers who are just like me—who live one way during the day at work or school, and would rather their nonBlack classmates or coworkers *not* know they live completely differently online. Completely authentically.

I walk past the woman in bone armor and spot a character in a dark gray hooded robe that extends about thirty feet behind him. He's wielding a katana in each hand and has the words JUSTICE FOR TRAYVON written across the back of his robe in bloodred. Not going to lie, his outfit is pretty legit. When text on clothing was enabled, I just wrote EMERALD down the leg of a lime-green jumpsuit I had stuffed in the back of my inventory. The text was impossible to line up with various articles of clothing, so I ended up giving up on the function, and now I'm wishing I'd written something meaningful instead of my name, because it'll be awhile before I'll have time to sort that feature out.

The entrance to Fairbanks Arena is everything I'd

imagined a Hollywood movie premiere to be. Neon-blue and purple strobe lights are creating a faux aurora borealis across the night sky and across all sides of the building. At least I hope people recognize it's the aurora. It looks a little like a sloppy watercolor potion, which I guess is okay since this region is full of witches and magicians. It's much easier to mix potions when you live right next to the mines, where the crystals are—in yellow, blue, and pink.

The purple carpet leading up to the front steps only appears thirty minutes before a tournament duel, mostly to alert players in the area who don't check the schedule that a tournament duel is about to happen. Players can initiate a regular duel at any time, anywhere, by sending a request to any character they wish. But the tournament duels are where the *real* athletes come to play. Those are the duels that get spectators. I hike up my dress out of habit, since it's immaterial and poses no risk of tripping, and race up the steps. My green gown flies behind me, and I pound the + button on my virtual screen, allowing my character to grow to ten times her size so people know I've arrived.

The minute I step through the front door, having to duck just to fit into the arena, the people in the stands roar to life. I look up and around the arena in awe. The stands reach so high into the rafters that I can't see the top on account of the light from the moon, which is directly above us in the night sky. Characters jump and scream, waving veils and scarves and jangling bracelets and jewelry. Anything to attract my attention. I can't stop looking around. Everyone's configured their characters to be different shades, from Zendaya to Lupita, and I am living for it. There's forehead jewelry and face paint, flowers, feathers, beads, glitter, Afros the size of small vehicles and braids as long and thick as pythons. I spot dashikis, Mursi lip plates, otjize clay, Ulwaluko blankets, Marley twists, Michael Jackson's glove, and a man in a purple cape twice as tall as me in the front row who's trying a little too hard to be Prince. And this splendor, this orchestra of Black magnificence, extends all the way up to the ceiling, beyond my vision.

Steph would cry tears of joy if she could see this.

To make my way up the steps to the middle of the arena, I march my VR-socked feet against my rug—the rug I asked for last Christmas to cover up the sound of me dueling. In the middle of my bedroom, I raise my gloved hand and Emerald's hand shoots up in the air. The conversations of over a hundred thousand people dissipate into immediate silence. I don't think I'll ever get tired of that satisfaction.

I raise my index finger and see the virtual white-gloved hand slide my virtual keyboard from the right side of my screen.

"Welcome, kings and queens," the text above my head reads. I wish I could use a mic, but there's no way I'd be able to keep up the whole "secret identity" thing in a house with walls this thin. The crowds roar to life again, and I keep typing.

"Tonight, we await a fierce match between two of the

greatest magicians in the Tundra. Our very own civil war."

The applause doesn't stop. So many people so excited to be here. I can't even.

"In one corner of the ring—some call her a Voodoo queen, some call her a dark witch, and others just call her the Shadow. Please welcome . . . Zama!"

I extend my hand toward the Western Gate as a cacophony of cheers and boos melds into an uproar. Zama speeds from the gate under a bear-size wolf pelt with her head tucked down low and bare arms extended like airplane wings. Her tail extends twenty feet behind her as she glides across the arena floor and around the ring. She runs as gracefully as a bird flies, so fast that the whole pelt stays off the ground. Her fans—mostly from the front rows—erupt into soulful howls that echo all the way up to the invisible ceiling. Zama finally turns and races up the steps to the ring where I am, and raises her hands to her worshippers, who continue to howl their respect.

I've seen Zama duel before. She must be a professional martial artist in real life, with access to an entire gymnasium of space, because she can flip across the whole arena and roundhouse-kick her opponents clean out of the ring. Once, in the Rain Forest region, I saw her leap into the air, grab a vine that was hanging in a loop above the arena, and ninja-kick her opponent hard enough to knock six hundred points off the board in a single blow. Her agility and mastery of the cards earned her immediate popularity in *SLAY*, and now that she's climbed the ranks to the top of the Tundra warriors roster, her fans have crossed over from a fan base to a cult following.

"And in the other corner," I type, "we have a wild card of a warrior. They're mighty, they're unpredictable, and they have a whole book of tricks up their sleeve. Please welcome PrestoBox!"

More applause and booing as I gesture to the Eastern Gate, where a black disk emerges and slides across the floor. It's like a shadow, but with nothing creating it. It slides right up the steps, headed straight for me. Just as I think it's going to stop, it slides underneath me. I glance over my shoulder as it emerges from under my sparkly green train and stops beside me. The cheering hasn't stopped, and it hums louder as a mountain of black lumps rises slowly from the disk, which is shrinking. The lumps slowly take shape into shoulders and a head. Then a face forms—one with a Guy Fawkes mask and a black Zorro hat—they look a bit like No Face from *Spirited Away*. The body is just a nondescript black cloak, concealing whatever tricks lie underneath. I've never seen Presto duel before, but I know rumors have been circulating about them since they joined six months ago. Presto has been accused of hacking because they've discovered spells so rare that Cicada was convinced nobody would ever figure them out. To create a spell in *SLAY*, you have to find specific ingredients, combine them in your inventory in a specific order to make a spell base, and enter codes to add certain qualities to the spell so you can actually use it. Presto managed to unlock a spell that allows you to fly—or more accurately, hover—and everyone flipped out and assumed that since no one had seen it before, it couldn't be real. But it's very real. To get it, you have to combine a Pink Crystal from the Tundra region, an Ostrich Feather from the Savanna region, and a rare Foxblood Flower from the Forest region. Then you have to find four numbers on the back of a framed photo in one of the pyramids in the Desert region and enter them into the spell code box backward. Cicada's idea. She wanted the coolest spells—the ones that let you teleport, see through walls, become invisible, levitate objects, and summon thunder—to be almost impossible to figure out. But they're very real, just waiting for players to discover them, and of all the spellmasters I've seen duel, Presto has the most potential to find them first. PrestoBox is silent and makes no movement, so I begin typing again.

Before I can enter my next sentence, a loud thunderclap explodes through the arena and a shadow appears over the ring, startling even me. I gasp and suddenly hope my mom didn't hear me from the hall. PrestoBox has raised their arms and thrown their cape fifty feet in all directions above my head and Zama's, consuming us in darkness. I look over at PrestoBox, who has revealed their body underneath the cape. They're wearing the standard black stretchy shorts that every character gets by default, since we can't have characters walking around naked, and they have gorgeous skin, the color of raw umber, with white body paint made to look like a skeleton from neck to toes.

The crowd can't get enough. If PrestoBox had fans before walking in here, they have at least double that now.

As quickly as they'd flung the cloak over the whole ring, they retract it, sucking it into their body like a Shop-Vac sucking up motor oil. PrestoBox takes a bow and raises a black lump to the crowd in a wave. I grin at their style, which has turned out to be as magnificent as their reputation.

I click enter.

"Kings and queens, you know the drill. We are here first and foremost to celebrate Black excellence in all its forms, from all parts of the globe. We are different ages, genders, tribes, tongues, and traditions. But tonight, we are all Black. And tonight, we all *SLAY*."

I raise my right arm for dramatic effect, and the audience members jump up and down in their seats. A shrill voice in the front screams, "I love you, Zama!"

"The rules of duel engagement are simple," I type. "Each dueler will draw six cards—two Battle cards, two Hex cards, and two Defense cards. Once the cards are drawn, duelers will have ten seconds to determine the order in which they want to use their cards. Duelers will fight using two cards each per round, in any combination they choose. In regular duels, Dueler One will launch attacks at the same time as Dueler Two. But because this is the Tundra Semifinals, and because luck makes everything more interesting, for this match, the dueler who draws the higher initial card will be allowed to use their first two cards five seconds before their opponent in round one. Defense cards beat Battle cards. Battle cards beat Hex cards. In rounds two and three, duelers will launch attacks at the same time, as per normal duel rules. The scores will appear on the Megaboard as the game progresses, and the drums will signal the beginning and end of each round. Is everybody ready?"

More cheering and hollering from the crowd. Everyone is so hyped for this online world. I wonder how many of these people ran home from school just to log on and watch.

"Duelers," I type, "face your opponent."

Zama and PrestoBox turn to stare each other down as I navigate to my inventory and pull out the deck of gold-plated cards. They come in three colors—Hex are purple, Battle are red, and Defense are blue. For the initial draw— the one that determines which dueler will go first—I keep them scrambled. I hold my arms out on either side of me, right here in my room, and watch the virtual cards shuffle theatrically through the air over my head in a shimmering arch. I look up, spinning them in all directions until they fall like a stack of leaves neatly into my hand. The crowd has gone silent as I whip my arm in front of me, casting the cards across the ring until they're sucked up into two piles, one at the feet of Zama, and one at the feet of PrestoBox.

"Duelers, draw your initial card to determine who will go first."

PrestoBox levitates their card into the air and flips it over so I can see it.

"It's the Innovation card!" I announce. I look at the Megaboard behind me, a TV screen the size of a football field floating in midair. PrestoBox's Innovation card appears enormously, in great detail, on the screen. The light bulb pictured in the middle of the card is another donated piece of artwork. It's a Hex card, the lowest ranking of the three categories. Zama draws a card from the top of her deck, glances at it, and then hands it to me.

"It's the Representation card!" I declare, watching the card appear on the Megaboard with the image of three identical silhouettes, since it duplicates the dueler times three. "A Defense card! Zama goes first."

An eruption of howls from Zama's fans drowns out the applause and booing. Zama and PrestoBox continue to stare at each other. I point to the ceiling and pull my trigger finger lightly, pulling me up into the air like I have an invisible grappling gun. I watch the ring grow smaller below me as I type with my free hand.

"On my count, the duelers will have ten seconds to study their six cards—two Battle cards, two Hex cards, and two Defense cards."

I arrive at my seat, which is high above the Megaboard where I can see a hundred more rows of stands. I programmed a holographic projection of the stage a hundred rows high so people too high up to see the floor can still see the match clearly. I prefer to watch from up here because it's much quieter, and I can watch the match under the stars. It's a game of strategy and timing. Zama and

PrestoBox stare each other down like cats about to rip each other apart. Each has three stacks of cards at their feet— one red, one blue, and one purple, all with that iconic *SLAY* golden trim.

"Ready?" I type as I gather my gown around my feet and sink into my thronelike chair, which would fit two of me. "Go!"

Zama kneels, snatches up her deck, and flings cards one by one onto the ground in a two-by-three formation, faceup. PrestoBox's cards move on their own, six arranging themselves in the same way.

The Megaboard counts down from 10 . . . 9 . . . 8 . . .

Zama studies her cards and slides all six of them around on the ground in front of her. Presto calmly moves just two of theirs to different positions. Both duelers can see their own cards clearly—the titles, the stats, and the artwork. But Cicada and I figured out pretty fast that characters in the front rows could see some of the cards with more striking artwork, ruining the surprise. So to those of us who aren't dueling, including me, the cards look like solid gold rectangles. No text, no art, nothing. Not until Zama or Presto decide to use them.

The voices of a hundred thousand characters chant along with the Megaboard: "Three! . . . Two! . . . One!" And then those drums thunder through the whole place, signaling the end of Zama's and Presto's chance to study them. All twelve cards on the floor between them flip over, facedown. It's up to the duelers to remember the order they chose and be prepared to fight with them, two cards at a time.

"Duelers," I type, "have you studied your cards?"

Zama raises her fist and releases a mighty roar among the howls of her fans. PrestoBox lifts an amorphous lump from under their cloak and waves it up at me. I'll take that as a yes.

"Excellent," I type. I have the next part memorized now, but it took me forever to write at first, jotting down the words in notebooks, on napkins, and in my phone until they clicked perfectly. "These are the rules of tournament engagement: Using the unique powers indicated on each card, duelers will battle each other until their powers run out and they return to the state in which you see them now. Then we will progress to round two. The dueler left with the most points at the end of round three wins the match. Attacks in rapid succession *are* permitted—duelers may deal as many strikes as they want before the timer runs out and their powers disappear. Duelers *may* use items and spells during game play. The restrictions are few: in-game betting on opponents, hacking, lag mechanisms, and unapproved mods to characters, skills, and environments are strictly prohibited. In general, no—"

The audience yells it as my next text appears:

"Tomfoolery!"

I grin as I type the next part:

"And finally, remember that little queens and kings are watching. Opponents, respect each other in words and in actions. No trash talk. Let your skills speak for themselves. Now, are you ALL READY?!"

The crowd roars to life and Zama begins hopping up and down to loosen up. PrestoBox widens their stance under their robe.

"Duelers! On my count, flip your first pair of cards! Ready? Three . . . two . . . one . . . Flip!"

Zama flips the two cards closest to her. Two cards flip on their own in front of PrestoBox. The four cards appear on the Megaboard, and I hurry to read their names so I can type.

"Zama has chosen the Gabby Douglas card and the Twist-Out card for a deadly combination. Very nice, but will it withstand PrestoBox's selections, the Jimi Hendrix card and the Swerve card? We'll find out in three! Two! One! And begin!"

Those drums thunder away through the arena.

Zama taps the Twist-Out card first, and her hair grows into two monstrous ropes as thick in diameter as Thanksgiving dinner plates, ropes that deal no damage but can render the opponent immobile if they catch them. They fly straight for PrestoBox, who ducks and rolls out of the way, just barely escaping their grasp in time as the two ropes untwist into four. Presto reaches their hand out from under the inky black cloak and touches the Jimi Hendrix card, and an electric purple haze falls over the ring, descending from the sky like a tropical rain. I debated between calling this one the Jimi Hendrix card after his song "Purple Haze" or the Prince card in honor of "Purple Rain," but in the end, it looked more like a "Purple Haze" to me, and since it clouds the opponent's vision by 75 percent, the name stuck.

Zama begins to stumble amid the violet fog. The crowd is loving this, and I'm loving it along with them. Even though I have all the cards' stats memorized since I wrote most of them, I never know for sure how a match will end. The outcome depends on so many factors besides luck of the draw—aggressiveness, patience, reverse psychology, game theory, character strength, and frankly, how skilled the person behind the character is at using VR equipment. It's impossible to tell who has the upper hand, and I realize I'm holding my breath.

Zama's untwisted ringlets split into a flailing spiral of fifty locks of hair. The crowd gasps as all tendrils zoom straight at PrestoBox, who can't escape them this time. Presto is sucked up into a jet-black bouquet of gorgeous natural hair that I'm envious of. My twist-outs have been stuck at my shoulders since junior high. Presto squirms fruitlessly as Zama leaps forward into a handspring with one of her hands on the Gabby Douglas card, and her feet follow effortlessly. She tumbles and flips across the ring with such speed and strength that people are rising out of their chairs in awe. A swift roundhouse to the face sends PrestoBox flying mask-first into the ground.

I gasp and realize I'm clenching my fists, and then I take a deep breath and remind myself that none of this is real, and that Presto isn't really hurt, and that my animations are just that realistic. I steal a glance at the Megaboard. That blow gave Zama a whopping twelve-hundred-point lead.

"Come on, Presto," I urge. My heart skips as I realize I've said it in real life, and I lift one headphone to listen to the quiet of my room, just to make sure Mom hasn't heard me.

PrestoBox is off the ground, tapping their second, and last, round one card—the Swerve card, one of my favorites, marked by a black steering wheel as the artwork, since it comes from the expression "swerve," which means "step off" or "stay in your lane." It blocks 80 percent of opponent damage. To use this as a round three card usually means the player has given up on offense and they want to block as much damage as possible in a last-ditch effort to stay in the game. Using the Swerve card in round one means Presto anticipated Zama would take the offensive out the gate and is giving themselves time to catch up. The crowd erupts in boos, and Zama shrugs, circling the ring with a raised hand to calm her supporters down. Her twist-out is still billowing behind her. With Zama's back to the ring, PrestoBox glides across the floor in her direction. I smirk at Zama's carelessness. We're only two minutes into round one, with sixty seconds left. There's no way she should be this confident yet. If there's one thing that'll get you flattened in the ring, it's pride.

Presto leaps through Zama's hair tentacles and engulfs her in that inky black cloak until both duelers are a tangle of hair, wolf pelt, and shadowy blackness under a purple haze. I can barely make out anything through all that, so I watch the Megaboard as Presto's points tick up and up and up. Three hundred, four hundred, five fifty, six fifty. It's thirteen hundred to eight hundred as Zama breaks free and sics her hair on PrestoBox again. Presto reverts to shadow form, sinking into the floor until they're a pool of black zipping all over the ring. Zama's eyes can't keep up, and she looks ridiculous tap-dancing around in her regal wolf cloak to keep her feet away from the shadow.

I can't help it—I burst into laughter.

My mom's voice comes instantly.

"Honey, I hope you're studying in there," she calls.

"Yeah," I holler, probably a little too fast. "I'm just taking a quick break."

"Well, dinner's almost ready anyway. You can take a break with us."

"Is Dad home already?" I exclaim. It can't be. It's only—

I glance at the clock in the corner of my navigation panel. 3:45. What in the world is Dad doing home so early on a random Thursday?! Why, of all days, did both my parents decide to show up early from work *today*? I'm only halfway through round one of the Tundra Semifinals. I can't just leave!

PrestoBox is flipping Zama over their shoulder now and slamming her flat on the ground. It's time for me to chime in again. I begin typing and talking at the same time, which is always dangerous. I type: "A spectacular move by PrestoBox! What a show!" at the same time as I say, "Fine, just let me finish this show," instead of what I *meant* to say: *Fine, just let me finish this assignment.* I scramble to correct myself. "I'm writing a report on *The Fresh Prince of Bel-Air* and its impact on Black culture in the nineties. I'm kind of in the middle of a train of thought here."

"Yes, well, you won't be able to think if you don't get some nourishment," calls Mom.

"Yes, ma'am," I say begrudgingly, knowing a fight with my mom over dinner will not end in my favor. I listen to the ensuing silence until I'm sure she's gone, and then I focus back in on the match. Zama is swinging her staff, knocking away sickle-shaped darts flying out from under PrestoBox's cloak. We're nearing the end of round one, and the Megaboard reads 1500–1300, with Zama in the lead. It's so close, but there's no way I'll make it through to the end of round three without Mom pounding angrily at my door with the news that dinner is getting cold.

I call in the only reinforcement I can count on: Cicada.

I slide my chat panel out on my VR screen and open a private convo with her, relieved to find her name lit up in green.

Me: Please tell me you're watching this.

Cicada: Zama and Presto? It's past midnight here and I have a final exam tomorrow. In other words, wouldn't miss it. :)

I smile. I don't know where Cicada lives, but she's somewhere in the Central European Time Zone, putting her somewhere south of Norway and north of Nigeria, which doesn't narrow it down much. I don't know a lot about her, really, since most of our conversations are strictly business—related to game updates, new cards, landscape artwork, or server maintenance—but I know that I can trust her. She's been on this *SLAY* train since the beginning, faithfully moderating matches when I can't, and it works, since she's somewhere on the other side of the world. She's awake when I'm not.

I type a reply into our private chat box.

Me: Thank God. Listen, it's dinnertime and if I don't get out there soon, my mom is going to have a liter of kittens.

Cicada: ☻ Spell-check? Or did your mom take "Kittens in a Blender" too literally?

I manage to contain a laugh and send a crying laughing emoji right back, and a grateful **IOU a major one.**

Then I navigate back to my announcement panel and type to the masses just as Zama reciprocates PrestoBox's earlier body slam.

"Attention, lovely kings and queens, I leave you in the capable hands of Cicada. Be conscious, and be well."

I don't want to log off. The score is tied 1700—1700, and Zama's hair is weakening its grip from around Presto's amorphous form. The purple haze is fading. Round one is ending in a tie. The crowd is roaring as the imminence of round two sinks in. I see Cicada's name light up in the stands on the opposite side of the arena, and freestanding, glowing white text appears above her bald head in a floating holographic speech bubble. It says "What a maneuver! Moves like that only come from the Tundra, am I right, kings and queens?"

I love her gown. It's all white, off shoulder with white fur lining the neckline. A single strip of black fur lines the hood, which is pulled elegantly over her head. Her face is actually devoid of makeup. She just has the base-model face. But sometimes, if she's feeling spunky, she'll don the Princess Mononoke mask—the red and white one with the brown eyes. So badass. She's sitting in the stands, so I can only see her from the torso up, but I've seen the gown in all its glory before. She looks like an ice princess. I wonder if she's bald in real life too.

"Kiera!"

The yell makes me jump, and I scramble to log out, kill the power, yank off my headphones, headset, and gloves, hop across my carpet as I pull off one sock at a time, and get all my equipment back into the drawer before the knocking starts.

"Hold on!" I holler. I try to keep my keys as quiet as possible while I lock the bottom drawer.

"Dinner is getting cold!"

"I know, just—" I'm trying to catch my breath after being startled, so I don't emerge from my room a raging ball of nerves. I'm already sweaty from the excitement of the match. I don't want to look like I've just run a marathon while I'm supposed to be watching *Fresh Prince*.

"Just, get started without me. I'll be out in five."

"If you think you're going to leave your father and me to listen to this rant about African American Vernacular English by ourselves, you've got another think coming."

I smile and shake my head, wiping the sweat from my forehead and turning off my computer. As I open my door and follow Mom down the hall toward the dining room, I wonder which cards Zama and Presto will be using in round two.

I stack three more peas onto my fork and try not to imagine what other incredible tricks PrestoBox has up their sleeve.

Steph is talking at us again, this time recalling a debate she had with Holly Little, the treasurer of Beta Beta, about Martin Luther King. I love my little sister, I really do, but she could talk about Dr. King for hours if we let her. Literally hours. There are few things I'd like less than to listen to that right now.

"And so then," Steph says around a mouthful of rice, "I asked Holly if she'd ever actually *read* anything by MLK, like *really* read it, because if she *had* read MLK, she'd know he wasn't the patron saint of complacency like she was insinuating, and that he made it clear that there's a time and a place for revolt. So then Holly asked me if I was advocating for the destruction of infrastructure—you know, like when Black people loot stores after an unarmed Black person is killed and their killer is acquitted, and do you know what I asked her?"

Before any of us has a chance to guess, she's answering her own question.

"I asked her if she thinks it's worse than when white people loot stores after their team loses a big game."

Steph throws her hands up as if she's inviting the rest of us to test her.

"Boom," she says, picking up the spoon.

I eat my peas and cut into my chicken with the edge of my fork. It's tender and melts right off the bone, and when I put it in my mouth, it's salty and buttery. My mom has managed to redefine the concept of baked poultry, and one day I hope to learn how she does it. Auntie Tina can do it too. Granny could make it. In fact, I'm sitting here realizing that every woman in my family knows how to make this chicken but me, and I'm hoping it's genetic and one day I'll just *know* how to make it. I've considered adding some kind of chicken-related *SLAY* card to the game, maybe as a Hex card, because I swear it's like a drug. But people would riot. I can hear them now:

Chicken isn't necessarily a Black *thing!*

Some of us are vegetarian!

All this talk of Black excellence, and you reduce us to a chicken trope!

I take another bite of chicken and realize Steph is talking about Beta Beta now.

"New member initiation is next week, and I'm *so* excited. There's a sista joining us. I don't know much about her, but her name is Jazmin, and I know we're going to be best friends because she loves A Million Ways like I do, and she knows all the members and all their choreography. I know that much from Holly—"

"The same Holly that you had to set straight about Dr. King?" asks Dad. "If she's confused about Dr. King, how can you trust the rest of her sources?"

He somehow finds a way to get his opinion in with Steph when Mom and I fail to, which I always find impressive. He's an analyst at Gutenberg Enterprises, one of the largest paper manufacturing plants in the continental US, and I can't imagine what he's paid to do as an analyst except analyze things to death all day. Maybe that's why he gets along so well with Steph.

"I mean . . . ," says Steph, looking at the ceiling with both palms up, as she always does when she's thinking too hard about something, "she already, like, *knows* Jazmin, so I trust her. And I know Holly. She wouldn't lie about A Million Ways."

I look at Dad now, sitting at the head of the table, his hazel eyes looking at Steph through windshield-size glasses, thinking.

"That's a valid assessment," he finally admits. He takes another bite. His salt-and-pepper mustache swishes side to side as he chews, and he shakes his head.

"Mm-mm-mm," he marvels. "Are y'all eating the same chicken I am? Is nobody going to thank your mother for this gift from the cornucopia of Demeter?"

"Thanks, Mom," I laugh. Steph nods and covers her

mouth to say politely, "Thanks, Mom. This is really good."

Dad knows how to get a smile out of me, Steph, and Mom, whose face is glowing now.

"Oh, it's just a li'l salt." She shrugs humbly, her eyes cast down to her plate as she slides her knife through the middle of the chicken like butter. "Li'l mayonnaise."

"If you gave me salt, mayonnaise, and chicken, I wouldn't bring back something like this," Dad says with a smile. He shakes his head and does that thing where he looks like he's wincing in pain and then he jerks his head in a weird way and lets out a *"WHOO-WEE!"* like it's just so good he can't physically contain himself. Corny. But it gets Mom going.

"Stop it, Charles," she says, grinning. He wiggles his shoulders and cuts another piece.

"Can't wait to see what's for dessert," he says. I almost spit out my chicken with laughter. Steph looks at me wide-eyed and erupts in giggles. Mom's eyebrows are at work again, rising up as if to say, *I taught you better than this,* but she's also struggling to stifle a laugh as she changes the subject.

"So, Kiera," she says, and then pauses as if she's forgotten something. "Actually, hold on a minute."

She slides her chair back from the table with half her food left on her plate, which is unheard of in this house. Nobody leaves the table until their plate is clean. That's the rule. That's *always* been the rule. What is going on?

I look to Dad for answers, but he's taking advantage of

the fact that Mom's out of the room to check his phone at the table, which is also strictly prohibited. Steph is following suit with that hot-pink cat phone case of hers with the round baby blue Care Bear dangling off the end. I still haven't figured out what that's for. I suddenly remember the text I got earlier that I forgot to check. It's hard to remember to text real-life people back when there's a world of dueling magical beings in your room. I unlock my phone and realize the text is a mile long. Of course it is. It's from Harper.

Harper: Hey ☺. Mind helping me with polynomials? Even my app isn't picking it up 😩. I even asked Wyatt 4 help, and u know how desperate I have 2 be 2 do that, but he wouldn't even look at it!!!! He says he's "too busy" playing Legacy of Planets!!! Like WTF dude???! ☹

Outside of tutoring lessons, Harper is always asking me for math help. Not because she can't understand it, but because she doesn't take the time to hash it out. When we studied trig last quarter, I refused to help her with the first problem of any of the sections until she'd sat there looking at it for at least two minutes, which didn't really work because she always whipped out her math app well before the two-minute mark. Everyone uses the Mathdeco app, and the website version of the app for homework, and I'm pretty sure the teachers have figured that out, because you can't use either of those on the tests, and this year the tests are worth 100 percent of our grade, and the homework is worth zilch.

I manage to send off a single unpunctuated text before I hear Mom's shoes coming back down the hall toward the dining room.

Me: Sorry YES I'll help u later g2g

I should have thrown in a heart emoji to cushion how short the text was. Harper loves emojis, and I mean she really can't get enough of them. Last Halloween she wanted me to be a heart eyes emoji, while she was the crying laughing emoji. She asked Malcolm to join us, but he said he'd only do it if he got to be the eggplant emoji, which I thought was funny. Harper called the whole thing off at the very suggestion.

I can hear Mom from the hall.

"Kiera, I'm sure you've been wondering all evening why we're all home early." She comes back into the room, still wearing her blue scrubs, holding a huge blue-and-white envelope against her chest like it's a newborn baby. I look at her face, at those pearly white teeth in that smile a mile wide, and I realize what the letter is.

Steph blurts out a startlingly loud "Is that from Spelman?!" before I can say anything. I just sit in my chair, petrified, staring at the envelope. My hands feel sticky, and I'm suddenly not hungry. I think I'm both nervous and excited at the same time, but both those emotions feel like nausea and heart palpitations, so it's hard to tell. I think of what I should text Malcolm if I get in. I think of what to text Malcolm if I *don't* get in. Mom is holding the envelope out to me with a smile, expecting me to take it and rip it open like it's Christmas morning the way Steph did when she got the election results declaring her president of Beta Beta Psi.

I reach up and take the envelope and realize my hands are shaking. What am I so afraid of? A yes means I'm going to Spelman! I get to be with Malcolm in Atlanta while he goes to Morehouse! We'll be going to historically Black colleges in Atlanta that are literally two minutes apart. We've even talked about getting our own place together on either campus. It's what we've always wanted. It's all he's been talking about lately—being with me. I can envision it now: he'll wave at me across the street between classes, we'll make out in the plaza over lunch break, just the two of us on the grass in the hot Atlanta sun, and we'll share a bed at night. The idea is so romantic it sends a flutter through my chest.

But a no would mean all kinds of things I'm too afraid to think about, namely Malcolm's disappointment. I didn't tell him I applied to Emory, which is also in Atlanta, as a backup school. If I can't attend the historically Black college next door to him, I might as well try for the sub–Ivy League school down the street, right? So we can at least be close to each other? But shortly after I sent out the last of my college applications, he and I found ourselves lying under the stars on the trampoline in my backyard, dreaming together, when he looked over at me and asked where I'd applied. Something deep within me—call it intuition, call it vibes, call it psychic powers—guided me to answer simply, "Spelman."

He rolled over to face me, barefoot, in a T-shirt and sweats, with his legs curled up and one arm tucked under his head, smiling at me, and said, "I only applied to

Morehouse. I ain't going nowhere but an HBCU." Curious, I asked him why. He sucked his teeth and said, "Any non-HBCU would be a continuation of Jefferson." And then, when I smiled at him, because I totally feel him on that assessment, he reached up and brushed my cheek and said, "If I can't learn around my people, I can't really learn," and pulled me close and kissed me. But as I melted against him, I couldn't help but be lost in thought. Emory might be another Jefferson, but I'd go through Jefferson all over again, just to be with him. I know he'd do the same for me, although he got his letter from Morehouse last week, so he won't have to. Now our dreams hang in the balance with just me, with whatever is inside this envelope.

Steph's next outburst sucks me back into the dining room. Everyone's forks are down, and all eyes are on me.

"It's a thick envelope!" she exclaims. "They only send you a thick envelope if you got in, so they can tell you all about the college and what to expect on your first day, and how much scholarship money they're giving you—"

Mom clears her throat exaggeratedly, and Steph stops midsentence.

"I'm just trying to make her feel better," whines Steph. "Go on, Kiera, open it! Let's see!"

Even Dad, who's been noticeably quiet this whole time, is watching me in anticipation.

"If it's a no," I begin, tearing away the corner of the envelope, "you guys are going to feel really ridiculous. It's just a letter. Whatever it says, life goes on."

As much as I'm saying this to my family, I'm also saying it to myself. It's just a letter. But the pounding in my throat says otherwise. I tip out the contents of the envelope onto the kitchen table next to my plate and pick up the top sheet with the big blue Spelman letterhead. My eyes zoom to the very first word under *Dear Ms. Johnson*:

The word *Congratulations*.

I can't breathe. I don't know what to do. Steph is wearing the face of someone awaiting a birth in the next room. Mom is keeping her composure, but her hands are clasped tight and her eyes are wide.

"Well, Kiera, what's it say?"

I look at Dad, whose mouth is pursed together. He nods.

"What's it say, punkin?"

"I'm in," I say, forcing a smile. Why am I not happy? Why am I not relieved? Both my parents and Steph launch into a dance of whoops and hollers around the dining table like they're all going to Spelman *with* me. I sink lower in my chair with my hand against my forehead, but Mom yanks me up and pulls me into a tight embrace. Dad comes up behind me and adds his big bear hug to the mix. He smells like discount cologne and the room smells like my mom's special chicken, and Steph runs up and throws her arms around all of us while jumping up and down.

"I *knew* you could do it, Kiera, I knew it! Told you! It's all about the size of the envelope!"

Mom pulls away and cups both her hands around my cheeks and gives me a big peck on each one. She smells like coconut oil, and I love it. That smell reminds me of getting my hair pressed on Easter Sunday mornings when I was little, and it was cold outside, and everyone was ready for spring and it was almost my birthday.

"I'm *so* proud of you," she says. There are tears in her eyes as she says it. My dad hugs me again from behind and kisses my head, which I can still feel through my day five twist-out. His kisses are *that* strong.

"Love you, sweetie," he says, squeezing my shoulders. I smile and enjoy the moment right up until I see Steph bursting forward and throwing her arms around my neck.

"I'm so excited!" she squeals. "Spelman! My sister is going to an HBCU just like me!"

"Didn't know you were dead set on going to an HBCU," I say, since I actually wasn't aware until just now. Steph is super smart. She's ambitious, even for a junior. Not only is she president of her chapter, but she's a Scripps National Spelling Bee winner, and she already won a partial scholarship from a robotics project she built as a sophomore last year. Pretty sure she could get into Harvard if she wanted to.

"Duh," she laughs, flipping her hair over her shoulder. "I'm down for the cause. I want us to succeed."

I'm going to Spelman for two reasons only: First, Malcolm. My love. My life. The only boy I know I can be myself around. The only one who gets me. Second, I'm sick of white people. Actually, that's not true—I love all people. I'm sick and tired of being the only Black girl among *all* white people. I want to be around people who understand me and don't expect me to answer asinine questions every day. Steph and I, as the only two Black girls at Jefferson, are the be-all and end-all authority on all things related to Black culture. Steph's popularity attracts inquiring minds, and since she "only answers ridiculous questions with ridiculous answers," as she puts it, they flock to me as a second resort.

Lucy Ingwall, a freshman, the oldest student I tutor after Harper, once asked me, *If I wear this headdress to this festival, is it going to offend people?* I told her I didn't know because I'm not Native and am therefore unqualified to answer that question. She became increasingly insistent that I was the only one who could provide credible input into her outfit, because she needed the opinion of a person of color and she didn't want to talk to the only Native American kid at Jefferson because she didn't know him that well. And then she asked me why the phrase "person of color" is okay, but "colored person" is not. *I'm just trying to figure out what the difference is,* she'd said, as if she expects me to just *know* how to define terms that generalize my cultural history generations back.

In *SLAY*, all I have to explain to people is how the game works. I don't have to explain the cards. If you play the game, you understand. All this time, I've imagined a similar world at Spelman. So where's the warm, fuzzy sense of accomplishment I thought I'd feel reading this letter? Where's the relief? My hands are shaking. There's a knot in my stomach. Whatever I thought I'd feel after tearing open that envelope and reading that blessed word "Congratulations," it wasn't this.

Later that night, as I'm tying up my twist-out into a pineapple and Steph is trying to gab at me with her mouth full of toothpaste foam, I stare at the bathroom counter, wondering if I should add more cards. Zama was wielding Twist-Out like she'd used it hundreds of times, and pairing it with the Gabby Douglas was a stroke of genius. Nobody wants to fight an Olympic gymnast wielding sentient hair. PrestoBox used a Defense and a Hex in round one. Only a professional chooses not to come out guns slinging with at least one Battle card in the first round. They both knew their cards too well. It's time to write more.

The last time Cicada and I launched new cards, we tried to give everyone a voice via a poll. We put fifty card options on the board and asked chat to vote for the top twenty results. The comments section blew up immediately. Everyone had an opinion. Every card on the board was antiprogress or tropey, or cheesy, or insulting, or boring, or inapplicable to everyone. I've always tried to choose concepts that edify all of us, but it's getting harder and harder to think of things every single one of us can relate to. People in Kenya may not identify with a good ol'-fashioned Tennessee barbecue, and people in the US may not understand the nuances of an Ulwaluko ceremony, and when you have to memorize six cards in ten seconds, the less you have to google, the better. Characters were fighting, and nobody was voting, and I got so fed up that I pulled the whole thing, picked my own favorite cards, and posted a message in the next update that read: *We are a diaspora. We span hundreds of shades, religions, traditions, and cultural nuances. If you don't understand what some of these cards mean, blame the slave trade.*

"Are you even listening?" came Steph's voice, and suddenly I'm back in our little pink bathroom, staring at the mirror. Steph has finished her teeth and started pinning up her hair for bed.

"What?" I ask. Her eyebrows sink, but she can't lift her eyes far enough to glare at me properly, since her head is down while she adds another pin to her hair.

"I'm sorry," I say. I resolve to really listen to what she's saying this time. She probably thinks I try to ignore her on most days, but the reality is that I've created an entire universe in my room, and the responsibility of maintaining it gets distracting.

"Never mind," she says airily, reaching for another pin.

At first I think she's being petty, like I don't deserve to hear the rest of her monologue, but then she continues with a grin, "I forgot what I was talking about."

I can't help but laugh, which gets her giggling. Her eyes fly open.

"Oh!" she exclaims. "*That* was it. I was talking about AAVE. When did you stop listening?"

The "African American Vernacular English" thing. Right.

She's been dying to tell me this all day, and the honest truth is that I haven't heard a word. For the sake of my sister's feelings, I take a deep breath and offer up my sanity with a generous, "Why don't you just start from the beginning?"

"Okay." She shrugs. "So, I was talking to Holly and Harper about this new rap song Holly was listening to. I don't even remember who it's by—some no-name guy with a mixtape—and Holly actually asked if I could *translate* for her. Get this. From 'Ebonics,' she said. *Ebonics!* She asked if I could translate it into something 'plain English.' I just left. I walked right out of the room."

Steph rolls her eyes like she's trying to get them stuck facing the back of her head and lets out the most exasperated sigh I've heard in a while.

"I mean, *come on!*" she continues. "And *then* I got to thinking how racist the word 'Ebonics' is. Well, maybe not racist, but marginalizing! Otherizing! I mean, if I claimed everybody on *The Office* was speaking 'White-a-nese,' they'd feel pretty called out. But somehow, *we* need our own language. Asking that it be called something dignified like 'African American Vernacular English' is the *least* that can be done."

Steph has been getting louder and louder this whole time, and I debate whether to point this out, likely prompting an even louder *Did you even hear a word I said?!* or let her keep jumping decibels on her own until one or both of my parents creak open the bathroom door and scold us. I find an alternative to both.

"Sounds like you have your Spelman essay topic for

your application next year," I say. I have a finite amount of energy, none of which I intend to spend on debating what to call the framework of Black American colloquialisms. I care more about erasing the stigmas *around* how some of us speak. I realize all over again just how bad an idea it would be to show Steph the game. I can see her now, psychoanalyzing every word in chat, overthinking everything about the environment, every card, applying science where there's currently raw passion and joy. What about *SLAY*ers who haven't caught the AAVE train yet? I can see her now, correcting people's word choices, with the best of intentions, of course. But if everyone found out it was my sister, *Emerald's* sister, policing everyone's language left and right, my reputation could dissolve instantly. I shake my head just as my phone buzzes in my pocket. My heart skips at the possibility of a text from Malcolm inviting me to share a FaceTime call tonight. I suddenly regret washing off my makeup so soon. I reach for my phone, unlock it, and realize the only notification is in WhatsApp.

Cicada: Zama wins with the Hustle card! 👊

Not the damn Hustle card again! It's one I wish I'd never let Cicada add to the game, but she'd insisted. The Hustle is the name of a dance popular in the seventies, which was apparently my mom's signature dance the few times she went on *Soul Train*. *Hustle & Flow* is the name of a movie on BuzzFeed's list of "100 movies you must see to keep your Black card," and although I've never seen the movie, Cicada has. She confirmed that yes, it should be on that list. She convinced me the word "Hustle" warrants a card, but it's arguably the dirtiest one in the whole deck. It steals 50 percent of the opponent's points, and Zama used it in the last round! I suck my teeth and type out a furious reply:

Me: That's BS! Using a Hustle card in the last round with a game this close? I thought these two were professionals! 😡 Sometimes I think we should delete that card.

Cicada: I mean, hey, she was dealt a Hustle card. She had to use it. Wouldn't you save a Hustle card for the last round too? It's really the smartest strategy.

"You look mad. Is it Malcolm again?" asks Steph as she massages night cream into her face.

"Why would I be mad at Malcolm?" I ask, trying to keep my composure. Why is she always trying to be in my business?

"I'm always mad at Malcolm." She grins, carefully pulling her bonnet over her freshly pinned hair and snatching her phone from the counter.

"You know," I begin, testing the waters, "you and Malcolm have similar opinions on HBCUs. You both want to attend one. You might like him if you gave him a chance, Steph."

"Oh, I'm sure," she says, smoothing the last visible smears of cream into her eyebrows. "Let me guess. He thinks HBCUs are the *only* way to go because"—she dons her mockingly deep Malcolm-imitation voice—"that's how we Black folk woulda been learning before the 'white man' got ahold of us and colonized our minds."

Something about her tone—the exaggerated drawl—sets off alarms in my head, and I suddenly feel myself getting angry. Malcolm talks like he grew up in SoDo. He doesn't shuck and jive like a damn minstrel performer. I suddenly regret even trying to smooth things over between the two of them. Maybe it's hopeless. I force myself to stay quiet. But Steph's face softens, and she turns to look at me, seemingly surprised at herself.

"Sorry," she says. "Here I am talking about tone policing and 'otherizing' language and then I go and make fun of Malcolm's accent. I didn't mean to, and I'm sorry."

I smile, and relief washes over me at the faint glimmer of hope, but it's short-lived.

"But," she says, twisting the lid back onto her night cream and tossing it in the top drawer, "I stand by what I said. He thinks HBCUs are the way to go because he wants to live in this fantasy world where white people don't exist. I, the realist, think HBCUs are the way to go because they give funding and opportunities to Black prodigies worldwide, and because we need to take care of our own. I said I'm always mad at Malcolm, and I meant it. Mostly because I don't entertain illogical conspiracy theories or believe straight men are the center of the universe. And I don't trust a man with ashy ankles."

I roll my eyes.

Once I brush my teeth, floss, and apply my nighttime moisturizer, I climb into bed. As I lie under the covers, scrolling through Instagram, I think back to what Steph said earlier, about HBCUs: *I'm down for the cause. I want us to succeed.*

I keep scrolling without really looking. Steph is convinced that she's proving something by pursuing an HBCU—proving that she's down for the cause, that she's rooting for everybody Black. Does she think that in order to be "down for the cause," I have to go to an HBCU? To want us to succeed, I have to go to an HBCU? Is that right? What if I hadn't applied to Spelman at all? As Malcolm—and apparently Steph—doesn't know, there are probably woke Black girls at Emory, too, who are "down for the cause" and support Black businesses and maybe even program Afrocentric video games. What if Emory says yes to my application and I go there instead? What would Steph think of me?

What would Malcolm think of me?

I navigate to my texts and pull up our convo from earlier.

Malcolm: See you tomorrow. Until then, listen to this and miss me.

And then that song he attached. We should be FaceTiming right now. He should be singing this song to me right now in that corny faux R & B voice of his. I'm kind of miffed at him for teasing me like this, *knowing* he couldn't come over tonight, but I also miss his voice, and I'm sure he's lying up in bed at his house, probably reading. I could always ask him to FaceTime, but it wouldn't even do me much good. I wouldn't be able to focus. My heart would be in it, but my head would be on that letter from Spelman. Instead I open our texts again.

I type out the words *I got into Spelman* and then delete them, and then type them again.

If I tell him, he'll want to talk tonight, about how excited I am to be going to one of the most prestigious historically Black colleges in the country, about how grateful I am to be going to a college that's a sweet relief from the burden of being Jefferson's resident Black culture consultant. But I don't feel any of that. Not right now. Maybe it hasn't hit me yet, the weight of it. Maybe it's like finding out you've been crowned homecoming queen. Maybe the bliss of it won't sink in until I'm up there onstage at my high school graduation in a cap and gown, and the principal is announcing to all those kids and parents that the first Black girl to graduate from Jefferson is going to study among her own people now, because she's done her time and deserves some reprieve. I'll tell Malcolm about it later. Besides, it's already nine thirty. I have to be up and well rested tomorrow for a keyboarding test in the morning, which I completely forgot about until now because when you run an MMORPG with over five hundred thousand members, a typing test becomes something to laugh at. But I do at least have to be awake to take the test, so no time to chat.

And worse than Malcolm wanting to talk, I'm afraid he'll fall asleep reading again and he won't even see the text until tomorrow morning. He's done that before, and there's no worse feeling than waking up and scrambling to check your phone in anticipation of a reply and finding nothing.

I delete the message and lock my phone. I roll to my side and pull my blanket up to my shoulder, and I shut my eyes for maybe thirty minutes, but then it crosses my mind that I don't know how close the Tundra Semifinals was, or how the preparations for the Desert Semifinals are going. Whoever wins the Desert—either Anubis or Spade—will fight Zama in the finals tomorrow night, at two a.m. my time. We scheduled it so most players who live in the West, Central, and East Africa time zones can watch between ten a.m. and twelve p.m. their time, and so Cicada can officiate at eleven a.m. her time.

I pull my phone back out and navigate to WhatsApp. In Cicada's time zone, it's already six thirty tomorrow morning—Friday—and she's lit up green. It shouldn't take her more than ten minutes to recount the duel highlights, right? I can spare that for Cicada, even the night before an exam. It might even help me finally get to sleep. I start typing.

PARIS, FRANCE

My name is Claire, and today I'm especially happy I live alone.

"Yes!" I whisper-scream at my desk in the corner of my little flat. "Yes, yes, yes!"

Zama, my favorite *SLAY*er, has won, and will go on to fight the victor of the Anubis vs. Spade showdown happening in the southernmost corner of the Desert region in fourteen hours.

I've seen Anubis duel before. He's athletic, making strategic use of his environment—the guardrails, the stands, and even his opponents. In the duel I saw, using the Michael Johnson card, he sprinted toward his adversary—Orlea, a scorpion from the western part of the Desert region—did a handspring off her shoulders, grabbed her venomous tail, jammed it firmly into one of the sandy blocks that make up the arena wall, and landed squarely on his feet. It was sick! He might be into parkour in the real world. Give the boy a Battle card that has anything to do with agility, and it's over for Spade. But I've seen Spade battle too, and his greatest weapon—often underestimated—is his impeccable timing. He's used cards most people throw away in game-changing moves, like the Anansi card, which gives you eight limbs and two enormous fangs that will paralyze the opponent for five seconds with each strike. Most players who are new to the Anansi card don't know how to operate eight limbs with just two real live arms, but you don't command them with your arms— you command them with your fingers, and the thumbs control the fangs. Maybe the player behind Spade is a world-famous pianist. But I'm not worried. Zama has the agility of a jungle cat, and she knows every card I've ever seen her dealt. She won't give the finals away to either of these boys, especially with the howls of the Wolf Pack behind her.

I'm so excited I almost forget to breathe. I know as a game mod, I'm not supposed to have a favorite player, but I do. I adjust my headset and begin typing.

"It's a Zama victory! Zama wins! Zama wins!" I smile as the crowd howls to the stars in her name. Zama pulls back her wolf-head hood and exposes her gorgeous black locs speckled with gold jewelry. She raises her fists into the air and begins her victory walk around the perimeter of the ring. PrestoBox is kneeling in the center, face turned downward. I hope Presto doesn't feel too bad. I looked up their stats before the match and realized it's Presto's very first tournament. To lose 2200–2000 in the semifinals against a renowned champion is a feat to be proud of!

I look back to Zama. Oh, she's beautiful. Between her dreads, wrist bangles, abundant gold rings, and wolf pelt, I could walk the streets of Paris for miles and not find a look as striking as hers. I keep typing.

"Zama will represent the Tundra region in the finals against the Desert champion. Both warriors will face off in the duel of the century on Saturday morning, eleven a.m. West Africa Time, so be sure to log on then. Until then, be conscious, and be well."

I immediately pull out my phone and text Emerald. **Zama wins with the Hustle card!** ✊🏾

I glance at the clock. It's one thirty in the morning already. The match ran long, and my math final is in a little over six hours. Even though it's a three-hour final, I know I'll ace it. I'm not worried. My chief concern is getting back to my flat in time to prepare for Anubis vs. Spade by eight thirty tonight, since my last class ends at seven. I pick up a few almonds from the bowl in the corner of my desk that I keep handy for snacking, toss them into my mouth, and navigate to chat. I type in *A-N-U-B-I-S*.

He must be one of the oldest *SLAY*ers in the game. That's the only way he could've gotten the name Anubis. *Everyone* wants that name. There's also a BetrAnubis, whose name Emerald wanted to flag because she thought it was disrespectful, but I insisted we leave it. The name "Anubis" is not owned by any one man. My *SLAY* name was almost Nubia, but I chose Cicada instead because I didn't want Anubis coming after me thinking I was flirting with him. Emerald said that's going to happen anyway because my character wears a gown. She goes through the same thing, even when she's wearing her emerald-green horns.

I don't know much about Emerald even though we met three years ago when the game started, but I know she's braver than I am, in almost every sense. When people pop up with questionable usernames, she's not afraid to let them know, kindly—unless they keep with the tomfoolery, and then she's not afraid to bring down the ban hammer. My official title is "mod," short for "moderator," but I avoid conflict whenever I can. To each their own.

My teakettle begins to whistle behind me, and I slip off my goggles and stand up to get it. My VR gloves are impressively insulating, and waterproof, so any splashes from the hot water don't burn my hands. This kettle is getting a funny smell to it, no matter how long I leave the lemon water inside. I even went to Monoprix and bought a huge bottle of lemon juice and tried boiling it full potency, which didn't do anything for the kettle smell, but it made my little flat smell fresh and clean. It beats the scent of lavender laundry detergent that lingers here no matter what candles I light.

My neighbors have rented out their flat, since they're in London through the weekend on a business trip, and the current occupants are clearly tourists. I've heard them through the walls speaking mostly American English with some broken French sprinkled in, the word *bonjour* appearing every other word. We Parisians don't say hello to each other *that* often. They also behave like they're keenly aware they're vacationing in the city of love. The woman was wearing a baby-pink tutu and a red bow with a blue blazer as if the only insight into French culture she's ever had is from *Madeline*, and last night they were having the most enthusiastic sex I've ever heard—on the balcony! Right outside in the open! The man walked past me in the lobby yesterday evening when I left to get a snack while on study break. He looked at me and nodded and smiled. No marveling, no strange looks, no asking me how I'm getting along in this heat—you know, since so many white Parisian natives assume I'm from Africa. No surprise at my fluent French as I greeted the doorman, since I was born here in Paris. The Americans assume I'm supposed to be here, and I like that.

Emerald told me about a year ago that she's American, but I figured it out well before that when she said once that she was eating Easy Cheese on saltines for a snack. I had to google what the hell "Easy Cheese" was, but once I did, I realized only an American stomach could survive digesting cheese from a spray can, and due to the time difference, I know she's somewhere on the West Coast—I'm assuming Southern California, since everyone on the West Coast seems to live there. California must be lovely with the sun always shining, always something to do, and so many people. More importantly, so many Black people. I imagine it's like a real-life *SLAY* world, where everyone has special powers. Los Angeles is full of so many stars and starlets, so many incredible people of color. I want to go there one day. I want to talk to them, to know what it's like to be famous.

I look around my two-hundred-square-foot flat, at the pictures all over the wall behind the string of lights above my tiny mattress. I'm running out of wall space. My bald brown head is easy to find in all the photos, usually posing next to a friend who has come to visit for a couple of days, or fellow students at their graduation before they fly off somewhere exciting or home to their families. My university takes only two hundred students per year, and only 10 percent of those are native Parisians, leaving me here in Paris alone in the summer, or in Florence, Italy, with Mamma. Since she got sick, the amount of time I spend in Florence has slowly dwindled. More money for her treatment equals less money for my travel.

But I have one photo of us together—me and Mamma—on my desk in a little pink frame she bought me last time I was there with her. I stare at it now, with both of us holding so many shopping bags, they're crowding the shot. I'm wearing a grin from ear to ear, with my thick brown hair falling in waves over my shoulders, back when I used to wear it long and straighten it. She has striking black doe eyes, thick eyebrows I've always been jealous of, and thick, wavy hair a deep chocolate brown—well, *had* thick wavy hair a deep chocolate brown. Last time I visited, it was duller, much thinner, and her eyebrows had faded to gray. I could call her later today when she might be awake, but that's hard to gauge, since her sleep has been unpredict-able lately. Dr. Ricci insists she's sleeping so much because chemo takes a lot out of her body, but I suspect she's sleep-ing so much because it's taking a lot out of her mind.

I sigh and resolve to distract myself with maths. I'm studying for no reason except to make myself feel more prepared. I read and read until my eyes grow tired and dry, and I press my palms against them and yawn. My back and hips ache, and my neck is stiff from sitting too long.

I sink back into my desk chair and take a couple sips of tea, which has long gone cold, and notice I have a new message from Emerald in WhatsApp. I'm thankful for the distraction.

Emerald: Hey, tell me more about the duel. Did Presto have a fighting chance?

Oh, did they! I can't type fast enough to keep up with my brain.

Me: Presto attacked with the Weave card in Round 2, RIGHT after Zama fin-ished her Twist-Out power. Countering a natural hair card with a weave card? Petty AF. In round three, Zama used the Wobble card, which looks really funny when your opponent is wearing a cape. Presto just looked like a drunk guy at a toga party with that robe. Hey, why don't we have a Bald card? Some of us are bald.

I smile and wait for her to reply, those little dots pop-ping up on my screen. I wish she could've seen the Weave card in action. It's a rare one that functions just like the Twist-Out card in that you can wield long tendrils of hair, but it's slightly less versatile—yes, that's intentional—and deals twice as much damage—not intentional, but accurate in many cases.

Emerald: We could totally have a Bald card! Nobody rocks bald like we do ✊🏾. Wanna write one up for the next tournament?

Me: What would a Bald card even look like? Would a brown bowling ball roll out of the wall and attack?

Emerald: 😃 WTF no. Idk, but I know you'll come up with something good. Anyway, back to the fight. What else happened? Tell me everything.

So I recount the rest of the fight—every move. Especially PrestoBox's luck at being dealt an Innovation card. I designed that one. Since innovation takes whatever you have and makes it better, the Innovation card boosts whatever card you use with it by 20 percent. PrestoBox used it with a Shout card, which Emerald had to explain is something done in Southern churches in America. Anyway, the Shout card rattles the whole arena, shaking 25 percent of the opponent's points right off the board. It was a devastating blow, but Zama stole them right back with the Hustle card and won the day. Now she'll play either Anubis or Spade in the finals.

Me: Who do you think will win the Desert?

Anubis is from Kansas City, and Spade is from somewhere here in France. I know this because they both put their location in their profile, which Emerald and I urge players not to do every chance we get. For players' protection, we encourage everyone to keep themselves anonymous.

Emerald: Definitely Anubis. Have you seen the coin on that man? Over a million.

I blink in surprise. Over a million? I put my phone down, turn back to my computer, and click on Anubis's name in my "most recent" list. Sure enough, his *SLAY* coin count reads 1,305,200. That equates to months and months and months of game play, hundreds of duels won, and thousands of items sold. Curious, I check his inventory and realize he's full up on armor. He must be forging it in the Desert somewhere and selling it to players in other regions. It makes sense. Sand lends itself to crafting, since it can easily be turned into metal, and the Desert provides few other resources on which characters could thrive. Harsh living conditions and abundant sand mean high barriers to entry, and low-cost manufacturing.

Either that, or he's got real-life friends who play, and they've all pooled their money into one character to boost their economy of scale. In-game merchants will usually offer deals on large numbers of items sold at a time, tossing in extra items for free. Carrying a lot of *SLAY* coins at once can also boost your in-game influence. People are a lot more likely to trade items with or do favors for a character who has a lot of *SLAY* coins to give away, or use to buy them things. I've seen that happen too.

Emerald is typing again.

Emerald: He could buy every single card in the game if he wants and study them.

She's right. Players can learn the cards one of three ways: using them in duels and learning as they go, trading cards with other players for resources and outfits, or buying access to the cards outright with *SLAY* coins. It's why Emerald and I rarely battle anyone but each other. Since we have editing rights to all the cards, it wouldn't be fair to other players. Most of them haven't even seen all the cards, since they can cost anywhere from two hundred coins, for something common like the Innovation card, to half a million coins for something rare like the J's card—the one with the big picture of glistening white shoes with gold wings on the sides. Basketball shoes have a cultlike following in the US, so Emerald insisted the card should have a similar following, and it's a useful card too, boosting jumping ability by 70 percent.

Me: But then why is Anubis in the tournament? What's he playing for?

The prize is 100,000 coins. What in the world does Anubis, Sir Rich AF, need another 100,000 coins for?

Emerald: Maybe he's just greedy? Maybe he's trying to overthrow me because he doesn't know how programming works? No idea. Can't sleep. Wanna battle?

My heart sinks as I look at the clock again. *Merde*, it's already seven o'clock! Did I really study that long? I only have thirty minutes to make the forty-minute journey to class!

Me: Can't, sorry. ☹ I have to get to class. But I'll be back online in time to officiate the desert semifinals tonight, promise!

I hope she's not too disappointed. There's nothing I love more than battling Emerald, when I have the time. But I don't even have time to wait for a reply. I put my computer to sleep, slip my denim vest with the cutoff sleeves off my chair, and slide into it. I grab my backpack and I'm out the door, down the stairs, and running through the streets of Paris to get to the train at Gare d'Austerlitz. I live in the thirteenth arrondissement, and my university is in the fifth arrondissement, so I have to sprint, with my schoolbag bouncing against my hip the whole way to the train, to make it on time. I can't get Anubis out of my mind. I've never seen a balance that high. Maybe we need to start offering more purchase incentives? Or increase the price of upgrades?

It feels strange to wield that kind of power from the comfort of my flat—to be able to change the economics of an entire virtual community with a little coding. Emerald addresses every *SLAY*er as a king or a queen. "We're all royalty," she always says. I guess if everyone in the game is royalty, that makes me and Emerald kind of like goddesses.

I smile at that idea as I dart onto the train and spot an empty seat next to a slender older woman with a gorgeous red Louis Vuitton handbag. She doesn't see me. She's immersed in a book called *Amour et Fantaisie* with a gold-imprinted cover. I look around to see if anyone else is going to take the seat, and when I decide to take it for myself and let go of the pole, she looks up at me. At first I think she's looking over her glasses to see me better—they might be reading glasses after all. But then she takes that gorgeous Louis Vuitton, slides it on over into the empty seat, stares up at me again, and turns her attention back to the book.

I turn around so she can't see my face flushing, hoping to keep up the illusion that I didn't want the seat anyway, that I was just getting situated and now I'm on my phone not caring. The train lurches forward, and the inertia throws me backward against a middle-aged man in a suit, and I hurriedly apologize, *"Excusez-moi. Vous allez bien?"* and he looks up at me and nods with a smile and a courteous *"Pas de problème! Votre français est parfait. D'où êtes-vous?"* which translates literally to "I'm fine. Your French is perfect. Where are you from?" or, more loosely, "Where are you from, since obviously you're not native to Paris?"

My cheeks are burning, and my eyes are getting cloudy, and I wonder if everyone in America is as nice as that couple in my neighbor's flat.

Sometimes I think I relate more to tourists than native Parisians.

"La putain de toundra," I say.

The fucking Tundra.

The keyboarding exam goes exactly the way I expect it to go. I finish in fifteen minutes and sit there slumped in my seat for the last forty-five minutes of class, staring at the computer desktop, unable to look at my phone, unable to ask Cicada how the turnout for the Desert Semifinals is looking. She was supposed to finish up renovations to the Desert arena before the duel, but I haven't heard yet what she's actually done. Harper glances over her shoulder at me, as if she's trying to absorb exam answers via diffusion. I shake my head and try not to laugh. It's keyboarding. We're taking it as seniors because even the senior version is the easiest elective we could pick.

The hardest question on the whole exam was *Which finger is correctly used to operate the backspace key?* and by "hardest," I mean the only question on the exam to make me pause before marking my answer.

Harper finally lets out a sigh and minimizes her screen,

indicating that she's done, just as the bell wails from the hall. I have no idea if she's actually done, or if she just realized she was out of time and decided to quit.

I ask her in the hallway on the way to lunch.

"Oh, you know," she says, her answer when she has no answer or just isn't paying attention. She's totally engrossed in something on her phone. "So, Kix," she continues. I think she's about to launch into that question about the dreadlocks again until she thankfully says, "I saw you finished in, like, five minutes."

I don't know what she wants me to say to this, so I let her keep talking. I think that's partially why we've been friends for so long—she fills the spaces I would otherwise leave silent.

"I feel like these exams are getting unfair. I mean, how do you make the exams a *hundred* percent of our grade and then make them *that* brutal?"

A voice chimes in with a laugh from behind us. "Did I just hear you say you think keyboarding is brutal?"

We both turn to see Wyatt just before he throws his arms around both our shoulders. He smells like hair gel and way too much body spray, and I shove his hand off my shoulder.

"Uh, yeah, I did," says Harper, shoving his other hand off her shoulder and brushing her bangs off her forehead.

"And you've got nerve to laugh at us," she continues, popping a piece of gum into her mouth. "You're in junior keyboarding. Wait till you're a senior next year, and they'll hit you with these weird-ass *hard* questions, and I won't be able to hear you whine all the way from my dorm at Princeton."

"Doubt I will." He shrugs, pulling his own phone from his pocket. "It's just keyboarding. Let me know when they start asking C++ or Java questions. Then I might actually need to study. Maybe if you played more *Legacy of Planets*, you'd be as good with computers as I am. Oh, hey, Kiers, when are we doing that interview?"

I cringe inside and consider pretending I didn't hear him, but before I can even open my mouth to protest, he's talking again.

"Harper and I really don't know if it's okay. She wants to know so she can actually *get* dreadlocks, and I want to know because the *Jefferson Weekly* hasn't had a really good article in forever. I mean a *really* good article. Something funky and unique, new and different."

He wants to interview me about a hairstyle that's been around since the dawn of time, for an article that's "new and different."

I look up at Harper, who's looking at me like she wants to apologize for asking the question in the first place. Then I shoot Wyatt a look before turning my attention back to the door at the end of the hallway. The moment of silence is brief, interrupted by a deceptively apologetic Wyatt leaping in front of me and walking backward as he maintains this unwelcome conversation.

"Aw, don't be like that, Kiers." He smiles with one hand resting on his chest. "I'm asking because I got curious last night and found an article in the *Atlanta Star* about how white people wearing dreadlocks is cultural appropriation, and I thought you might have some opinions about it for the *Jefferson Weekly*."

"I do have opinions about it," I say as we step into the cafeteria, and I leave it at that. If I tell him I think white people look ridiculous with dreadlocks, it's just going to escalate the conversation to places I don't want to go. If I tell him white people should be allowed to wear dreads, he gets to use me in all his arguments from here on out with, "But my Black friend said . . ."

Wyatt drops it for now. Long enough for me to read the menu, anyway. It's sloppy joe day, my favorite, and I quickly hop in line. The food at Jefferson is actually pretty good. When they say it's sloppy joe day, you can expect the cafeteria to smell like actual sloppy joes, and the entrée to actually *look* and *taste* like a sloppy joe. It could do with some hot sauce, but at least it's sweet and tangy like sloppy joes are supposed to be. I won't touch the cafeteria chicken, though. They make baked chicken exactly as you'd expect it to taste—like nothing. Just sad, dry chicken. Mom might transfer me back to Belmont if I bring her home a plate. Sometimes, it's tempting.

Wyatt orders two sloppy joes and double fries, no salad, because screw nutrition. Harper gets the exact opposite— sloppy joe filling without the bun, half the fries, and a gigantic salad, because #FitLife. My phone vibrates in my pocket and I shift all the weight of my tray—sloppy joe, fries, salad, apple, and milk—to one hand just so I can fish it out of my jacket pocket. I'm praying it's a message from Cicada, but the one I see instead sends my heart palpitating.

Malcolm: I see you, Queen.

I look around, searching the throngs of students in the cafeteria like I'm searching for a lion among tall grass, because I know that if the word "Spelman" comes up, and we start talking, I'll have to fake being the ecstatic ball of excitement I know he'll be expecting. But then I realize Malcolm might be the perfect diversion, the only way for me to escape Wyatt's asinine questions. So I keep searching, trying not to look too desperate to find him. Five hundred fifty-five of the students at Jefferson are white, leaving just twenty-five students of color estranged and unfamiliar with each other. Most are Indian and East Asian, a handful are Latinx, two are Filipino, and one is Sioux. Only four of us are Black—Me, Steph, Malcolm, and the new member of Beta Beta, Jazmin. When your demographic makes up such a tiny slice of the pie, it feels weird to reach out to the only students who look like you. It makes you look desperate. It makes you look shallow. It makes you wish you could retreat into a world where just once you don't feel like an outsider. It's why I created *SLAY*. I may have to deal with Jefferson all day, but when I come home, I get to pretend I'm not the minority, that my super-curly hair isn't "weird" or "funky" or "new and different." White kids read so many books and watch so many movies about white teenagers "just wanting to be normal." How do they think I feel?

I spot Malcolm. He's sitting in the far corner of the room, under the TV that's playing the local news—they *always* show the news—no games, no daytime TV, just depressing stuff. He's slouched against the wall in a plain white T-shirt and jeans, locs tied up, lineup looking clean, staring at me with that grin of his. Even after three years of dating, he still gives me butterflies. I can't help but smile back as I slip my phone into my pocket, and just as I'm about to start in his direction, Wyatt snaps me out of my thoughts.

"Hey, where ya sitting?"

With someone who won't ask me a million questions, I want to say.

"With Malcolm," I say instead. I glance at Harper, who is staring at me like she's been wounded.

"I thought you were going to help me study polynomials," she whines. "Come on, Kix, I can't do this without you. Can I come over tonight or something?"

Cicada and I are supposed to battle tonight before the tournament finals, since tomorrow is Saturday and I can sleep in. It's one of those rare times when she and I, with our knowledge of all 1,245 *SLAY* cards, can battle it out and come up with new card ideas. My favorite thing to do in the entire world.

"I . . ." I glance at Malcolm, whose smile has fallen, probably wondering why I'm looking at him, maybe interpreting it as a silent cry for help. His eyes are darting between me and Harper and Wyatt, and he stands up. I know he's about to intervene and make sure I'm okay, like he did at Belmont, unless I hurry up and defuse this. I don't need Malcolm to get confrontational and show everyone in this cafeteria that the only Black boy here can't resist a fight.

"Okay, Harper, I promise we can study tonight, okay? My place. Eight o'clock."

I hate having to cancel another duel with Cicada. So much of my time logged in is spent programming and moderating players. It's rare that I get to let my hair down and duel for fun anymore, and I know Cicada feels the same. But if it keeps Malcolm out of trouble, it's a small price to pay.

"And I'll come too," chimes in Wyatt, "so I can get my burning questions about dreadlocks answered."

Malcolm's deep voice booms from behind me as I feel his enormous hand on my shoulder.

"What *are* your opinions on dreadlocks?" he asks smoothly. "S'this for that article?" I can hear the hesitation in his voice.

"Hey," I say, intertwining my fingers in his. My phone buzzes again and I suddenly regret occupying both my hands. But it's not long before Malcolm's fingers leave mine and travel to my belt loop instead, and I can check WhatsApp.

Cicada: SOS! SOS!!!! ANUBIS IS OFFLINE.

I look up at the cafeteria clock. How is Anubis offline two minutes before the Desert Semifinals? Cicada is panicking, but I'm not. In a way, this is easier. Cicada and I get to announce a forfeiture to his would-be opponent, Spade, and move on to the finals. But people don't carve time out of their schedules to watch a forfeiture. They want a fight.

"Hey, uh, babe?" I try to keep my voice steady, so Malcolm doesn't pry. "I'm going to go sit and eat."

"Did you hear what just came out this muhfucka's mouth?" Malcolm asks me in a clearly restrained tone. I look at Harper, whose eyes are wide with panic, and then at Wyatt, with his impish smile. What *did* he just say? I had completely checked out and missed what he said.

"Sorry, Wyatt, I wasn't listening."

He shrugs.

"I just said that in some cases, white people rock dreads better than Black people."

Oh, shoot. Of all the ignorant things Wyatt has said in the years that I've known him, this might be the thing that'll finally get him knocked out. My phone buzzes in my hand, but I maintain eye contact with Malcolm instead to show that he has my full attention this time. I silently plead with him not to make a scene.

He seems to have understood me, because he says to Wyatt, "You keep thinking that," and escorts me back to his table.

I steal a glance at Cicada's next message.

Cicada: Help! What do I do??? Cancel the final round? Forfeit? ☹

I set my tray on the table, and as I'm lowering myself onto the bench beside Malcolm, I fire off a message that says, Just reschedule g2g sry.

I feel guilty. I'm abandoning her at a time of extreme

confusion. I don't blame her for panicking. She's got over one hundred thousand logged-in users waiting to watch a duel between the two reigning champions of the Desert region—the biggest region on the map. I don't know much about Cicada, but I do know she hates disappointing people, especially me. But I can't just text Cicada the whole time Malcolm is sitting here trying to talk to me. He'll get curious. He'll ask questions. He'll be hurt at the fact that I'd clearly rather text someone else than talk to the man I claim to love, right here in front of me, in the flesh.

"Ay, was Wyatt bothering you? 'Cause you know I'll lay him out," says Malcolm, wrapping his arm around my waist protectively.

I glance around the cafeteria before stealing a kiss. His lips are plump and soft, and I wish we could pause time and make out right here on this table. When it's over, I look into his dark eyes and run my finger along his jawline playfully.

"Hey, Queen," he says. His voice is soft but strained, as if he's wishing the same thing.

Another text from Cicada comes through. My lunch tray amplifies the buzzing.

Malcolm takes notice this time. He gestures at it with his chin. "Who's that?"

There's no way I'm telling Malcolm about Cicada. The first question he'd ask about her is whether she's Black. If I say she is, he'll ask questions like *How did you meet her?* and *Can I meet her?* and *What are her opinions on X, Y, and Z?* If I lie and say she's not, he'll ask questions like *Why in the world are you friends with her?* and, every time I pull out my phone, *Why are you talking to her instead of me?* although more subtly (and more likely): *S'that your new white friend?*

"It's Steph," I lie. "Boy trouble." I've been getting good at stretching the truth lately. It's becoming part of who I am, and I don't know yet if I'm okay with it, but I pop a couple fries in my mouth and layer on details to make it sound more believable.

"She's talking about this boy. Matt. Goes to Harper and Wyatt's church. I told her if he makes her happy, he's got my approval."

I take a bite of my sloppy joe and hold it level, managing to keep it all from leaking out the back of the bun. It's sweet and hot and tangy and delicious, and I already want to put two more on my plate.

"Matt," he repeats, stealing a fry off my plate and eating it. "That don't sound like a Black name."

He takes two more fries.

"Where's your food?" I ask, hoping this change of subject isn't too obvious. He has no tray, no drink, nothing. "Did you eat already?"

"Yeah," he says. He leans back against the wall, picks up his black snapback from the bench next to him, nestles it on his head, and slides it down over his eyes.

"Tired?" I ask between bites. I glance at him and his hat bobs up and down as he nods in reply. I would bet money he stayed up all night reading. In fact, Malcolm does little else at home unless I'm over. He's rarely on social media because he says it lets the government track our whereabouts, and he calls TVs "propaganda machines." He's a weirdo, but I love him. And he's not a "conspiracy theorist," as Steph says. He just entertains weird theories sometimes. He's open-minded.

"So this Matt," he continues as I shove a forkful of salad into my mouth. I take a deep breath and brace for the interrogation. "He's white, ain't he?"

"Actually, he's brown. I don't really know specifics."

This lie is quickly getting out of control, and I try to think of a new subject, but the question he asks next piques my curiosity.

"That wasn't the *first* question out your mouth?" he asks. I roll my eyes.

"Does it matter?" I ask.

Normally, I'd drop it. I don't like the idea of expending energy debating the validity of a hypothetical relationship between my sister and a possibly nonBlack boy who doesn't actually exist. But I'm curious why Malcolm thinks this is so important, so I prepare to listen.

"Hell yeah, it matters," he says, leaning forward on the table and lifting his snapback to reveal his eyes. I can feel him looking at me, and I try to focus on my salad, but the silence chips away at my resolve, and eventually I'm looking at him.

"That's exactly what the world wants, babe," he explains. "They want to *divide* us. They want to break us up. The whole white world is after the Black nuclear family. Black kings are out here with these Latina and Asian women, saying they 'don't date Black women,' and Black queens are out here deserting their kings for white dudes. And the media encourages it! That's all you see in movies anymore! 'Oh, look at this Black queen defying all odds and going to get her a white man!' Implying 'you can too!' It's sad."

If only Malcolm would *SLAY* so he could see the Black Love card. If only I could tell him just how much it means to me to build up mutual respect and adoration between Black men and Black women. If only I could show him instead of telling him.

"I get it," I say, leaning in for a reassuring kiss, "and I love my Black king."

His eyes are smiling, and he flashes me that handsome grin before snatching a few more fries off my tray and popping them into his mouth.

"That's all I'm sayin' then," he says. "Black folks wanna be out here claiming they 'down for the cause' with a colonizer on their arm. Shit makes me sick."

Wait, is he saying you can't be for the advancement of Black people if you're dating someone who's not Black?

"Uh," I begin. "What?"

He looks at me in confusion and blinks a few times before answering, "You can't truly be for us if you don't love us."

"Just because a sister or brother dates outside their race, it doesn't mean they don't love Black people."

"Prove it."

I roll my eyes. "There's nothing to prove here, Malcolm. You're confusing correlation with causation. Yes, there are Black men out there who date nonBlack women, and vice versa, but that doesn't necessarily mean they *hate* them. You can be Black, and date outside your race, *and* advocate for everybody Black."

He pauses, and the silence becomes uncomfortable. I finally look up at him as he replies, "You saying you'd date a white boy?"

What if I would? Would that instantly disqualify me from the Black advocacy Olympics? I mean, I don't think I could date a white person, solely on the basis that whoever I date would have to understand me on a level that only someone who shares my experiences could. Malcolm knows how it feels to be a Belmont transplant at Jefferson. He knows what it means to code-switch, as best as he can anyway. He knows what it means to have every word he says cross-referenced with the stereotypes already well established in the music and movies and minds of these Jefferson kids, and to be prepared to explain himself if they don't match. Malcolm gets me on a level that no other boy possibly could. Doesn't he understand that? I have to smile at how threatened he feels by this entire conversation, and I decide to lighten things up.

"I mean, I don't know, Malcolm. Have you seen that kid Avery lately?"

Avery, the boy who picks his earwax in class and eats it.

Malcolm isn't smiling with me, though. Finally, he tears his eyes away from me and pulls out his phone.

"Don't even play," he finally chuckles, but it's one of those *I can't believe this shit* chuckles, and not a *ha-ha* one.

I roll my eyes. Whatever. At least I don't have to worry about dating. At the rate Malcolm and I are going, we'll end up in Atlanta together, married one day, with little Black babies, and I won't have to think about dating outside my race and "betraying my people." It's what I want more than anything. It's what I've always wanted. The reality of it will sink in, I'll be able to share the good news about Spelman with him, and we'll both be happy. As I unfold my milk carton, the TV on the wall above Malcolm fades from a black screen, signaling the end of a commercial break—back to the news. An earnest-looking news lady is staring at the camera as if she has the news story of the century, and I read the banner flying across the screen below her that says: *Nigerian rebel leader to meet with president for peace talks.*

I sigh and take another bite of sloppy joe. More people getting killed in Africa. Malcolm says I shouldn't be shocked anymore at how often US news networks feel the need to remind Black people how much worse we would've had it if we'd stayed in Africa, which is, of course, bullshit. He thinks it's the establishment's way of driving home the idea that we should be grateful for what we have. It's their way of keeping us submissive in America.

I tend to think it's to keep us from unifying across the

diaspora and becoming as powerful in real life as our *SLAY* characters.

The banner now reads something new that strikes me.

Boy shot in his sleep over video game.

My chest tightens at the reminder of how cruel people can be. As a game developer, I'm not just an artist. I'm not just a coder. I feel a certain responsibility for the people who play my game. Their characters are an extension of them, after all. I see them all every night. We compete, we barter, we trade, we converse, we create. There are real people behind those characters, and I suddenly feel sorry for whoever developed the game behind this murder. I watch and wait to see which game it is, although I suspect it's *Legacy of Planets*, that MMORPG Wyatt always plays. That game has millions of players, some of whom have died of pulmonary embolisms from blood clots that can develop after sitting still and doing nothing but playing for days in a row. With how seriously people take *Legacy*, I wouldn't be surprised to hear of someone being killed in real life over it.

The camera pans to a reporter standing in front of a mess of caution tape, and I take another bite of my sloppy joe. I can feel Malcolm lean forward behind me and suddenly begin kissing my neck, which he could've waited to do because my mind can't focus on both the deliciousness of this sandwich and the deliciousness of Malcolm. I force a giggle, trying to look as cute as possible with a mouthful of sloppy joe, and soon I really am laughing because of how ridiculous the whole situation is.

I pick up my napkin and wipe sauce from the corners of my mouth and my fingers. Malcolm is kissing my temple as I'm swallowing and trying to stop laughing so I don't choke. He's laughing against my neck now, which makes the hair on my arms stand up.

"You gon' let me come over tonight?" he asks, his kisses making their way up to my cheek. "I miss talking to you like this, just us."

Talking. Right.

I'm suddenly tempted to text Harper that we can study math another time, that a girl has needs, and that if she's actually my friend, she'll understand. But as I'm staring up at the TV without really processing how the video-game story is playing out, the closed-captioning appears below a boy who looks a few years younger than me, tears streaming down his face, gesturing hysterically behind him toward a section of the road cordoned off by the caution tape.

It was over a damn game, man. It was a game! That's my brother in there.

And what game is that? asks the reporter.

S'called SLAY. *Homeboy and I been playing every night for forever.*

The words freeze me where I sit, and I read them again to make sure I'm not imagining it. *SLAY.* It's written in plain English on the screen, but my mind can't process the words. It takes me a moment to realize my jaw is clenched, and I suddenly feel like throwing up. By now, Malcolm has noticed the panic in my face and turned his attention up to the screen.

"Black kings been out here getting killed over money for millennia. Now we gettin' shot for *fake* money."

Malcolm looks back at me, but I'm barely paying attention as I read the screen. A middle-aged, overweight, dark-skinned woman with a cheap wig peeking out of her hair bonnet is sobbing uncontrollably, held by a man who looks to be the same age. I hear Malcolm's voice somewhere that sounds far away.

"And they gotta make sure to show these queens out here disgracing themselves by wearing them hair-hats," he says, clasping my hand, which is still sticky with dried sloppy joe sauce, between both of his. "It reminds me how lucky I am to have you."

I silently hope the cringing my insides are doing doesn't show on my face.

My phone buzzes again, but I can't get to it without pulling away from Malcolm's hands, which would be rude. He's being romantic, and the last thing I want to do is direct his attention to my conversations with Cicada.

I lean into him and kiss his cheek to distract him as I read the next text on the screen. The news is back to the boy now, and the captions spring to life again.

We ran a hustle together. We spent hours SLAYing, dueling, stacking coins. We pooled all our coins in Jamal's account so he could buy [expletive] for us. He tried to hold 'em for ransom for real dollars, and . . . this dude we never shoulda been playing with, he's bad news, man. Came and shot Jamal. He shot Jamal in his sleep for hijacking damn game coins, man! That was my brother! Jamal was my brother!

A photo overtakes the screen, this time a mug shot. Another boy who looks to be about seventeen—my age— with cold, dead eyes and a clenched jaw is glaring at the camera with blood pooling at the corner of his mouth. His skin looks sullen, dull and ashy, and his gray sweater collar looks overstretched on one side, like it came to blows just to get him to the police department for a mug shot. The name Jeremiah Marshall is plastered under the photo, above the title *SLAY Murderer*. This guy had a *SLAY* account—*has* a *SLAY* account. He has a character somewhere in the game, and a virtual wallet with *SLAY* coins in it, and he took the life of another human being because that person wouldn't return his coins—his game livelihood—after they struck some kind of deal. He murdered a child over something I created.

It all washes over me so fast. I feel dizzy.

"I'm sorry, Malcolm, I think I might be sick," I say. I snatch my backpack up from the seat, scramble out from behind the table, and before I can leave, I hear Malcolm's voice behind me.

"You bed' not be pregnant," he grumbles.

I don't even have time to be mad at him for that. I can't decide whether I need to make up this sudden departure to him later when I finally do invite him over, or demand an apology from him for that disgusting comment. With trembling hands, I pull my phone out and scan the three consecutive messages from Cicada.

Cicada: He's been offline since the quarterfinals.

Cicada: I'm rescheduling for next Thursday at six thirty p.m. your time.

Cicada: Is that okay? I'm so sorry.

My fingers fly across the keyboard as I navigate through the swarms of students and vanish down the hallway to the bathroom, where I shut myself inside a stall, lean against the wall, and try my best to breathe. I think about going to my next class, but I'm too shaky, so I decide to do what I almost never do. I'm going to skip class and go home.

Me: Cancel. I know what happened to Anubis.

Does this make me a murderer? Did I kill Jamal?

I've been staring at my VR screen so long my eyes are dry and itchy. My back and feet hurt from standing for too long. My hands are sweaty inside my gloves.

Anubis is standing in front of me. I found him on the top floor of an adobe in the Desert, where he has a bed, a nightstand, and a shelf full of armor, exactly where his human—Jamal—left him. His head is that of a short-haired black dog with a long, strong nose and glowing white eyes, and his blinding-white robe and gold sash make him look misplaced in the humble clay house.

He's moving slightly, swaying slowly from side to side as if he's real.

Have I killed him? Was it me? It feels so painfully real now to remember there are actual people behind the characters I see in my headset. This Egyptian god of a character that stands before me, who's an epic warrior here in the *SLAY* universe, is just a kid in the real world—around my age. *Was* a kid. I can't stop shaking. This is my fault. I should've been more careful. I should've included in the list of game rules that you can't trade real money for *SLAY* coins. Maybe then, Jamal wouldn't have tried to hold his tribe's *SLAY* coins for ransom once they pooled them into his account. Not like it would've done anything. People do what people do. But . . . I can't shake this feeling, tight in the pit of my stomach, that I could've done *something*.

I think back to that day I came home from Harper's house three years ago, when we both played *Legacy of Planets*—it was the very first time I was called a nigger. After I had finally customized my character, who had to be a dwarf if I wanted to make her skin tone as dark as mine is in real life, I went to the first character I saw on the map—I don't even remember his username—and he took one look at my character and whipped out that word. I never told Harper or Wyatt because I didn't want to ruin the game for them. In fact, I kept playing that day. I kept playing that week, that month, and the rest of that year. I wanted so badly to love *Legacy of Planets*, because who doesn't love the idea of having a virtual miniature them who can go on campaigns and fight dragons and gorgons with no stakes except for virtual character damage and loss of items or coins? Who doesn't want to have a world at their fingertips—where you can do whatever you want within the limits of the game, where your actions have no consequences, and where you can hide behind a keyboard without being held accountable for what you say and do? Everyone wants that freedom. And whenever I played *Legacy*, I'd hear all the things that people wish they could say to people in real life.

Even when I played as an elven princess with snow-white skin, I'd encounter parties in the woods with red armbands threatening to lynch the dwarves, the only dark-skinned characters in the game. Behavior like that goes unregulated, and I can't blame the developers. With a game as big as *Legacy*, with millions of players worldwide, it's impossible to police the words exchanged between characters. The most they can do is encourage users to report abusive behavior, but by the time anything happens to the troll, they've either vanished or created a new account altogether. And this problem isn't just in *Legacy of Planets*—it's symptomatic of the whole online multiplayer universe.

I once tried playing *Mummy*, a game similar to *Legacy* except that instead of a Lord of the Rings high-fantasy world with dragons and elves, it takes place in ancient Egypt and you can *actually* play as a dark-skinned character. Things were going fine for days. I had acquired basic armor, basic weapons, and a few spells. Then, one day, well after I should've quit, I tried to intervene in a creepy séance in the woods when the campaign leader invited me to join their ritual, and I said no, and that they should probably disband before they got in trouble. That was back when I was fourteen and thought saying "please" and "thank you" would actually get me anywhere in an MMORPG like *Mummy*. That asshole—who could very well have been an eight-year-old in real life—and his gang attacked my character and stripped me of every item I had in my inventory. My armor, my shields, my potions, my Diamond Gauntlet that I'd been saving up coins for since day one. Gone. That was the last I ever played *Legacy* or *Mummy*, and the day I downloaded the Voyage engine and googled how to add my first skybox.

I remember creating Emerald, making her skin my shade, just a few shades shy of passing the paper bag test. I designed her clothes and built her a house, wondering how I could share her with everyone I knew who needed a world like this. I created a Twitter account under a fake name and sent links to every Black person I followed, urging them to join me on the forum I called *SLAY*. I never thought the game would get this big, this time-consuming, or this dangerous. I never thought a boy would lose his life because of me. I stare at Anubis, still swaying slightly in this little clay adobe, looking directly at me. I hold out my hands and look down at them, at Emerald's hands. Would I still have created her if I had known? A message from Cicada appears in the corner of my screen and I navigate to it.

Cicada: This is my fault.

Me: How?

Cicada: If I hadn't been late coming back from class, I could have noticed Anubis was offline sooner. I could have reached out to him. I could have made sure he was okay. And maybe if I'd named myself Nubia to begin with, we might have become friends and I would've known even sooner that something was wrong. . . .

All her logic is ridiculous, but I can't tell her this.

This is part of who Cicada is. She blames herself for just about everything that goes wrong in the game. When we opened up the Swamp region a few months ago, she fell through a hole in the terrain and apologized for unearthing the hole, even though the terrain was *my* design and the hole was *my* fault.

I can't convince her this isn't her fault, but I can try to assure her that this was unpreventable.

Me: There are over 200K active players and another 300K inactive. That makes 500K human beings with SLAY characters. How many of those do you think have died in the last three years?

Cicada takes a long time to reply. I'm hoping my question helps to console her instead of making it worse. When I'm distraught, I find comfort in logic and numbers. If I hadn't gotten into Spelman, I would have wanted someone to remind me that I've still got my application to Emory, and that all hope for my romantic life isn't lost, even if Malcolm and I wouldn't be on the same campus. Even if I have to convince him that Emory wouldn't change me.

If Cicada were in such a situation, I think she'd want someone to sit there with her and just listen, and remind her that all is not lost, and that it's not her fault.

Then I think of the next best thing I can do.

I take one last look at Anubis's face and slide the *SLAY* chat panel out from the right side of my screen until it completely covers his face. I click Cicada's name, and the game shoots me at light speed over the Desert, over the dunes and the caravans and the yurts and cacti and houses and camels and the occasional oasis. I fly over the grasslands, where I spy a herd of hippos splashing through river water, a pack of hyenas close behind them, and I keep flying until the snow begins to swirl around my face and I'm looking at white mountain peaks in the distance.

Cicada: Can I tell you something?

I type *of course* but then delete it as those three dots pop up, indicating she's still typing.

Cicada: I know we never really talk about personal stuff, but Jamal's death made me realize that life is too short to miss getting to know someone like you. So here goes.

Cicada: I live in Paris.

Oh God, that's personal. What if I were a serial killer or something? What if news of where she lives got out into the *SLAY* universe? Part of me is nervous, even knowing this information. Paris. But the other half is curious, and honored that she trusts me. Paris! I smile. I've always wanted to go to Paris one day. I wonder what it's like to live there. I want to ask her, but she's still typing.

Cicada: You know I go to school, but you don't know that I'm in my second year of college at the École normale supérieure, a Paris Sciences et Lettres institution. They take only 200 students every year.

Cicada: I love school, but my parents love it more.

Wow, she's a sophomore in college! Why did I think she was my age? I reread her messages as I descend and my feet land in the snow. I begin to walk, my socks silent against the carpet in my room, and the snow crunches with each step I take up to Cicada's white cube of a house, camou-flaged among the snowy hillsides.

My green gown flies behind me as I run up to her door. Her messages are coming rapid-fire now.

Cicada: I've never dated anyone.

Cicada: I've never traveled outside Europe.

Cicada: I love Vegemite.

Cicada: I'm a Cancer.

Cicada: I've never played Candy Crush, and I think I was the only person in the world to hate "Gangnam Style" and "Nyan Cat." I'm not on social media, and I only recognize a handful of memes. In fact, I'm just generally bad at the Internet.

I'm smiling now as I knock on her virtual door. It swings open and there she is, still wearing her white gown. She did a fantastic job creating a white gown that somehow doesn't look like a wedding dress. The fluffy black fur-lined cloak helps. It looks editorial, very high fashion. Very Parisian. Her text appears above her head now.

"It's rude to come over unexpected," she says with a grin, "but I've been expecting you."

She turns and welcomes me into her house. I've only been here a few times. In her living room, she's arranged just about every yellow item that exists in the game. Yellow sofa, yellow chairs, yellow rug, creamy yellow carpet, yellow drapes, yellow dishes, yellow vases and sunflowers—everything in the room is some variation of yellow.

Cicada: So you're not mad at me?

Me: For what?

Cicada: The whole Candy Crush thing. You're not going to take away my mod rights for being unqualified to run a video game, are you?

Me: If I hired you knowing only your name and credentials, how am I going to fire you for never having played Candy Crush? If I didn't bother to ask, that's on me. But had I known . . .

I take a look around the living room just as a loud *ding!* rings out from the kitchen. She seems to float to the oven, from which she pulls out a huge loaf of bread—bigger than the oven, actually. Why did we make it that big? It's comically huge. We did make it look good, though. I can see the steam rising from it, and I take a big deep breath, wishing I could smell it. My room smells instead like lavender and shea butter.

Cicada: It's on the news here in Paris, too.

She holds out a piece of bread to me and I take it and eat and watch Emerald's energy meter tick up and up, even though Cicada's message exhausts the real me.

Me: I haven't turned on the news since. I don't know if I can.

Cicada: Jamal Rice was only sixteen. God, I've been crying all afternoon. Why can't I stop crying?!

Only sixteen. A year younger than me.

Cicada: Can I tell you something that might ACTUALLY get me fired?

I hear a doorbell ring. As Emerald, I turn around to look at Cicada's yellow door, which is closed, and then I remember she doesn't have a doorbell. I rip off my headset, gloves, and socks and hear the faint creak of our front door, and my mom's voice following shortly after with, "Hey, Harper, how're you doing, baby? It's good to see you."

Shit!

I glance at my clock: 8:05 p.m. I forgot to tell Harper not to come over tonight to study. I need time to process this—*all* of it—Jamal, the news, what to do with his character, Anubis, all these messages in my inbox. Careless, so careless of me! I yank the headset back onto my head, my thumb accidentally catching and ripping out a few hairs right at my temple. I wince and crank out the message:

Me: I'm SO sorry g2g a friend came over uninvited. B back latr.

Eyes still teary, I rip off the headset again and throw it, the gloves, and the socks back into my bottom drawer and run to my door just as it swings open and Harper's face appears before me. At first she looks happy to see me, and then she looks confused.

"What the hell happened to *you?*" she asks, stepping past me into my room and making herself comfortable on the sofa under my elevated bunk bed.

"Nothing, why?" I ask, focusing on catching my breath.

She's wearing a smug grin. "You look like you just got some *some-some* with Malcolm, except I don't see Malcolm anywhere."

I roll my eyes at her use of "some-some," whatever that is. I think she meant some'm-some'm, but I let it go. I'm not in the mood to correct her pronunciation any more than Harper's ever in the mood for correction. She's on her phone now, her thumb scrolling, meaning she's not really looking for an explanation into why I'm so sweaty. I can throw some BS at her and change the subject.

"I was practicing my dancing," I say. A story she'll buy. "You know I still can't do the Running Man?"

It may sound unbelievable, but it's the truth. I really can't dance. Mom can, and Steph can, but while Black Jesus was kissing the foreheads of other Black babies and bestowing upon them the gift of happy feet, he somehow missed me and my dad.

"No, but seriously," Harper says. "If Malcolm is here, let me know. I won't care, but things might get weird if Wyatt comes in here."

"Wait, is Wyatt here?"

She looks up at me and shrugs one shoulder. "Of course he's here. He said he'd be here. He's out in the hall, waiting for permission to enter the girls-only zone. I told him to be polite and ask first—"

As if on cue, a knock sounds at my bedroom door, and before I can protest, Harper replies, "Permission granted!" I'm not prepared for his interview questions. I'm not prepared for *him*.

"Yes, come in." I shoot Harper a look for bringing him into my house. The door swings open, and I've never been so relieved to see my little sister in my life, still wearing her shoes and backpack. She smiles at me and then notices Harper.

"Hey, girl, heyyy," she sings. She and Harper exchange an elaborate secret handshake I didn't know they had.

"Heyyy," replies Harper.

"Did you get the flyers printed for pledge?"

"I got Jazmin to do it. We'll see how she does."

"Brilliant."

Steph and Harper sit down on the sofa and I sit criss-cross on the pouf in the corner. While they launch into conversation, probably more Beta Beta Psi logistics, I pull out my phone and open WhatsApp.

Me: Sorry ☹. A friend came over unexpectedly and I had to log off. What were you going to say?

Then the app responds for her.

Cicada is offline.

I let out a frustrated sigh before I remember I'm not alone in my room.

"You okay?" asks Steph.

"I mean, it's a really sad story," says Harper. "I don't blame her."

"Blame me for what?" I ask. I'm trying so hard to sound interested while I wonder if Cicada has had enough of me leaving her hanging. Emerald is still standing in her kitchen, meaning I left my character taking up space in her house. I know it's all virtual, but it still seems inconsiderate, somehow.

"We were talking about that kid, Jamal, who was killed over a video game," says Steph. "Did you hear about that?"

I look up at them, now trying not to look *too* interested. My hands are getting clammy as I pull my shirtsleeves over my palms.

"Yeah, it was on the news today."

Harper's eyes get huge. "Isn't it so sad?" she asks. "I

can't believe how selfish humans are sometimes. We as a species should be past this."

Why is it that whenever something like this appears on the news, people want to zoom out to the species level? People who want to get to the root of a problem, the source of the cancer—don't they zoom farther *in*?

Another knock echoes from my door, and my parents don't knock, leaving the only person left in the house. Again, Harper shouts, "Permission granted!" But this time when the door opens, an impish face with a huge, mischievous smile appears, and I take a long, deep breath.

"Hey, ladies," he says, shutting the door a little too hard and glancing at me apologetically. "Hey, Kiers."

He's holding a notebook, already prepared to begin the interview. On one hand, I'm glad to be done talking about the game, but on the other hand, I'm dreading having to answer questions about whether white people are allowed to wear dreadlocks, as if there aren't thousands of Black professors who teach the nuances of this stuff every day. I wonder what he thinks his article will be contributing to the conversation.

"Shoot, I forgot my pen," he says, feeling around in his pockets.

I'm relieved but only for a moment, right up until Steph says, "We were just talking about the *SLAY* murder."

My chest tightens. That's what they've nicknamed it? The *SLAY* murder? That would make Jamal the *SLAY* victim—the victim of my creation. To think that if it weren't for me, Jamal would be alive—it washes over me like a wave, the weight of it sinking into my chest. Jamal had a family, he had friends, and all those people on TV are now missing a piece of their lives, their futures, because of what I did.

I suddenly feel nauseated, and I want to leave the room and lock myself in the bathroom until they leave. Cicada would cry if she could hear this.

"Oh, the kid who was shot over that racist game?" asks Wyatt.

Did he just call *SLAY racist*? I turn and catch him rummaging around in my desk with his arm in my bottom drawer, and panic grips me. I forgot to lock it!

"No, no, what are you doing?" I demand, jumping up and running at him. He yanks his fingers out of the way of the drawer just as I slam it shut and pull the key from my pocket to lock it. "Do you keep pens in your bottom drawer? They're in the pencil cup on the desk!"

My hands are trembling as I turn the key and hear the click, and then I glare up at him the hardest I've ever glared at him.

"Do you keep your tampons in there or something?" he says with a smirk.

My chest pounds, and I feel that sickening rage boil up inside me. Behind me, Steph clears her throat and changes the subject with what might have been my follow-up question, had I not had the first layer of my biggest secret almost exposed to the world.

"You said the game is *racist*?" she asks. "How?"

The room is silent, and I turn around to observe the answers from the two kids in the room who didn't think they'd be getting interviewed today. Harper goes first.

"I mean, they said on the news that you have to have a passcode to get in, and only Black people have the passcode, and only Black people are *given* passcodes. Sure sounds like the game excludes people based on race. That's the definition of racist."

"How is it even legal?" asks Wyatt. "If I made a video game and said it's only for white people, I'd be publicly ostracized, expelled, and probably fired from my job."

Harper shrugs. "First of all, *what* job? Second, it *isn't* legal. There are laws against that kind of discrimination. Right, Steph?"

Steph sits there with the smuggest grin and says, "It's not racist."

Harper and Wyatt look at each other in surprise, but I just smile. I've seen that smile of hers before—the one that always appears right before she drops knowledge on somebody. Her debate face. She stands up and makes her way to the middle of the room, and I get ready to watch the show.

"I want you to imagine for a minute," she begins. "I know it's going to be hard for both of you, but just imagine—that literally nothing was made for you. Your parents were denied a house because of their skin color, your grandparents were sprayed with fire hoses and ripped apart by dogs in the streets, your great-grandparents were housemaids and mammies and barely paid entertainers, and your great-great-grandparents were slaves. Every movie in your life is majority Black, all the characters in your favorite books have been cast darker in the movie adaptation for no reason, and every mistake you make is because of your skin color and because of "your background" and because of the music you listen to. You are the only white kids at a school of five hundred Blacks, and every Black person *at* that school asks you to weigh in on what it's like to be white, or what white people think about this or that. It's not fun."

Holy shit, I've never seen Steph talk to Harper and Wyatt like this before, but her voice is impressively calm as she says all this, and apparently she's not done!

"I've lived my entire life like this. *Kiera* has lived her entire life like this. If Black gamers want their own space online away from the eyes of the majority, let them have it. Y'all have *Mummy* and *Legacy of Planets*. Do you need to have everything?"

I'm smiling so big and my heart is so full. Steph has never sounded more grown-up than she does right now, standing in the middle of my room in jeans and a high-school sorority T-shirt. Maybe Steph understands me more than I thought she did. She really *has* been listening. Harper is staring at her in shock, like she doesn't know her anymore. Wyatt is looking at me.

Harper clears her throat and says, "It's not about needing their own space, Steph."

I don't like the way she says the word "their," but I stay

silent because I want to hear how she could possibly refute the magic that my sister just spoke.

"It's about the principle of exclusion," she continues. "Haven't we *all* been working toward desegregation for decades now? Haven't we already determined that separate is not equal?"

"Forget all that," says Wyatt. His face is pink, and his eyes are wild. "It's about fairness. This is a free country. We can't exclude them, and they can't exclude us. The playing field stays level."

I fold my arms and take a deep breath to calm my nerves. I'm shaking as I speak. "Video games *do* exclude us," I say, finally. I can't take being silent anymore. "Weren't you listening? Haven't you been paying attention? Think about the character selection in *Legacy*. The only way to play as a character with dark skin is to be a dwarf—an ugly, hog-nosed troll with big floppy ears and an underbite. That doesn't count."

"Oh, this is about skin color now, Kiers?" he hisses. "You're going to stir up all this hate because you can't play as a character with dark skin? Is that it?"

"No, Wyatt, that's not *it*," I snap. The rage is bubbling up in me like hot oil and if I don't let off some steam, I'm bound to burn everyone in the room. "Most fantasy games are also Eurocentric. Castles, dragons, princesses, elves, Greek and Roman gods—all of that is *your* history—"

"Whatever," he says. "That stuff is universal. Everyone knows European fairy tales, and game developers make what people know and want more of. Wasn't *Mummy* Black enough? It's set in Egypt, for God's sake—the whole point was to defeat the gods and escape the pyramids with the Sun Ruby, remember?"

"Oh right, Wyatt," says Steph. "A game set in *one* country in Africa. Our mistake for asking that Black people—12 percent of the American population—get a little more than that, maybe something about what it's like to be Black in America? Specifically, what it's like to be Black in America if you're *not* dealing drugs, soliciting sex workers, or breaking out of prison?"

Wyatt keeps talking as if he hasn't heard a word of what Steph and I just said.

"Whatever. If the developers really wanted to show us what it's like to be Black in America, they wouldn't have hung a big sign on the log-in screen that says 'No whites allowed,'" he grumbles. "And it's a video game, not Area 51. It's only a matter of time before someone hacks in, tracks down the developers, and sues the shit out of them."

The room goes dead silent. Wyatt is a bit redder in the face than he was when he walked in here. Harper is staring uneasily at her brother, and Steph is looking at me like, *Do you see this mess?*

I must be giving her the same look, because she clasps her hands together and asks, "Who wants a snack? Let's all go to the kitchen. Kiera, want to meet us there in a few?"

I nod as she swings open the door and ushers Harper and Wyatt out of my space just before I hear Wyatt's voice fade down the hallway, saying, "But seriously, when Dad comes home, I'm going to ask him about talking to Duncan."

I don't have the energy to even care who Duncan is—probably one of their dad's rich coworkers. As my door clicks closed, I send a silent *thank you* into the air, grateful for Steph's ability to see just how uncomfortable all this is making me, even though she doesn't know the extent of the *why*. I lean my head back against the wall and take in the silence.

But all I can think about is Jamal. What do I do? A boy is dead because of me. His friend has announced on national news that our beloved world, the *SLAY* universe, exists. My game has been called racist. I, by extension, have been called racist. My sister is the only one who has my back, but she doesn't even know I'm the developer. I have a friend in Paris I know nothing about, who is probably sick and tired of me being unreliable. Spelman is already disappointing me, and I don't know why, and if I don't go, I'll be disappointing my sister and my boyfriend, the two most important people in my life.

I open my phone, take to Google, and search his name—Jamal Rice—which brings up dozens of photos of the same Black boy with narrow eyes and a button nose. Most of them are the same grainy photo of him standing on one side of a Ping-Pong table in front of a faded yellow wall with yellow lighting that makes it look like he might be at a gym or a Boys & Girls Club. He's staring piercingly at the camera with a Ping-Pong paddle in one hand, making a peace sign with the other. I have to look away for fear of crying, but I can almost feel his eyes still on me. Without me, he would've had a chance to grow up.

I realize my hands are clasped hard enough to cut off circulation. My jaw hurts. My head hurts. I'm hungry but I don't feel like eating.

I feel like escaping.

I slip my phone into my back pocket, lock my door, unlock my bottom drawer, don my VR gear, and dive into the game. My inbox has burgeoned from six hundred messages to over sixty thousand, and I already know it's going to be full of stress. The subject lines confirm my suspicions.

> *ANUBIS IS DEAD??*
> *WHERE'S ANUBIS????*
> *WAS THE BOY ANUBIS?*
> *Anubis = Jamal?? Domino = Jeremiah??*
> *Vigil for Anubis @ Desert arena*
> *#BlackLivesMatter*
> *#Justice4Anubis*
> *#Justice4Jamal*
> *Orisha Tribe Forever* ✊🏿
> *Jamal Rice—Never forget*
> *Ban Domino!*
> *KING ANUBIS IS DEAD. LONG LIVE*
>   *THE KING.*

My eyes are getting cloudy with tears again and I close out of my inbox, but not before one message catches my eye. I reopen the inbox and find it again. The subject is simple and soothing, like medicine.

Wanna battle?

I click on it. It's from a player named Q.Diamond. I can't reply *yes* fast enough. I need a break. I need to pretend for a few hours that everything is back to normal, that Jamal is still alive, that Harper and Wyatt won't be back at my door soon asking why I haven't joined them for snacks. My plan right now is to holler through the door that I'm not feeling well, and Harper and I will have to study another time, wait for them to leave, and then hop back into the game when Cicada might be online, so I can finally ask her what she wanted to tell me about herself. I hope she was joking, and that I won't actually want to fire her after she tells me what it is.

I decide to send a follow-up message to Q.Diamond.

Me: I'll battle you on one condition. Promise not to ask questions. Especially about Anubis. I need a break for a while.

Q.Diamond: You need a vacation. I get it. I won't ask questions, but I will say this isn't your fault and I know you'll get us through this. You've gotten us through a lot.

It melts me. The *you've gotten us through a lot* part. And the *us* part. Who is *us* exactly? I know they're probably talking about everyone who SLAYs. But I hope they don't also mean *us* as in, the Black community. My throat closes at the thought. I'm just a game developer. I'm no pioneer. I'm certainly not qualified to lead the global crusade of Black people to victory. But I can't help rereading that word "us," and feeling something warm and tingly settle in the pit of my stomach. Responsibility? Pressure? The expectations of over half a million people? I don't know what to say back, so I just click *Start Duel*.

Me: Where to?

Q.Diamond: You pick.

Me: No preference. I know them all.

Q.Diamond: Swamp region. It's my home.

Me: Done.

I scroll through the list of all six regions, ranked by popularity—Tundra, Desert, Savanna, Forest, Rain Forest, and finally, the Swamp. My heart begins to pound as I click on it, and the three Swamp arenas appear in a drop-down menu—Beyoncé Bayou, Bluegrass Basin, and Drinking Gourd. I select Beyoncé Bayou, and the trees spring up in the murky water around me. An alligator swims across the screen behind Q.Diamond, but it's just a shell—not dangerous if you fall into the water during a match. Mosquitoes buzz in my ear. Cicada has made them sound a little too real, but I guess nothing can really be too real in a VR game. I have to remember to compliment her when she's online later.

The square dueling ring rises up from the water under me, and then Q.Diamond appears. Their face is covered up with a jet-black mask. They have two long, dark elf ears *and* bright red deer antlers, and their hair is long, pin-straight, and paper-white. Their eyes are sky blue, they have the muzzle of a dog, their arms are purple tentacles, and they stand upright, balancing on a hot-pink-and-green mermaid tail.

They're truly a sight. I don't think I've ever seen a character so . . . unique. Not what I would've chosen, but it's somehow a relief to see the really out-there characters show what they can do and let their imaginations run hog wild. Although I can't imagine why a character this magnificent would want to live in the Swamp region. Most characters who live in the Swamp are beginners, because it's an easy place to start the game. Anyone can find fish bones and turn them into arrowheads. It's a great way for novices to make fast money. Most of the more advanced characters who make their homes here weave baskets from vines and turn the sturdy wood from these trees into canoes to sell to those who live near water in other regions. They almost always wear browns and greens to blend in with their surroundings, as many aren't in the game to duel, but to make a virtual life for themselves, like you can do in *Legacy of Planets*. But I don't know what Q.Diamond is doing living in the Swamp. They have absolutely no camouflage.

They reach up and remove the black mask, and I realize their face is painted in vertical rainbow stripes, a design I released for Pride Month last year. It didn't cause as much of an uproar as I suspected it might, which was a pleasant surprise. I'm happy it made Q.Diamond happy. I'm grateful for little reminders like this, reminders that this game wasn't a mistake.

The deck of golden cards shuffles itself in the air between us before distributing our six cards, and then the timer begins counting down from ten seconds. I click and drag my cards into pairs at random without really looking at them, since I know all the cards and I want Q. to have a fair shot. I reach up and stretch my arms high above my head and yawn.

My phone buzzes in my pocket, and since Q. is still sorting their cards, I slip the goggles up onto my forehead, take out my phone, and unlock it. I expect it to be a text from Steph asking if I'm okay, but it's from Malcolm. My throat closes as I read it.

Malcolm: I better not find out you play that shit.

Malcolm is a lot of things, moody being the most annoying, but he's never aimed his raw anger directly at *me* before, and my blood is jumping. I reread his text. *I better not find out you play that shit* . . . or what? I think of Atlanta. I think of our life together at Spelman and Morehouse and all the nights we've spent in each other's arms, dreaming of a future in which we can live surrounded by people who won't treat us differently because of how we look, and I wonder if Malcolm would give all that up if he found out I play video games. All our plans, gone? Just like that? I glance at my door as if I half expect him to be standing right there. It suddenly feels colder in my room, and I toss my phone on the soft carpet and try to focus on the match.

But I can't stop imagining what Malcolm would say if he knew I *SLAY*—or what he might do if he finds out I created this.

NEW ORLEANS, LOUISIANA

My name is Jaylen, and I can't believe I'm about to start round three of a duel with my celebrity crush.

Most people wouldn't consider her a celebrity, but I do. Most people haven't named themselves after a precious jewel because she did, but I have. She's as magnificent up close as she has been in the arenas. I've tried replicating her algae-green dress so many times, but I can never get the design right. Mine always ended up looking like tacky prom dresses. So eventually I gave up and gave myself a huge black robe instead, kind of like PrestoBox.

I still think Presto was robbed in that duel against Zama. Who uses a Hustle card in the last round of the semifinals? A bad sport and a crybaby, that's who. Cruel.

I look at the cards I've got for round three. Emerald's cards are already on the floor in front of her, and her fingers hover over the one on the left. I'm in the lead, 1200–800, and I might have a shot at this if I can use these last two right. I wipe the sweat from my forehead. I got these gloves at a garage sale. They're fabric, and there's a hole in the left index finger where one of the sensors keeps popping out, but I can't afford new ones, so I've got to work with what I got.

I couldn't ask for better round-three cards. The Mumbo Sauce card and the Louisiana Barbecue card, which don't really go together in real life, since mumbo sauce is mostly found in the DC area, and it's almost impossible to find authentic Louisiana barbecue anywhere but Louisiana. You'd never see sweet and tangy mumbo sauce at a Louisiana barbecue, but Q.Diamond does what she wants, and today she's serving Louisiana barbecue with mumbo sauce.

I kneel and touch Louisiana Barbecue first, using my right hand since my left glove is prone to act up. The card flips over, and I whip out a giant brochette from under my robe. I look at it and take a moment to appreciate the artwork. The meat looks juicy enough to eat. The barbecue sauce glistens so pretty I could lick it right off. I want to tell Emerald how beautiful it is and ask her if she lives in Louisiana like I do, but I don't have time to open my keyboard before she calmly, like the goddess she is, touches her card and holds out both her hands facedown. Then she points at my feet. I look down.

My feet have sunk into the floor of the dueling ring, which has turned into a thick, bubbly yellow mess that looks like lava. Then her card flies up and appears in the corner of my screen.

Mom's Mac and Cheese.

I try to move my feet, but the floor is too thick and gooey. How appropriate. She's hexed my Louisiana Barbecue with Mom's Mac and Cheese. If I were on my deathbed and had to pick a last meal, I don't know which one I'd ask for.

"Well played, Queen," I say aloud. I suddenly hope nobody heard me upstairs.

I'm tempted to take off my headset just to check for footsteps coming down into the basement, but Emerald is moving again. Her hands produce fireballs hovering just above her fingers, and her second card flies up into the top corner of my screen.

Fuck. Another Battle card. Good ol' Alabama Sunshine hot sauce kicking my ass again.

My dad thought it'd be funny to put a hit of that in my juice bottle at a cookout when I was little. I barely remember it, but Granny loves talking about it. She always follows that story up with, "My Louisiana baby boy grew into a hot-sauce man."

She still doesn't know I'm a *she*.

Nobody knows, and I can't imagine when I'll be able to tell them. Sunday after church never seems like the right time, and weekday evenings after class at my Christian high school don't seem right either. My parents both work Saturdays, and so do I, and I absolutely cannot tell them over the phone or by text, because then the anger will just build over the course of the day, and the whuppin' will be even worse.

Emerald isn't throwing fireballs at me and I wonder if she's having connection issues. Doesn't feel right clubbing her with a meat kabob while she's stuck, so I send her a message.

Me: Go on! Don't go easy on me!

Emerald: Thought you might be having connection issues.

Without warning, my screen erupts into a burst of fiery fury, knocking me back a couple of steps. Certain parts of my parents' basement creak, and the explosion from the fireball is so loud in my headset that I can't tell if I stepped on a bad floorboard.

I don't have time to check. I swing my brochette as hard as I can, but she just leans back to dodge it. My feet are still stuck in this mac and cheese, but I dodge fireballs like Muhammad Ali. I was so happy when the Muhammad Ali card got approved. I'm the one who proposed it. I hope she holds another poll soon. More fireballs. I can hear them whizzing past my ears, and I'm so glad I spent the extra ten dollars on a binaural headset instead of the regular one, which transmits sound equally through both headphones. It makes this feel so much more real.

I glance at the board. That damn fireball blow cost me four hundred freaking points, and now we're tied 800–800. My other card—Mumbo Sauce—is sitting there unused. I consider canceling the brochette and switching to the Mumbo Sauce so I can have something to throw at her, and I'm grumbling to myself.

Why did I put both my Battle cards in round three?

It's a rookie move, which I thought would give me the element of surprise. Once Emerald looked at my stats, I knew she wouldn't think I'd leave both my Battle cards for the last round. Reverse psychology usually works in this game. But then again, it didn't work out so well for PrestoBox, either.

I grab my Mumbo Sauce card, stack it on top of my Louisiana Barbecue card, and start swinging, hurling globs of that sweet, tangy goodness straight at her. I don't hold back, swinging an invisible baseball bat in the middle of my parents' basement, trying to be as quiet as I possibly can.

She can't dodge fast enough! She ducks and leans and jumps out of the way, but eventually one hits her square in the chest and she goes flying backward off the edge of the ring and splashes into the murky water.

I'm grinning so hard my face hurts as I look at the score-board: 800 – 500, and the clock is ticking down the seconds.

3 . . . 2 . . . 1 . . .

Yes! Yes, I win! I'm so happy I start dancing, listening to those sweet victory drums pounding in my headset. I can't describe how spectacular it feels to beat the developer of *SLAY* in a duel. She's climbing out of the Swamp, and I extend my hand to help her back up into the ring and pull her into a hug.

I'm sure I look ridiculous standing down here in the dark by myself with my arms in a weird hugging position, and I know there's no one here with me, but I still feel like I can *feel* her somehow. I mouth the words "thank you," and my cheeks burn with tears. I don't think she'll ever understand what she's done for me. To have a place like this where I can be who I am is indescribable. It feels like waking up for the very first time.

"Jaylen!"

The voice startles me so bad, I rip off the headset and hurl it—I don't even know which direction—until it makes contact with my computer screen. Glass shatters and shards make a tinkling noise as they scatter all over the room, and everything goes dark.

Oh, my God. No, no, no. No!

I scramble to find the headset, kneeling and feeling my hands along the floor. The gloves and socks protect me from the glass. I just have to be careful not to set my knees down as I move. The light flickers on, bringing everything to life again, and I jump to my feet and look across the room to the stairs, where my mother is standing in her nightgown, holding a cigarette in one hand. She told me she quit.

"Just what are you *really* doing down here at that computer, Jaylen? Huh? At eleven at night while you're supposed to be sleepin'?"

I swallow and try to keep my breath calm. I can feel my pulse in my throat as I watch her walk down the stairs toward me. A tear falls. Dammit. I can't wipe it away or she'll know. But if she comes closer, she'll see and tell me that men of God weep for nothing.

"Now, I'm not mad at you."

That's a lie.

"But I already know what's going on, and I think it's time you and I had a talk about what you do in the dark."

I know what she thinks I'm doing down here, and this time, that's not what's happening. I've never been caught watching porn, but I'll admit to doing that if it can keep her from finding out about *SLAY*. And if I'm ever able to afford another monitor.

I wonder if my character, Q.Diamond, is standing as shit scared as I am right now in the middle of that ring in the Swamp. I wonder what Emerald is thinking watching me. I wonder if I'll ever see her again.

Mom gets close enough to touch me, and panic tingles all through my body. I know I can't dodge her hands nearly as well as I can dodge Emerald's fireballs. She yanks her hand up into the air and lunges at me, and I reflexively go reeling backward into the couch in my room, my arm catching the lamp in the corner.

"I'm sorry!" I scream. "I'm sorry!"

Her eyes are wild with rage, her backhand still raised threateningly, but the corners of her mouth tip upward for a split second, and I realize there's a hint of triumph in her face. There's a satisfaction at seeing the fear in my eyes.

My terror melts into anger. Anger at myself, for giving her that.

"You let me catch you down here looking at naked girls on that computer again and I'll drag your ass to the church steps and beat the love of God into you, y'hear?"

"Yes, ma'am." I'm sobbing now. I can't help it. I'm curled up on the couch with my eyes shut tight, listening to her footsteps getting fainter and fainter and creaking up the stairs. I listen for her to slam the door before I grab the only pillow down here, which smells like cat pee and mothballs, but I don't care right now. I bury my face into it and scream all the air out of my lungs as loud as I can, until my toes curl and I can feel my blood pulsing through my body.

I scream for Emerald, for Q.Diamond, and for me.

I know when I'll be able to tell my parents who I really am.

When they're dead.

I woke up this morning—Saturday—to a message from Cicada. I was so happy to hear from her, itching to ask her what she wanted to tell me, that I didn't realize what she'd said until I read it three times:

Cicada: You're on the news.

Me: What?

Cicada: They're talking about you. Look.

There's a YouTube link. My questions for her can wait. I click the link and watch as two white newscasters—a man and a woman—begin assessing the validity of my game with a middle-aged Black man on the other side of the screen.

"We have Dr. John Abbott on our show tonight," says the white guy, whose shoulders look like he could use a long massage. "He's a professor of African American studies at MIT. John, thank you for joining us tonight. This game called *SLAY* . . . what is it? Where did it come from? And is it racist?"

There's a moment of silence as the sound transmits from the newscaster to John, a Black man in his fifties or sixties with square glasses and worry lines in his forehead, and I hold my breath, wondering which side he'll end up on, wondering if he plays in secret or if, like Steph, he'll advocate for it anyway.

"Yes, the game is called *SLAY*, and although I've never played myself, I understand it's very violent. If you remember *Tokyo*, the card game of monsters and violent duels, it's a lot like that. Players log in, they create a persona, and then they fight each other to the death. It's quite gruesome."

I'm really getting tired of these ignorant-ass people who don't even play weighing in on *my* game. This wasn't even for them. It was for me. I should have kept Emerald to myself.

"As far as whether it's racist," John continues with a shrug, "I haven't played, so I cannot weigh in on whether it's exclusionary, but if it is, then of course it's racist—"

What? I want to throw my phone. A new banner message pops up from Cicada at the top of my phone that says, **What do we do now?**

The female newscaster, with long brown hair and hazel eyes, starts asking questions.

"But, John," she begins, "when a new user goes to the site and tries to set up an account, they're met with this image."

I'm horrified to see the *SLAY* log-in screen, with those big green letters, appear on my phone—the ones I wrote:

Welcome to SLAY. To create an account, you'll need a passcode from a friend who already SLAYs.

"So, it is exclusionary then, Jan," says the male newscaster.

"Yes, and a local mom has written to us about this with her concerns, saying, 'My son asked a friend in his class if he plays *SLAY*, and his friend said yes. But when my son asked for a passcode, his "friend" told him, "You can't play because you're white."'"

The male newscaster looks shocked and appalled, as if Black kids aren't treated unfairly every day in *Legacy of Planets*.

The professor is impressively calm as he replies, "Do we know, Derek, if this is a reflection of the game's official policy, or an isolated incident?"

I make a fist and mouth the word "yes" as I'm silently rooting for Dr. Abbott. He may not *SLAY*, but at least he's looking at this situation with some damn common sense. Let's go with the isolated-incident theory and wait until white people forget about this so we can go back to our Nubian realness in peace.

Jan says, "Mr. Abbott . . ."

I imagine an alternate universe in which Professor Abbott interrupts her with, "That's Dr. Abbott."

But in this reality, he doesn't, and Jan continues. "There have been several cases like this all over the state of Washington. We've been getting e-mails since this morning, when Jamal Rice was murdered, bringing to light this underground community. This is the boy in Kansas City who was caught in the cross fire of a disagreement between two friends over ownership of coins in the game. According to his brother, Jamal's tribe of three pooled their coins into Jamal's account so they could buy every single *SLAY* card in the game, but Jamal changed his mind in the middle of the deal and held the coins for ransom in exchange for real US dollars, and that's when things went sour. Derek, we've got 'tribes,' we've got 'coins,' and now we've got a murder. This is sounding more and more like an underground Internet gang! And this violent game is excluding white players on the basis of race. I just don't know how you can entertain the argument that this isn't racist."

A *gang*! I growl and pace across the carpet in my room. They actually called us a gang! Malcolm says this always happens when Black people gather in large numbers, no matter what it's for. "Where one Black man is, there is a thug," he says. "Where two or more are gathered, there is a gang. So sayeth the word of the white man."

I laughed when he said it, but I'm beginning to wonder if he's right.

Come on, Professor, I urge.

"I think the factor that we're missing here," he begins, "is the lens of gaming while Black. When I was a young man, I used to play video games. Sometimes I watch my little nephews play *Legacy of Planets*, and the number of times I hear expletives hurled at them would make you sick. The number of times I hear the *N* word aimed at them—they're six and eight years old—should make you angry. I think what we're missing is the understanding that the world of online gaming is naturally cruel, naturally dog-eat-dog, very exclusive, and in some cases, hostile toward people of color."

Derek opens his mouth, and I find myself holding up a silencing finger just like Dr. Abbott does before he continues.

"I think Black gamers deserve to have a safe arena in which they can play freely without having to deal with racial slurs and the threat of violence to them should they win a campaign."

I can't help but laugh at his use of the word "campaign." He must know *something* about *Legacy of Planets*. He'd probably love *SLAY*. I hope he's lying and actually plays. We need more people like him rallying for us.

And then he goes and disappoints me.

"As for the question of the game being racist," he continues, "we absolutely cannot solve this problem with more division in the gaming community. What we need right now is unity and constructive discourse to develop a solution that doesn't exclude anyone, especially on the basis of race."

This man is really trying to *all lives matter* my game. I want to click the home screen. I feel like I can't watch any more without popping a blood vessel, but I remember that I'm listening for them to talk about me, Emerald, so I sit back down on my sofa and kick my feet up on the pouf.

"I think we're all on the same page here," says Derek, clasping his hands and looking directly at the camera. "And we're learning now about the game's elusive creator, known only as Emerald. All we know of him is that he created the game three years ago, as 'a fabulous mecca of Black excellence in which Nubian kings and queens across the diaspora can congregate, build each other up, and SLAY.'"

What about that quote could they possibly find threatening to their existence? Who, in a court of law, would challenge that mission statement as discriminatory? They didn't even want into our world until they found out about it.

"I mean, the very *name* of the game seems to incite violence, right?" asks Derek. "SLAY—it just sounds so vicious, doesn't it?"

"It absolutely does, Derek. Frankly, I'm offended by the silence of this mysterious developer, Emerald," affirms Jan. "He's the one we should be tracking down and demanding answers from."

I swallow and grip the phone harder.

"Well," continues Jan, "we thank you, Professor, for your time. Parents, if you're as disturbed by this news as we are, be vigilant about what your kids are playing online. In these times, we need to be more careful than ever. I'm Jan Fitzgerald with Derek Bennett. Thank you for joining us tonight. Join us Sunday night at eight for an exclusive interview with Dr. Brandon Cannon, associate professor of civil rights law at Sutton University, to help us determine whether this 'game' is a step in the right direction for diversity, or discriminatory."

The fact that they even have to *ask* that question makes my heart race with rage. I close the app and resist the urge to throw my phone across the room. I've gotten another couple of messages from Cicada that I hadn't noticed.

Cicada: I can't believe these people.

Cicada: Emerald? I'm sorry if that video upsets you. I didn't mean to freak you out. I'm sorry.

Cicada: It's just that I'm so freaked out myself right now. I can't believe they're actually trying to hunt you down! Have any local news stations contacted you yet?

Cicada: What are we going to do?

Cicada: I'm sorry. I should never have sent this to you. You're probably panicking about this, and there's nothing we can do about it. This doesn't fix anything. It was so inconsiderate of me. I'm sorry.

First of all, in the mind of the news, I'm still a *rumor*, so there's no need for us to panic, even though that's easier said than done. And second of all, once again I find myself having to remind Cicada that she hasn't disappointed me.

Me: It wasn't inconsiderate. I'm actually glad you sent me this. I need to know what's going on, even if it's not happy news. Thanks, Cicada. I appreciate you.

Cicada: You're not just saying that? You're not mad?

Me: Have you ever seen me get mad at anyone for stating facts? ☺ I really do appreciate you sending me this. Thank you.

Cicada: Thank God. ♥

I *do* need to know what the news is saying about me, and I *am* grateful to Cicada for having my back and sending this to me, but my hands are definitely shaking. I don't even know how these people would track down and identify me. All they have is my username and a masked IP that I've set to keep shuffling so my location changes every thirty seconds. Technically, if they took me to court or something, they'd be suing Emerald, not me, which matters. I remember when the CEO of NoonMoon was outed and the company was sued for plagiarizing a game ironically named *Moral Hazard*. NoonMoon no longer exists, but the CEO still has his house in the Hamptons. I'm sure it also helped that he probably had top-notch legal counsel.

Then I realize what I need to do.

I climb out of bed, get dressed, grab my backpack and a granola bar from my top drawer, slip my feet into my shoes, pick up my phone, and head out the door and down the street, trying to breathe deeply and enjoy this cool Saturday morning. I read Cicada's next text.

Cicada: So then, what now? I'm following your lead here.

Under her message, I add my reply:

Me: We're going to get a lawyer.

BOSTON, MASSACHUSETTS

My name is John, and when it comes to playing video games, I have no idea what I'm doing.

When my brother and I were kids, we used to bike home from school, pick up a box of Milk Duds from the corner store, and play pinball at the nickel arcade. It was easy. There were exactly two buttons and only three instructions: Pull the pin. Click the levers. Don't let the ball fall in the hole.

But *this*? This thing I'm watching the boys play? *Legacy of Planets*? There's a headset, gloves, socks, a computer screen, *and* a controller with fifty buttons. I've heard them talk about riding rhinos, building watchtowers and catapults, crafting lizard suits, mixing elixirs from crystals in the mountains, and yesterday they dueled some guy who apparently hailed from a tribe of man-size cobras. There's an entire world in that game, and I don't even know where to begin in understanding it.

Joshua and Asher are standing side by side in the living

room, each with a lime-green headset over their eyes. Asher, my eight-year-old nephew, is at the helm, navigating through a settings screen, modifying a series of what look like health bars, talking to Joshua like they're on another planet. I'm watching the computer screen from the kitchen, as if they're playing a regular PC game without VR. But the boys can see the same world through their goggles, fully immersed in *Legacy of Planets*. Apparently, the goggles are optional. You don't *need* them to play the game, but Asher made it clear last Christmas that playing *Legacy of Planets* without goggles is like playing basketball without shoes—it's possible, but not nearly as fun.

"Do we have enough coins for the cheetah suit yet?" asks Asher.

Joshua shrugs and adjusts his headset, which is too big for him and keeps slipping down on his head. They don't make them for six-year-olds.

"That's the king of the Savanna—Orion. I'm not gonna duel him," says Asher, reaching over and tapping his little brother's arm before pointing to the screen. "But this guy over here? BlackBeetlejuice? He's new. Look at him. Two cards, no armor, and he's won *one* out of eight duels. I can take him down. Give me your crossbow, and we'll split the coins fifty-fifty."

"I wanna duel the lion," protests Joshua.

Asher laughs and asks, "You really think we can take down Orion the Lion? That's *nuts*."

Joshua nods. "Maybe? What are our cards again?"

I smile at the sight of them getting along. Virtual reality

games seem to make everything a competition between them, but it also seems to foster collaboration. With the little I've heard them play, they've loaned each other weapons, pooled their money, and given each other tips as they duel other players. I smile and pick up my wineglass and take another sip, scrolling through my phone and resisting the urge to look up footage of my own interview. As a general rule, I don't torture myself that way. Whatever I said earlier, I said. Watching it later won't change anything. If my tie was crooked on live TV, I don't want to know. I hear my little sister, Candace, enter the room from behind me.

"Heyyy," she sings, gliding into the kitchen and reaching past my head for the bottle. "Saw you on the news looking like you *own* MIT. You did great! Saw the whole thing, didn't we, boys?"

She grabs the empty glass on the counter and pours until it's halfway full. Her purple braids are tied up into a loose ponytail on top of her head, and her face is makeup free, looking freshly washed. She's leaning comfortably against the counter in a gray sweatshirt that's two sizes too big for her, with holes eaten into the sleeves from excessive wear.

"Boys, did you say hi to your uncle when he came in?"

Neither Asher nor Joshua responds. They don't turn around. They don't flinch. Understandable, since I'm over so often now, this place is like a second home to me.

"*Boys!*"

They both jump, their heads whipping around, and yank off their headsets.

"Say hi to your uncle."

Asher greets me dutifully with, "Hi, Uncle John," but his smirk asks, *Why are you bothering me?*

He's getting to that age now. But Candace seems more than prepared for it.

"I told you—if you can't hear me with the headset on, it's too loud," she scolds, tipping the wineglass up and taking a long drink. Asher shakes his head, pulls his headset back over his eyes, and turns his attention forward again. Joshua is still smiling at me, headset in hand.

"Hi, Uncle John," he says sweetly.

"Ah, my favorite nephew," I say, holding out my arms as exaggeratedly as I can. Joshua runs to me and I get down from my chair and kneel so he can throw his little arms around my neck. Sure enough, this catches Asher's attention, but not enough for him to fully turn around.

"Nice try, Uncle John, but he already knows I'm your favorite."

"Whatever," says Joshua. I smile at him now. His bright little eyes turn back to his brother, transfixed on the computer screen again.

"What's *that* one?" he exclaims, darting back over and picking up his headset. He can't get it over his head fast enough.

"They're on that game all the time now," Candace says. She leans on the counter and picks at a hangnail. "I thought *Legacy of Planets* was bad, but all they ask for now is *SLAY*."

My chest tightens. My eyes fly from the computer to my

sister. They're playing *SLAY* right now? I clear my throat and climb back onto the bar chair.

"I know," she says, leaning in and softening her voice so they can't hear us across the room. "I *did* see the interview. I wish I'd never even let them create accounts. Asher's friend Noah gave him a code at school a month ago, and Asher gave Joshua a code, and before I know it, I'm coming home to them talking about Nubian gods and goddesses instead of dire wolves and dragons. I can barely keep up."

She tips the last of the wine from the glass into her mouth and pours herself another, this time filling it almost to the brim. She sighs deeply and presses her face into her hands in exasperation.

"Did you mean it, John?" I hear her mumble.

She looks up at me, and her eyes are wide, searching mine. I sigh and refill my glass. I'm not an alcoholic, but after long days like this, I appreciate the hum of a smooth wine in me. I swirl it around in the glass and smell it this time before answering.

"I always say exactly what I mean," I reply, but I know what she's really asking, and I lower my voice and lean in so the boys can't hear. "It's a game, Candy. Like any other video game, it can be an innocent learning tool, or it can be dangerous."

I see the disappointment in her eyes. I would love to sit here and tell her that this thing her children have fallen in love with is something she can write off as safe, that she isn't releasing her six- and eight-year-old sons into the cruel arms of interactive gaming. That they won't be parented by the other players. But as long as she's gone most of the day, leaving them to spend their free time however they please from the time school gets out until almost bedtime, she's giving up control to whatever and whoever is in that game.

"I just . . ." She picks at her fingers again. "I can't get that boy's face out of my head."

There's a lump in my throat now, and I take a sip of wine, which doesn't help. I stare at the counter, but I can feel her looking at me.

"Jamal Rice," she says. "That photo they keep showing of him playing Ping-Pong. He looks just like Asher. Just *like* him! He was only a baby. And someone shot him dead as he slept."

A tear falls from her face and lands very close to the spot on the counter I'm staring at. I shut my eyes and remember my words in the interview.

I think Black gamers deserve to have a safe arena in which they can play freely without having to deal with racial slurs and the threat of violence to them should they win a campaign.

I stand by what I said. With everything I am, I stand by it. I look up at my nephews now, playing side by side, the glow of the computer turning them into silhouettes. They're little men—little Black men growing up down the street from Harvard University and MIT. They have every opportunity before them if they want it, if they seize it.

Should they be allowed to play online multiplayer games? I don't know. Should they be allowed access to safe spaces should they *choose* to play online multiplayer games? Absolutely.

"Ooh, look at this one!" exclaims Asher. "Says it's . . . the Satchmo card?"

This catches my attention and snaps me from my thoughts. I look at the screen as the card appears, a bloodred rectangle with an ornate golden border. The card hovers in midair and rotates slowly, light glinting off the border and the glistening golden trumpet in the center.

"What's that about Satchmo?" I ask.

They both turn around, lift their goggles, and look at me in surprise, and then look at each other.

"It's uh . . ." Asher shrugs. "It's some jazz card, I think. It lets you play a trumpet super loud and knock points off your enemy in a duel."

"Well, of *course* it does!" I exclaim. I push myself away from the kitchen bar and step down into the living room. "If the card is named after *the* Satchmo, I bet it'll do some significant damage."

"What's a Satchmo?" asks Joshua.

I can only hope these boys at least know Satchmo by his real name.

"More like *who* is Satchmo," I say, lifting my arms. "The great Louis Daniel Armstrong himself."

The boys exchange glances before looking at their mother. I look at Candace in just as much surprise.

"You haven't told these boys about *the* Louis Armstrong? What kind of household are you running here?"

That gets her to smile and roll her eyes.

"I was too busy playing classic R and B around here. They may not know who Louis Armstrong is, but I made sure they know who was taking over for the nine-nine and the two thousand."

"Oh, for the love of God," I say. "Someone deal me in. Y'all gotta learn today."

I'm going to fail miserably at this, but what kind of uncle would I be if I let my two nephews wander this earth ignorant of the history of jazz music? So I walk my fifty-five-year-old ass into the living room and stand right between the two of them. Asher and Joshua look up at me like I just announced we're all going to pack up our bags, hop in the car, and drive to Florida for a trip to Disney World.

"Josh, give him your headset and stuff," commands Asher.

"Noooo," whines Joshua. "I wanna play with Uncle John."

"I'll play with each of you in turn," I promise, and after a spirited three-game tournament of Rock Paper Scissors, Asher relinquishes his headset, gloves, and socks to me. I'm impressed the gloves and socks are stretchy enough to fit me. They're disgustingly sweaty, and I wonder if they're even machine washable, and how long it's been since Candace washed them. The headset strap is somehow rubbing more against my left ear than my right, which I'm trying not to let bother me.

"Now," I say, adjusting the headset one last time, "what about this Satchmo card?"

I'm staring at a dashboard with a million controls, which

is now curved slightly as if I'm looking at one of those fancy concave TVs, as opposed to how it looked on the computer screen when I wasn't wearing the goggles. Looks like there's a calendar in the bottom left corner with an *X* marked on several upcoming dates, and an energy meter that reads sixty out of a hundred. There's a whole list of weapons and items, including a Basic Spear, a Wooden Bowl, a Ram Horn, a Bone Ax, and an Elephant Tusk, the last of which alarms me.

"You . . . kill elephants in this game?"

"Nope!" exclaims Asher. "You can't hunt in *SLAY*. You have to wait until animals die on their own. Usually another animal will take them down if you wait long enough. The Bone Ax and Elephant Tusk are *super* rare."

That's thoughtful of the developer. What did the newscasters call him? Emerald.

"You use cards in duels," explains Asher further. "Click the deck in the top left corner."

I see a large white Mickey Mouse cartoon hand reach forward as I move the controller joystick up, and I tilt it left until it hovers over the black rectangle with gold trim.

"To click it, you can either press A or click with your finger."

"Wait, click what?" I ask, looking down at the controller. The screen goes nowhere, and I remember too late that I'm wearing the headset and can't actually *see* the controller.

"Here, give me this," says Asher, and I feel the controller

being ripped from my hands. "Just use your fingers. It's easier."

I move my right hand around gingerly and watch the white hand move as mine does.

"Whoa!" I exclaim. This is actually pretty cool. I can feel a large set of adult footsteps join mine to my left, and I realize Candace has entered the living room to watch. She's silent, but I hope this is bringing her some joy in the midst of uncertainty about what her kids are playing.

"So, I just . . ." I say, poking my index finger forward, virtually clicking the rectangle. The deck of cards explodes across the screen in a slideshow, startling me into a reflexive hands-in-front-of-my-face, one-leg-curled-up-against-my-chest position as I let out a yelp of surprise. Both boys giggle, and Candace chuckles behind me.

"Cute." I nod. "Okay, what now?"

"Use your finger!" contributes Joshua.

"You can slide through the cards with your index finger," says Asher.

I do as he says, flipping through red, blue, and purple cards, all with that ornate gold trim, each with gorgeous artwork in the middle. I read them one by one:

Wobble.

Carefree Black Girl.

Bad and Boujee.

Innovation.

Langston Hughes.

Satchmo.

I grin and nod, looking back in Candace's direction, and then I remember I can't see her because of the headset. But she can still hear me.

"Candace, this game is all about Black culture?"

There's a long pause before she says, "Yeah."

"It's pretty cool," says Joshua. "My character is a wrestler!"

"You can't *actually* be a wrestler in the game," argues Asher. "That's not a thing. He's just got a wrestling mask. Calls himself 'TheNight.'"

"Your name is TheNight?" I ask with a chuckle at the idea of my littlest nephew calling himself something so ridiculously badass and menacing. "All right, li'l man!"

"Ooh, ooh, ooh!" cry both the boys together, startling me again. "Duel request!"

"What?" I scream, leaning back and then remembering to close out of the screen. Panicked that I'll be met mano a mano by some extremely ripped guy, I scramble to click the X in the corner, but to my surprise, I'm standing in the middle of tall brown grasses. The sun is blazing against a brilliant blue sky, and there's nothing but a few green trees in the distance. Looks like some footage off Nat Geo, and I half expect to see a cheetah run past me and pounce on a gazelle. The sound is back on now that I'm out of the menu screen, and I can hear the grasses brushing against each other, and a secretary-bird call migrate from my right ear to my left. Something groans heavily behind me, and I flinch and turn to see an enormous rhino standing there munching on some grass a mere ten feet behind me.

"Oh God," I whisper as if it might hear me, and I back away from it slowly. "Boys, there's a rhino here. It's *right here*. What do I do?"

They both erupt in giggles.

"That's Ananias," says Joshua.

"He's my pet," says Asher. "You're playing as my character, LitMus."

I don't like Ananias. He looks too real. "He's making me nervous. Just a little bit."

"He doesn't really do anything except get you around faster. Don't get him anywhere near water, or he'll start blinking all weird and fall right through the map. Respond to that duel request, though. Don't leave that guy hanging. Top right corner."

It's taken me this long to notice a flashing red button in the top right corner of the screen. I direct my arm to the right and click on it with my index finger. A window comes up that says:

> *Duel Request*
> *From*
> *SPADE*
> *Accept?*

"Holy *shit*!" exclaims Asher.

"Hey!" cries Candace. "Absolutely *not* in my house!"

"Asher, come on, man," I coax.

"Sorry," he says, "but it's *Spade*!"

"Spaaade, Spade, Spade, Spade!" squeals Joshua.

"He's the king of the Rain Forest! Why is he here in the Savanna? He's *never* out here. You have to duel him! Even if you lose, it'll give you some serious XP just playing him!"

I am *made* of questions. We're in the Savanna? Apparently there's also a rain forest? With a king? Apparently there are political hierarchies in this game—regional hierarchies contingent on how much "XP" one has?

"We're dueling!" yells Asher. Suddenly the white hand that I was supposed to be commanding flies to the accept button, courtesy of Asher operating the controller, and I explode in panic.

"No, no, no! Wait!"

"You're in it now, Uncle!"

Another window flies onto the screen out of nowhere, followed by another, and another, and another. Words are flying so fast across panels that I only catch pieces of phrases.

. . . uncle's playing.
. . . going down.
Energy.
Arena: Zulu.
Region: Savanna.
Spade vs. LitMus.
Duel begins in 3 . . . 2 . . . 1 . . .

THE GAME PLAN

I've never had to get a lawyer before. I'm sure my parents would be able to help me, but the whole point of getting a lawyer is to protect my identity from everyone, including my parents, so it's just me and Google today. I find the only Black lawyer in the entire city of Bellevue and call her office, and the conversation goes like this:

"Hi, you've reached the law offices of Annette Coleman. This is Michelle. How may I direct your call?"

"Hi, uh, I want to make an appointment for a consultation with Annette Coleman."

"Absolutely. Ms. Coleman does charge a consultation fee of one hundred twenty-five dollars per hour. Are you prepared to pay that at the time of consultation?"

"How long is the consultation?"

"That's entirely up to you, starting at one hour. Ms. Coleman's next availability is on June first."

"That's in three months!"

"The only sooner time available is in twenty minutes, at 1 p.m. I had another appointment cancel at the last minute."

"I'll be there."

"Okay, excellent. What's your name?"

"Can I stay anonymous? I don't know if this line is tapped."

"I have to put something down."

"Put down Wakandria."

And so here I am, Saturday afternoon, sitting alone on the light-rail toward downtown, holding a jar of money I didn't even have time to count. With these big round glasses, yellow sweater, maroon pants, and my hair still in jumbo twists, I look like Celie from *The Color Purple* would if she lived in 2019 and went to USC.

I'm trying to keep my head down to avoid the attention, but I can still feel the stares, and they make me keenly aware that I'm the only Black girl in this car. I think back to Derek and Jan's news segment, about what Jan said about me. *Emerald's the one we should be tracking down and demanding answers from.* I think of Jamal again. I think of his face, his piercing eyes staring at me across the Ping-Pong table, holding up that peace sign. I can't help it. I google his name again, this time under "news," and find a whole list of things I wish I could unread.

Honors Student Killed for Video Game Coins

SLAY: *Black History Game, or Virtual Reality Gangbanging?*

*Black Kansas City Teen Was Captain of
Entrepreneurship Club, Family Says*

*SLAY Murder: Elusive Game Developer
Emerald Silent*

Silent, it says. That word is a knife in my stomach. I quoted Elie Wiesel in my Boston University essay, and it's coming back up with a vengeance, like a bad case of heartburn: "We must take sides. Neutrality helps the oppressor, never the victim. Silence encourages the tormentor, never the tormented."

What is my silence saying?

I feel a little sweaty, and a little nauseated. I'm surrounded by staring eyes on this train, reminding me that there's an all-out media manhunt after me, demanding answers. Demanding my un-silence. What does un-silence look like? I open WhatsApp to see if Cicada is online. She's not, but I could use her company right now.

We're passing Lake Washington, and the sun is peeking through the clouds and glinting off the water. I love it out here, and I imagine the Atlanta humidity and hope it doesn't wreak havoc on my hair. My phone buzzes with a text from Malcolm, as if he can read my thoughts.

Malcolm: You never answered my question.

My chest tightens. It's been a whole day since we last talked, and his last text is still sitting there above this one: *I better not find out you play that shit.* It's not even a question. It's a threat. I realize I really don't want to talk to him, because I don't want to have to lie. How can I denounce the hundreds of thousands of people I talk to in *SLAY*? I remember my duel with Q.Diamond and their rainbow-striped face staring at me, and I can't deny how incredible it felt to realize what this game means to me, and what it means for others. After staring at my phone for a solid ten minutes, I finally figure out what I'm going to text back.

> Me: Play what shit?
>
> Malcolm: The shit that got that li'l king killed.
>
> Me: The video game? You know I don't have time to play video games.
>
> Malcolm: You females only start texts with "you know" when you lyin'.

I toss my phone in my backpack. He won't be getting a reply out of me until I see him on Monday. If he's lucky. I cross one leg over the other and tap my foot against the wall while I try to calm down. I love Malcolm, but I hate it when he gets like this, moody and disrespectful, throwing words like "females" around dismissively.

My phone buzzes three more times before my stop, and I finally cave and check it when I get off the train and start walking. But I tell myself it's okay to read the texts as long as I don't reply.

> Malcolm: I didn't mean that.
>
> Malcolm: I'm sorry. It just scares me to think you might be getting brainwashed playing it.
>
> Malcolm: If something happens to you, a nigga goin to jail.

I smile at the apology, although I realize he's just rerouted his anger from me to anyone who would hurt me. But I decide to reply anyway.

Me: You don't have to worry about that.

Malcolm: But for real, don't let them distract you. Stay focused.

By "them" he means white people. But "they" didn't make this game. I did. And now the whole damn American media wants my opinion about it.

Me: SLAY isn't made by white people, babe. The developer is Black.

Malcolm: And Carter G. Woodson, a Black man, created Black History Month.

He keeps typing as I reach the intersection and click the crosswalk button at the corner of Fourth Street and Bellevue Way.

Malcolm: Black people will create their own distractions using the white man's tools. You forget I used to be addicted to video games way back in the day?

The signal changes and I step off the curb. Malcolm once told me he used to spend every waking moment playing *Mario Party 2* when he was little. His mom has always been a working single mom, leaving him home all summer with nothing to do but hold a controller and try to beat his own high score against three CPUs. He didn't talk to anyone. He had no friends. Until he met me.

Malcolm: I could've spent all that time reading. I could've been decolonizing, undoing everything I was seeing on TV. I could've been surrounding myself with Black rhetoric.

Me: I know, babe.

Malcolm: Good. This game, SLAY, it may look like a step forward for us, but it's another way to keep us from being great. Don't let it fool you, babe. Promise me you won't try it, ok?

I take a deep breath and wonder if Malcolm will ever understand. He surrounds himself with Black rhetoric in the form of written words. I surround myself with the company of Black gamers worldwide. What's the difference?

Me: I gotta go babe, I'll talk to you later.

I find the brick building with the giant white letters that spell out THE LAW OFFICES OF ANNETTE COLEMAN, press open the heavy glass door, and step into a spotless, minimalist, chic New York loft–style office with white leather sofas, bamboo floors, and unfinished concrete walls. A dark, slender woman with high cheekbones, round eyes, and a natural hair updo greets me with a smile. She's wearing all black, long, drapey clothing that looks like something you'd see on a fashion show runway. Her style overshadows mine.

"Good afternoon," she says warmly. "Can I help you?"

"Hi," I say. I feel weird standing in this posh office looking like a runaway from the South Bronx, clutching a jar of loose change. "I'm here to see Ms. Coleman. Are you Michelle?"

Her eyes drift from my face to the jar, but somehow I don't feel like she's judging me—just assessing the situation. Her eyes are kind, and I'm shocked when she stands and holds her hand out to shake mine like I'm a bona fide adult.

"You must be Wakandria," she says warmly. "You're right on time. I'll take you to Ms. Coleman's office."

This woman isn't clueless, and neither am I. I know she knows my name isn't Wakandria, but she must get all kinds of hopeful clients coming through here with absurd names and even more absurd cases. As I follow her down the hallway with the almost-white concrete floor, I notice a gray smudge at the tip of my right shoe, which would otherwise be paper white, and I hope there's a box of tissues in the room that can serve as a stand-in for my toothbrush until I get home.

I don't want to admit it, but I'm nervous. What if she doesn't take my case? What if she doesn't answer my questions? What if she finds out who I really am and calls the police? Why am I so afraid of being turned in when I didn't do anything wrong? I'm not a murderer, but I feel responsible. If I hadn't created SLAY, if I hadn't shared Emerald with the world, that boy—Jamal—would still be alive. And then I remember Q.Diamond with the rainbow face again, and I wonder if giving Q.Diamond a space to be themselves, assuming they're not out and proud and surrounded by supportive friends in the real world, is worth the life of a sixteen-year-old boy.

As I follow her down the hallway and Michelle ushers me through a door into a tiny conference room, I try to tell myself that I'm not responsible for either of their lives, and that none of this is my fault.

I try, but I don't really believe it.

The lights are off, but it's bright in here. Natural sunlight is shining brilliantly through the gray blinds, and I wonder what the view would be like if we opened them. There's a wooden table in here with two black swivel chairs, one on each side. I slide one out and have a seat in its cushy flexible mesh. Michelle offers me a cup of water, and I gladly accept, and then she leaves me alone in the room to think. I feel out of place in here, especially with this jar, and I set it on the wooden floor next to my rolling chair. My pocket vibrates and I pull out my phone to find a message from Cicada, who is awake in the middle of the night in Paris.

Cicada: That thing I was going to tell you . . . I'm only half-Black. My mother is white Italian. I don't know when I could have told you that wouldn't make this awkward. I don't blame you if you don't let me keep playing the game. I should have told you sooner.

My stomach turns. Not at the revelation that Cicada is mixed, but at the idea that she might think I'm *that* prejudiced, that I might actually ban her from the game because she's only half-Black. I begin to text her back just as another message comes in.

Cicada: Am I Black enough to keep playing?

The door opens, cutting off what I was about to type, which would have been *Of course you're Black enough! What kind of question is that?*

"Hello, you must be Wakandria!" says Annette, beaming. I stand up to shake her hand. I expected her to walk in here in all black—blazer, pants, and shoes, like lawyers on TV always wear—but instead she's wearing a navy blouse with bold yellow flowers and a mustard-yellow blazer on top. She has black pants and matching black heels, her handshake is strong, and her eyes are sure. Her hair falls shoulder-length in the most perfect bell-shaped twist-out I've ever seen, and I'm suddenly very conscious of my jumbo twists. She's stunning. I look like I just rolled out of bed. I remember the jar on the floor, and I'm so impressed with how nice she's being to me.

"Hi," I muster. "Nice to meet you."

We both sit, and she opens a binder and folds her hands on the table between us, looking into my eyes, eager to listen to what I have to say. I don't have anything prepared. I just plan to tell her exactly what happened without giving her enough details to figure out I'm Emerald, if she even knows who Emerald is.

"So," she says, "Wakandria, it's so nice to meet you. I was thrilled when Michelle told me she'd booked a consultation with twenty minutes' notice. I hate last-minute afternoon cancellations that leave an hour open. They're too short to go get a massage, too late to grab lunch, and too early for dinner. Thank you for coming. I'm so happy you're here."

I like her already. I like her energy. She's already making me feel like hope isn't lost, which I guess is her job, but I like to believe she's being genuine. Under different circumstances, I might ask her the *SLAY* code question, "Do you eat meat?" so we can duel later, but she probably doesn't have time to play, and when it comes to my identity, I've sworn myself to secrecy.

"Before we begin . . ." She turns the first page in the binder.

She's about to ask me for money up front. I lean down, grab the jar, and hoist it into my lap.

". . . I want to review the terms of this consultation." Then she notices the jar, brushes her hand through the air with a grin, and says, "Oh, don't worry about that yet. We'll come back to that at the end. I want to make sure I give you the full hour."

I put the jar back down and feel heat creep into my cheeks. How ridiculous of me to assume she needed my little allowance money. Her blazer alone looks like it costs a few consultations.

"I do charge one hundred twenty-five dollars per hour for a consultation, but if it ends earlier, I prorate for low-income-qualifying clients. To inquire about our low-income options, please see Michelle. She'll be more than happy to help you. During this consultation, I can provide legal counsel with the promise of confidentiality. However, if the client—that's you—reveals explicitly or implies the intent to carry out an illegal act, I have the responsibility to report said intent to the appropriate authorities without notifying the client. If you agree and concede to these terms and conditions, please sign here."

She unclips a page from the binder and hands it to me along with a heavy, cold silver pen that feels expensive. Since I don't intend to do anything illegal anytime soon, I sign and pass it back to her.

"Wonderful," she says. "So, Miss Wakandria, what brings you into my office today?"

I take a deep breath to calm my pulse, and I think of Cicada, of how she's depending on me. I think of how boldly and cleverly Steph would navigate this meeting, and I try to channel her energy right now.

"Am I allowed to ask you questions in hypotheticals?"

She nods with a smile as warm as my mom's.

"If I created a . . . thing . . . that made other people feel like I was discriminating against them, could they sue me?"

"Hmm," she says, leaning back in her chair. "I'd have to know a little more about this thing. Is it a club? A fraternity?"

"Kind of like a club. It's an online club for . . . a certain demographic. Could they sue me if I didn't let their demographic in?"

"What's the nature of this demographic? Do you not allow low-income people to join your club? Is it for young people only? Only people who live in a certain area?"

"It's only for Black people."

She pauses and stares at her binder, so I keep talking.

"It's not . . . racist exactly, is it? I mean, the club doesn't talk badly about white people or anything. But you have to have a passcode from an existing club member to join, and all existing club members are Black."

"Have these existing club members been informed that only Black people are allowed to join this club?"

I stop and remember the mission statement.

A fabulous mecca of Black excellence in which Nubian kings and queens across the diaspora can congregate, build each other up, and SLAY.

"It says it's for Nubian kings and queens across the diaspora."

"Sounds like a fantastic place." She grins.

I wish I knew if she has a character. She'd SLAY so hard, and if she dressed her character like she dressed herself this morning, I'd have to cop her look.

"But it sounds like, hypothetically, you would be concerned about someone bringing legal action against you."

"Sort of. Against my persona. I have a username in the online club, and the person who is suing—who would be suing—would be suing my online persona. They don't know me in real life."

"You mean they wouldn't under these hypothetical circumstances." She chuckles.

Dammit, why am I so bad at making up stories? I've kept Emerald a secret for three years, but I can't keep up a hypothetical story about her?

"Yeah."

"Well, I think this online club sounds like a lovely place," she says, "but I think you may be right to be concerned. The American justice system does not take discrimination cases lightly, and from the information you've provided to me, the prosecution may have a case in this instance."

My heart sinks all the way through the floor. That can't be right. There's no way this can be legal. White people under Jim Crow legally kept their whites-only spaces, and to this day, Black-exclusionary spaces still exist, especially online. The fashion industry is predominantly white, Hollywood is still overwhelmingly white, and, as Steph once pointed out, white people had a monopoly on the word "nude" until recently. White people are the standard in so many different industries, but the minute Black people build something for ourselves, we're wrong for causing division.

I press my fingers against my eyes. I hear her set a cardboard tissue box in front of me, and I gratefully take two and dab my cheeks and eyes, pocketing a third for my shoes later.

"Thank you," I say. I want to thank her for being honest with me, even though I have no idea where to go from here. If someone does decide to sue, there's no way I can afford a lawyer without telling my parents who I really am. I can't just pay the settlement, whatever it is, because neither I nor my parents have thousands of dollars to throw away. I know Ms. Coleman means well by being honest, but she's essentially just told me that if someone sues, Emerald's secret identity can't stay secret anymore. The whole reason behind SLAY— wanting a private space for me to explore who I am—is gone. And whatever judge takes the case would probably force me to let the plaintiff play too, and then what's the point?

"And unfortunately . . . ," continues Ms. Coleman.

I force myself to look up at her, even though I'm not sure I can handle whatever is coming next if it's worse than finding out I'm going to have to out Emerald.

". . . I won't be able to take your case if you do decide to hire an attorney. I'm a family litigation attorney, not a civil rights attorney. I won't be able to help you."

Great. I've just spent all my money on a consultation with a lawyer who can't even take my case. I'm so mad

I want to overturn this table and run all the way home. I just stare at the tissue box, unsure what to say. I can feel a vein pulsing in my jaw, and I'm afraid if I open my mouth, something venomous might spew out and burn both of us.

"But off the record, please don't give up. I know you'll figure out how to navigate through this."

I nod even though she's wrong, and force a half-hearted "Thanks, Ms. Coleman."

I get up and turn to leave, and I hear Ms. Coleman stand too.

"Oh, Wakandria," she says, "I meant to ask you."

I turn to look at her.

She's got her hands clasped in front of her, and she asks me matter-of-factly, "Do you eat meat?"

I freeze. Did she really ask me what I think I just heard? "What?"

"Do you eat meat?" she asks me again. She definitely knows.

She *SLAY*s! This woman who became my ultimate style icon twenty minutes ago, and who probably drives a Bentley to her two-million-dollar mega-mansion on Mercer Island after work every day, plays *my* game! I want to scream! I want to cry! I want to hug her and ask her what her *SLAY* name is. This queen staring at me is a gamer? I can't believe it.

I laugh a little and say, finally, for the first time in real life, "We meet at dawn."

I look closer and realize there are tears in her eyes as she says, "Thank you. Thank you so much."

"For what?"

"For giving my son and daughter a place to go after school."

I don't know what else to do but nod. All I did was make a video game. Anyone can do that nowadays, by the power of Google and boredom. I haven't done anything spectacular. I'm not Nelson Mandela. I'm not MLK. I'm not Rosa Parks. I don't feel like I've done anything revolutionary. But this woman is looking at me like I saved her life somehow.

She thanks me again and assures me that I "needn't worry about the fee," that it's taken care of, and that I might need it if I decide to find another lawyer.

Hours later, after retiring to my room without dinner, I lie awake in bed, staring at the ceiling, thinking about everything Ms. Coleman said. I think about the fact that even she, an attorney with her own firm, has children with nowhere to go after school. And I know what she meant. I know she can afford to send her kids to the very best after-school programs on the Eastside, but that's nowhere to go if you're the only one who looks like you.

I can't sleep. I open Instagram to distract myself, and it takes only thirty seconds for me to wish I hadn't. There's a hashtag circulating—#Justice4Jamal—accompanied by captions like *If you are a gamer, you ARE Jamal Rice* and *Where are you, Emerald?*

I shut my eyes. I'm thousands of miles away from the

crime scene in my comfortable bedroom in Bellevue, doing exactly what *every* Black pioneer in history would condemn. I'm hiding.

I'm silent.

I close out of Instagram and take a deep breath, retreating to WhatsApp. Cicada is offline. Of course. Just when I'm ready to answer her question, which has been boring a hole into my conscience all day—*am I Black enough?* I consider answering now, while I have time, but then I begin to ask myself questions. Did she ask that because she doesn't *feel* "Black enough" or maybe doesn't believe in the "one-drop rule"—the idea that as long as you have one drop of Black blood in you, you can call yourself Black? Does she think *I* don't think she's "Black enough"? Does she think I resent her for having light-skinned privilege, or un-nappy hair? Wait, she might be bald in real life like her game character. Never mind. Still, though, these unanswered questions are enough to make me realize, maybe I'm *not* ready to unpack my answer. Maybe I'm not ready to talk about this yet.

Silent again.

I toss my phone to the end of my bed and shut my eyes hard, pressing my fingers into them. I want to open my eyes and go back to last week, before all this—before *SLAY*—got complicated. I've never wished so bad for Cicada to be online. Maybe if I could just say *something* to her, start talking, I'd arrive at some kind of answer for her. That's what we do best, right? We discuss things. We sort out the cards, we compare notes, we align, and then we run this game like the warriors we are. We figure things out *together*.

I don't know what I need right now. I need to relax. If things can't go back to the way they were last week, I need to at least *pretend* they are for a while. Just for an hour or so.

I climb down from my bunk bed and head to the computer.

I have a duel request from Anubis's semifinals opponent, Spade, who has a fro-hawk as far off his head as he is tall, making him a whopping twice my size. I can't turn that down. He also took advantage of my text-on-clothing initiative and made a pair of sunglasses that say RUDE in rainbow letters across the lenses with a big ol' sassy period at the end. I kick myself for not thinking of that.

We battle in the Rain Forest, among the vines and lush greenery, so close to the Chasing Waterfalls—yes, I called it that—that we can hear the rushing water so clearly it feels real. Toucans squawk somewhere deep in the jungle. They aren't really there in-game. It's just an audio track. But I like to imagine that they're real—perched on some tree, snacking on whatever it is toucans eat, watching the match. Round one is going okay. I just wish I could relax and focus on the gorgeous scenery while we duel, but Spade keeps bringing up my chat box, trying to talk to me the whole time with illegible abbreviated messages.

Spade: I cn't blieve Im actually dueling u rite now!

Spade: Thx 4 dueling me.

Spade: I may b king of rain4st but is honor 2 duel u.

A very kind person, and an expert dueler—his use of the 'Fro card is perfectly timed, encapsulating him in a giant Afro before I can deal the first blow. But I can't focus on dueling with all these messages flying at me, and my heart's not in this match. I'm tired. I'm hungry, but I don't feel like eating. I can't stop thinking about what Ms. Coleman said.

The prosecution may have a case in this instance.

My VR headset is fogging up inside with the heat of my tears, and I finally send Spade a reply at the end of round two.

Me: Hey, don't take this the wrong way, but I shouldn't have started this match. It's late and I'm tired. Mind if I forfeit?

He sends me back the most comforting message I could receive right now.

Spade: Not @ all. Go rest. U r a queen and this is ur game.

You are a queen, and this is your game.

I force a smile and a **Thanks**, and just as I'm reaching up to pull my headset off, a new message appears in my *SLAY* inbox, in the corner of my screen, from a player named Dred. It stops me cold.

Dred: It's me.

I just stare at it. I read it over and over. Who is *me?* I finally work up the nerve to type a response.

Me: Do I know you?

Dred: You had to expect me if you've been watching the news.

A chill goes up my spine. For a moment, I think this is the ghost of Anubis haunting my computer, and I wheel my chair back a few inches just in case I'm the next victim of the video-game version of *The Ring*. I look around my pitch-black room, which feels suddenly colder.

Me: What's your name?

Dred: Scott.

Scott. Do I know a Scott? Then I reread his last message. Dred: Scott. This guy has named himself after the Dred Scott decision—the infamous 1857 Supreme Court case that ruled a Negro was not entitled to sue for his own freedom even though he lived in a free state. The case that ruled Blacks were not, and could never be, citizens of the United States.

Me: Have we met before?

Dred: Not yet. But you had to know someone would lead the charge and take down this racist online dumpster fire of a game eventually.

Holy shit. Is this guy insinuating that he's actually going to sue me? Like, for real? I mean, I anticipated it happening eventually—I wouldn't have gone to see Annette Coleman if I didn't think it could—but I didn't expect it to happen a few hours after meeting her.

My forehead is clammy with sweat, and I briefly consider banning him immediately and kicking him off the server, but that would only give his case fuel. I decide that the best thing I can do is to keep him talking.

Me: How did you get an account?

Dred: Same way everyone else gets an account.

Me: What do you want?

Dred: I want to duel.

Me: Why?

Dred: Same reason everyone else wants to duel.

Me: I don't have time.

Dred: Fine. I'll just duel someone else.

Me: Why are you here?

Dred: Same reason everyone else is here.

I've already had enough of the word games. I click his profile and navigate to his character, and what I see scares me to death. He's chosen the lightest skin color possible, which almost looks white, he's shaved his head bald, and he's given his character a tiny black symbol that looks like a four-petal flower, right between his eyebrows. That flower petal is the closest thing in the game to a swastika, and I can't imagine that's not exactly what he intends it to be.

Me: If you wanted to be included, you've got what you want. You're here.

Dred: I said I want to duel.

Me: I said I don't have time.

Dred: I'll just find somebody else.

The audacity of this boy coming into my game and acting like he's not here to terrorize my kings and queens. I know what he means by *I'll just find somebody else*. He's not talking about dueling. He's talking about harassment. He's talking about stinking up my inbox. He's talking about making this game hell for me.

I could block him, but again, fuel for his potential lawsuit.

Me: Please leave me alone.

Dred: As long as I live in a free country, I can inbox whoever I want. I'm an equal player. All players are equal here, right? All you need is a passcode. If you don't like me, though, you can block me.

I'm not falling for that trap. Does he really think I'm going to walk right into that?

Me: Are you trying to piss me off? Because it won't work.

Dred: No. I'm trying to be the first thing you see when you open your inbox, and the last.

He's got me. I'm scared to block him, and I'm scared to keep typing, and I can't duel with his messages flying all over my screen. I can't take this. I log off and turn off my monitor, and the minute I put my headset, gloves, and socks back into the drawer and lock it and find myself sitting at my desk with that black computer screen staring back at me, the tears overtake me, and I cry. Hard. I fold my arms, rest my forehead on my hands, and let the sobs out. Granny used to say that the best remedy for a dry patch is a little rain, and I believe her. I feel better once my face has dried on its own, but I still don't know what to do with myself. I'm tired enough to sleep, but I'm awake enough to wish Cicada was online. If I text Malcolm, he'll assume it's a booty call and want to FaceTime, and even if I *could* manage to avoid all talk of the game and focus on him, I could never let him see me right now, when my face looks like it's been attacked by a hive of bees.

I don't have anyone I can call and talk to, just to talk. I could send Cicada an emergency text alert, but it's six thirty a.m. her time on Sunday, which is her only day off from class, and I don't have the heart to wake her up.

There's a knock at my door so soft I'm not sure I actually heard it, and that's when I realize I've been asleep. I look at my phone. Ten thirty p.m. I've been asleep at my desk for over an hour and my neck is killing me.

"Hello?" My voice feels like sandpaper.

"Hey," comes a whisper.

"Steph?"

I double-check to make sure my drawer is locked, and then I stand and feel my way to the door.

"You okay?" I ask her.

"Yeah, yeah, just let me in," she urges. She sounds concerned or rushed, or both, and I unlock the door and open it. The hallway light is on, and I'm sure I look exactly how I feel—like Black Dracula.

"Jesus Christ, what happened to you?" she asks.

"What do you want?" I force a smile.

"Can I come in?"

I have no one else to talk to tonight. I let my little sister in, and we sit down—her on my sofa, me on the pouf. After she clicks the lamp on, I can see she's staring at me with a smirk that says she knows something's wrong, and I'm trying not to look back at her with a face that admits she's right.

"Okay," she says, "you may have Mom and Dad fooled into thinking you're 'too tired' to eat, but not me. You don't skip dinner for anything, including sleep."

I just look at her in silence. I don't know what she wants me to say.

"So, I ordered a pizza," she says casually, crossing one leg over the other and folding her arms. "Pepperoni and olives. Your favorite. Now tell me what's up."

I try so hard to think of something believable—I'm on my period. I failed an exam. Harper and I got into a fight. But I asked Steph if I could borrow a tampon two weeks ago when I ran out in the middle of the school day, I don't fail exams, and Steph needs just one text from Harper to confirm that we're all cool.

She leans in close and whispers, "Did you step your white Keds in dog shit?"

The laughter bubbles out of me, and I cover my mouth to keep quiet. I'm grateful for her sometimes. She knows how to get me laughing, even if my world is falling apart— in this case, literally.

"That doesn't sound like a no."

"No, Steph. No, I didn't."

"Then what is it? Ever since that conversation with Harper and Wyatt last night, you haven't been yourself. Skipping meals, going to bed early, moping around all day like you and Malcolm are going through some—" Steph gasps and grabs my knee. "Did he hit you? Because if he hit you—"

"Jesus, Steph, no! He would never hit me."

"Good," she says. "I'd have to kill that boy."

Between the way she says "that boy" and the fact that she's wearing a hot-pink nightcap and matching satin robe, she's acting like Malcolm's auntie instead of a girl a year and a half his junior.

"Wyatt didn't say anything to you after we left the room, did he? Because I let him out of my sight for five minutes while he went to pee, and if he came back in here—"

"It's not Wyatt either, Steph."

She looks lost, her eyes searching mine like she's waiting for me to announce that somebody's dead. She leans forward and takes my hands, and I'm worried I'll start getting worked up again. I think of Dred and I think of Cicada. What if he sent her a message too? What if she quits being a mod and I have no one to back me up? What if I end up alone?

Steph's eyes narrow, analyzing me.

"You're afraid of something," she says.

How is she always right? I swallow and look away. Would she get it if I told her?

"You don't always have to be the voice of reason around here, you know," she continues, squeezing my hands between hers. "People forget that strong Black women need support too. I know I like to talk, but tonight I'm here to listen."

I look up at Steph and think of what a relief it would be to tell her everything. About the game, about Jamal, about Dred. I have to talk to someone, and besides Cicada, she's the closest thing I have to a friend. She wouldn't tell everyone about this if I really stressed that she shouldn't, right? She knows the gravity of the situation by now, with it all over the news, and with literal lives on the line. She wouldn't. I have to tell her. Steph is here, with me, in my room. She's real, and for once she's listening and not talking. I look into her eyes and imagine her sitting at her computer, typing this to people in chat. She's not policing what I'm saying, she's not here to reprimand me or judge my words. She's 100 percent support right now, and I want to believe she'd do the same if I let her into the game.

"Hey . . . uh . . ." I squeeze her hands. "There's something you should probably know about me, Steph."

"That you play SLAY?"

I'm not sure if my face looks guilty, shocked, annoyed, or impressed, but I'm all four. She looks so pleased with herself, like she's caught me in a lie.

"How did you know?"

"You don't get worked up about the news for just anything. The minute all this news dropped about Jamal, you changed. Every time the 'SLAY murder' comes up, you shut down. This game means a lot to you for a reason."

I think back to last night, right here in my room, when Steph led Harper and Wyatt to the kitchen to spare me having to continue that conversation. She could see just how much it rattled me, and now she deserves to know why. The whole story.

"I invented it," I say.

Her face goes flat. Her eyebrows fly up. "You invented what? SLAY?"

I nod.

"I don't understand. How . . . How did you 'invent' it?" She's using air quotes like I'm speaking in metaphors.

"I invented it, as in, I built and launched, and now maintain, the game."

There's a pause as her eyes get huge, but eventually one

hand flies over her mouth and she squeezes the life out of my hand with the other as the implications sink in one by one.

"Holy shit—you're Emerald!"

"Shh," I urge. Mom and Dad sleep lightly, and their bedroom is right above mine. She lowers her voice to a whisper, but she sounds like she's hyperventilating.

"Holy shit—no, no, we dueled! Like, last week! Do you remember? I'm Hyacinth!"

"Wait, *you* SLAY?"

"'Course I *SLAY*." She shrugs as if I should've known by now. "I'm a self-respecting Black queen who just so happened to beat you by six hundred points in the Savanna last week. Speaking of the Savanna, what's with the new gray rhinos you threw in there? They glitch out whenever they get near water and fall right through the ground."

My own sister *SLAY*s and I didn't even know it. We *dueled*, and I didn't know it. I remember her character now—a tall girl in all pink with flowers woven into a thirty-foot braid behind her. Her character is beautiful just like her, and smart just like her.

"How long did it take you to make?"

"Make what?"

"The whole game!"

"I've been working on it for three years now. Cicada and I have been using textures and character models from various players who are also artists and coders."

"I can't believe it!" she says, her eyes measurably brighter. "My own big sister is gamemaster of *SLAY*!"

"You're the only one who knows, Steph. This doesn't leave this room. Not for anything, understand? I can't tell anyone else. Now you know why people calling it the 'SLAY murder' cuts me so deep. It means a boy my age in Kansas City was killed because of me."

Even saying it makes my chest tighten up. My throat hurts. I want to say more, but I can't even bring myself to look at Steph right now. I keep my eyes to the ground, and my voice breaks as I continue, "His death was my fault."

"Jamal Rice?" she says, leaning forward and looking into my eyes. "His death was absolutely *not* your fault. Have you read anything at all about the killer? Jeremiah Marshall? His rap sheet is a mile long: grand theft auto, assault, illegal possession of firearms, and misdemeanor arson, whatever the hell that is. If it's arson, it sounds like a felony to me—"

"This is serious, Steph!" I snap. "A boy is *dead* because of a disagreement over something I created. There's nothing you can say that will convince me there wasn't something I could've done to prevent this. And people are calling me a racist! They're saying SLAY is an online gang! Some guy sent me a message earlier today threatening to sue me unless I agree to duel him—"

"What? What a pleb," she says, standing up and beginning to pace. "He wants in, you say?"

"Yeah, he's all up in my DMs and everything."

"Wait, you gave him a passcode?"

"No, he just *took* one! I don't know where he got a passcode from—some friend of his."

"One *coon*-ass friend of his."

"Steph," I hiss. She knows I hate that word. "I'm telling you this because I don't know what to do, and you seem to always know what to do."

"Have you gotten a lawyer?"

I shake my head. "I talked to one, just out of curiosity, when I went to downtown Bellevue earlier today. She's not a civil rights lawyer, but from what she said, Dred might have a case."

"Who's Dred?"

"The guy who keeps harassing me. Dred, as in Dred Scott."

There's such a long pause that I eventually look up at her. Her eyes have narrowed and darkened, and her mouth is hanging open.

"Oh, *hell* no," she says. "He doesn't know what family he's messed with. Where does he live? I know you can see his IP address."

"Actually, I can't see players' IP addresses," I say. When I created Emerald, I was thinking solely about how I could share her with the world, not about tracking geographical locations of eventual trolls. Oh, naive freshman me.

"But you're the developer! Can't you ban him?"

"I could, but if he wants to sue on the basis of discrimination, banning him might be the worst thing I could do, right?"

"So let me get this straight. The world is demanding justice for Jamal, demanding to know who you are, and you decided hiding in your room was the best way to handle it?" Steph is whisper-screaming at me. "Why didn't you tell me any of this sooner?"

"I'm telling you *now*, Steph, because I have no one else to talk to. Cicada is offline, my inbox has blown up, and Mom and Dad would know my identity. And you already know why I can't tell Harper and Wyatt. They'd think I'm a racist. All I ever wanted to do was escape into this magical world where for once I don't have to act a certain way because I'm Black, and where I don't have to answer certain questions because I'm the Black authority in the room, and where if I do something that's not stereotypically Black, I'm different."

Steph is staring into my lamp now quietly, thinking, until she says softly, "I see why you like Malcolm then."

I know why I like Malcolm. Malcolm has never treated me like the different one. Since he's the only other Black student at Jefferson—aside from Steph and her new Beta Beta recruit Jazmin—my relationship with him has always been based on sameness, and what we have in common. But he's more pro-Black than I am. He reads Baldwin, Walker, Ellison, and even Du Bois, who—God rest his soul—reads less like an anthem of the Black experience and more like a refrigerator manual. It's dense, it's hard to get through, and sometimes fiction just sounds more fun. Sometimes SLAY just sounds more fun. Malcolm makes me feel guilty for not being "Black enough," even with all his talk of rebelling *against* the concept of a "good Negro." He's pro-Black *and* antiwhite, two ideologies that sometimes overlap but are not the same thing. He's pro a lot of things, but to realize he's not nearly as progressive as I thought—that's hard for me to admit. The last thing I want to do is call my boyfriend a liar.

I don't hate white people like the news says I do. Harper and I have been friends since middle school, before *SLAY* was even a thought. I've been to all her birthday parties, and she's been to all of mine. But she exhausts me sometimes because even though we're friends, she'll never really *get* what it's like to be me. But now I don't think Malcolm will ever get what it's like to be me either. I think I love *SLAY* so much because we're a mutually empathetic collective. As we duel, as we chat, there's an understanding that "your Black is not my Black" and "your weird is not my weird" and "your beautiful is not my beautiful," and that's okay. It brings tears to my eyes if I think about it too long. And here I thought I wasn't a crier.

I say nothing to Steph for fear that my voice might crack, and instead I wait for her to keep talking.

"You realize what you have to do, right?"

I don't know what she's getting at. Knowing Steph, it's something drastic, like *hunt Dred down and kill him.*

"No," I say. She sucks her teeth in disappointment that I haven't telepathically reached the same verdict she has.

"Drag him."

"You want me to roast him in front of the *SLAY* community?"

"No, for once I'm not suggesting you use your words.

Battle him. This is your game! Who is he to come up into *our* community and demand anything?"

Spade's words come back to me now: *You are a queen, and this is your game.*

But logically, what would it prove? We battle, I win, then what? Maybe there is something to sister telepathy, because Steph answers the question I've just asked myself.

"You win, and he drops the threats and leaves you alone."

"And if he wins?"

"That's up to you."

Later that night, after the pizza arrives and Steph and I eat the whole thing and I'm finally starting to doze off under my covers, my phone buzzes with a text.

Malcolm: I'm reading The 48 Laws of Power. WYD?

Me: I'm in bed.

Malcolm: In bed or sleeping?

Ordinarily this would be the part where we open FaceTime and wish one of us were over the other's house. But right now, all I can think about is Dred. It sucks. I couldn't even finish my duel with Spade today because I was so distracted by real-life problems, and when I'm talking to real live people that I care about, people I've promised my future to, like Malcolm, I can't stop thinking about the game. How do I juggle both? Can I keep existing like this, as Kiera, and as Emerald? I don't know what else to say to Malcolm tonight.

Me: Sleeping. Sorry.

I lock my phone and roll over.

BEIJING, CHINA

My name is Maurice, and there's nowhere I'd rather be right now than in my tiny hotel room here in Beijing.

When I open the door and slip the key card into the slot to turn on the lights, I'm met with the scent of lemon and household cleaners. Housekeeping was here, even though I'm checking out in the morning.

I let the door shut behind me and step out of my brown Louis Vuittons, which at the time I thought were too expensive but am now grateful for. They're sturdy but soft inside, making my feet much less achy at the end of a long day than my old Nauticas. I spot a new bottle of water on the counter next to two new coffee mugs, empty the bottle into the kettle, and set it to boil. Although everyone in China assures me that boiling the tap water is safe enough, why take the chance when hotels eagerly replenish water bottles and tea bags every morning?

I shrug out of this enormous coat that fits me a bit weird

in the shoulders. It's March, and the weather outside is surprisingly cruel. I had to buy this coat from one of the shops that line the streets a quarter mile from the conference center downtown. I loosen my tie, slip off my blazer, and make myself a cup of English breakfast tea, which I'm shocked they have. This is the first time I've seen anything but green tea in my hotel room basket. I sink into the edge of the bed and sip it gratefully, letting it warm my insides.

The tea is gone too fast, and I set the mug on the bed, lean back against the pillows, and close my eyes. I could sleep like this if I let myself drift off—pants, dress shirt, belt, and socks still on. That number that's been running through my head all day crops up again. Six dollars and sixty-five cents.

Six dollars and sixty-five cents sounds pretty affordable, but when multiplied by sixty thousand, it's . . . not a good number. But Mr. Min insists that's the lowest he can offer, and as much as I want to keep haggling, it's the lowest offer I've gotten out of all fifty-some trips, and it's the factory with the most airtight safety regulations. As a responsible business owner, I should probably keep researching to find a manufacturer who's ethical *and* cheap. But I really don't want to come back to Beijing. I'm looking forward to spending at least a month straight with Sylvie, sharing cappuccinos at our breakfast table every morning, debating whether we should leave the parlor window closed so I don't freeze to death, or leave it open so she can hear the bluebirds while we eat.

A knock at the door startles me from my thoughts.

"Yes?" I ask into my empty hotel room. No response. I peel myself from the bed with the most hushed sigh of frustration I can manage and drag myself to the door. There's no peephole, so I unlock the dead bolt and crack open the door. Two women stand there looking up at me with big smiles. One has her hair in a short bob with bangs, and she's about a foot shorter than my wife, who's five foot ten. The other is my height, with her hair tied into a bun at the nape of her neck, her dark eyes looking exhausted despite her smile. They're dressed in matching white, short-sleeve button-up blouses that look freshly ironed and black pants, and they're each holding a neatly folded white towel.

"Hi," says the shorter woman in a soft, sweet voice. She holds out the towel to me and asks, "Massage?"

I look from her face to the taller woman's, and she nods in confirmation. First, exhausted, unthinking me considers whether I would actually like for two women to enter my hotel room, as a lone Black man in the middle of Beijing, where any man off the street speaks Chinese better than I do, and where I would have the worst time acquiring a lawyer, let alone talking to my cellmates in jail. And then I reply with my best pronunciation of *"Bù, xièxiè."* No, thank you.

They look at each other in surprise and contest my reply together.

"Free," they say simultaneously.

"Bù, xièxiè," I say again, with a shake of my head this time. The hotel manager must have added a free massage to my account to thank me for the several times I've stayed here. But free or not, I know how this might look to someone on the outside. I wish Sylvie were here. She'd love a massage, and I'd feel so much more comfortable with this situation if we were getting massages together.

The taller woman nods enthusiastically and backs away from the door, but the short woman stays and keeps staring up at me curiously.

"Uh . . . ," she begins, looking like she's trying to think of what to say to me. I know that face. I make that face all the time. It's the face of someone who doesn't speak the language they so desperately wish they spoke right now.

"Uh, I, uh . . . ," she says.

The taller woman says something to her in Chinese that I can't decipher.

The shorter woman spits a single syllable back to her: *"Shì." Yes.* She looks back up at me with wide eyes, visibly gripping the towel tighter before sinking down and setting the towel right there in the middle of the floor. Then she pulls her phone out of her back pocket and begins typing with trembling thumbs.

I'm so confused. What's happening? I begin to back away slowly and ease the door closed.

The short woman notices what I'm doing and exclaims, "Ah! Wait!"

I'm trying to be polite, but at this point I'm just wondering what else these two could want from me. The taller woman is looking at me so apologetically, I wonder if I'm about to become the next article in the murder column of the Beijing news tomorrow in a language my wife won't be able to understand.

Every instinct in me says to retreat into my room and shut the door before she can do anything unpredictable, but just before I resolve to do so, she's holding up her phone screen to me enthusiastically. Her perfectly manicured hand is shaking so badly, I have to hold the corner of it just to read what's on the screen.

The translator app says, *Can I take a picture with you?*

I look at her again. She has the eyes of a superfan asking a celebrity for an autograph.

I'm used to being asked for photos, actually. I'm one of maybe six Black men I've seen since beginning my excursions to China to find a suitable manufacturer. And I'm definitely the only one with a hairstyle that's a fade on the bottom and five-inch dreadlocks on top. A group of three waitresses once asked me in an Indian restaurant in Shanghai if they could take my picture because they said I look like Will Smith. I don't see a single feature between us that's alike, but if three beautiful women want to tell me I look like Will Smith, I'm not going to complain. But this question comes up at least once every time I fly out here, like I'm a damn circus act. I'm a normal human being in Paris, but as a Black man in Beijing, I'm a celebrity.

"Fine," I say.

Her whole face lights up and she talks a million words a minute giddily, squealing Chinese to the other lady, who has shrunk away halfway down the hall with embarrassment. But once she gets the message, her smile returns, and she comes back to sandwich me between the two of them in the selfie the smaller woman takes. I'm sure I look exhausted in the picture. My tie is loose, my shirt is partially unbuttoned, and my eyes are probably dull after a full day of factory tours, contract negotiations, and Chinese beer. I'm too tired to be doing this.

The shorter woman thanks me profusely before the taller woman shoos her down the hall and they move on to their next potential customer.

When I'm alone in my room again, I lie down on the bed feeling even more exhausted than I did just five minutes ago. At some point, I must have fallen asleep, because when I blink my eyes open again, the lights have automatically shut off from lack of movement in the room, and my neck feels stiff. My thoughts are racing. I think of Sylvie, of how much I miss being in the arms of someone who understands me, and I start texting **Réveillé?** That's "Are you awake?" in French. Then I realize it's five in the morning here, which means it's eleven at night in Paris and she's already put on her blue silk nightie and gone to sleep alone.

I love her in that nightie.

I cover my face with my hands and sink into my thoughts. This room is dead silent. My flight doesn't leave until noon, so I've got seven hours to kill before then. Who knows if I'll be able to get back to sleep later in the morning, but for now, to keep from missing her, or texting her and waking her up, I have to keep busy.

I look to my left, at my silver laptop sitting on the desk. I wonder if Emerald has fixed that rhino glitch yet so I can snag one and try riding it around. I wonder if my tribemate TandemTen has found that hornbill horn he went off in the wilderness to find days ago. I wonder if Zama ever found that blue crystal I asked for in exchange for all the raffia and bamboo we've got stored up for her in the Rain Forest.

I wonder if there's a new date for the Desert Semifinals yet.

I log in as my character, Spade, and see that screen welcoming me into a world where I can let go of the responsibilities and the stress of being Maurice Belrose and just be Spade. On trips two days or shorter, I pack lightly. But any longer than that, and I'm lost without my headset, gloves, and socks.

There's a character online this morning named KaepWuzRobbed7 who's already sending me a duel request, but they've got five hundred thousand *SLAY* coins, a complete set of bone armor, and nine hundred fifty-seven *SLAY* cards. This guy has stats almost as high as mine, and I'm not looking for a challenge right now. I want a good old-fashioned duel, just for fun.

I spot a character in the Desert who I haven't seen before. Username is LitMus, which immediately makes me grin. Six cards, steel armor, and nine duels won out of sixty-six.

I'll take it.

SKIN IN THE GAME

I don't know how Mom manages to come up with new pancake flavors every single Sunday morning. Today's are pear and goat cheese with crispy bacon strips on the side. Steph scarfs hers down, but I pick at mine.

"Excited for school tomorrow, you two?" asks Dad as he stuffs another forkful of pear-and-goat-cheese-covered pancakes into his mouth. "Steph, ready for your math test?"

Steph nods and takes a bite of bacon. "It's geometry. Shouldn't be too hard."

Shit. My polynomials test is tomorrow too. I haven't studied. Why hasn't Harper reminded me to study with her in the last day and a half? Better question: Why haven't I reached out to Harper? Why haven't I made sure she's prepared? I've been so preoccupied with Dred, and Cicada, and Malcolm, and Jamal, that I've neglected my best friend. That stops today.

"I'm going to the bathroom," I announce.

I sit on the edge of the bathtub and text her.

Me: Hey.

Harper: OMG I'm so glad you're okay. I wanted to say I'm sorry for the other day. I'm so, so sorry for what Wyatt said to you. He's so butthurt about that stupid video game.

I ignore the pain of hearing my best friend call my life's work stupid and begin typing.

Me: It's okay. I'm sorry I haven't been around to help you study for the polynomials test. Are you going to be okay tomorrow?

Harper: Yeah, I'll be fine. I'm more worried about you. You've been ignoring my texts since Friday, and I don't blame you after what Wyatt said. But Malcolm says you won't talk to him either. Even he's getting concerned.

Me: I'm okay.

Harper: I know you're NOT okay, but I won't ask you to tell me about it.

I'm surprised at how cool she's being about my absence, about my negligence. I take a deep breath and figure out a way to continue this conversation without sounding unnatural or stiff.

Me: How have you been? What's been up?

Harper: Been fine. All this talk about video games in the news made me dig up my old Legacy of Planets log-in. Wanna come over tonight and play a little? I'll pay you for a tutoring session and everything. Just want to hang out.

Guilt grips me. Harper is so worried about me that she's willing to pay me sixty dollars just to hang out. In all this whirlwind around *SLAY*, I've left Harper hanging for so long that somehow I've given the impression that I'll be more inclined to spend time with her if she pays me first. What kind of friend have I become? My immediate inclination is to say yes and tell her to forget the money. But as fun and nostalgic as a night of playing video games with Harper sounds, casually racist characters included or not, I don't know if I can bear to look at Wyatt right now, or deal with his interview questions.

Before I can answer, Harper texts me again.

Harper: Wyatt is at baseball practice tonight. He won't be around to bother us. No interrogations, no interview shit. Just you, me, Sheila, Zelda, and my homemade white cheddar jalapeño popcorn. I'll even bake you a batch of peanut butter cookies. Pleeeeease? I just want to make sure you're okay.

I have to laugh. I can't believe she remembers our characters' names from so many years ago.

Me: I promise I'm fine. And you don't have to bribe me with cookies 😎. I'll be over around 8.

Harper's house is at the top of a hill in Medina at the end of Lake Washington Boulevard, right on the edge of Lake Washington. I would've thought Steph would jump at the chance to drive me over here—at the chance to drive anybody *anywhere*—but she actually passed up a chance to hang at Harper's house because she was feeling sick. Probably from eating too many goat-cheese-and-pear pancakes too fast, or too much pizza last night. So here I am, sitting alone in the driver's seat of my parents' SUV, looking ridiculously out of place parked in the middle of this wraparound driveway that's the size of my backyard. I take a long, deep breath and lean my head against the headrest, listening to the light sprinkle of rain on my windshield.

Being over here is the least I can do for Harper, but my mind is far away. Every time I close my eyes, I see Jamal's face, staring at me across that Ping-Pong table. I found out earlier, after torturing myself some more on Google, that not only was he set to graduate a year early with a scholarship to Sutton University, but he was about to be named valedictorian, and he wanted to study engineering, with his hopes set on becoming an aerospace engineer. With a 5.0 GPA, he might have been able to.

I force the energy into my arms to swing open the car door before I start tearing up.

"Hey!" hollers Harper from across the driveway. I pull my backpack over my shoulder, slide my hood over my hair, and shut the door.

"Hey, girl," I say back. As I hurry across the spotless concrete, which looks like it's been recently pressure-washed, I catch the scent of something sweet and buttery.

"You didn't *actually* make me peanut butter cookies, did you?" I grin.

"Obviously," she says. "Well, Marie Callender made them, but I baked 'em, so it counts."

We step through the wooden double doors, out of the cool night air and into the climate-controlled foyer with hardwood floors and thirty-foot-high ceilings, and suddenly I'm relieved to be here again. Just Harper and me, with peanut butter cookies and white cheddar jalapeño popcorn, and maybe some *Legacy* if I can get myself to relax first. Then I remember something that might just get me to loosen up, something their personal chef used to keep in the back of the fridge just for us.

"Does Logan still keep those raspberry sodas at the back of the fridge?"

"Of *course!*"

Once, years ago, we thought it would be a good idea to mix those sodas with some tequila that had been left out after a party. That was the night I learned I'd make a terrible bartender. My pouring was so heavy-handed that Harper and I both fell asleep dizzy as hell in the middle of her living room floor, talking nonsense that I couldn't remember the next morning. Her parents didn't even care. They said Wyatt's bullhorn-assisted wake-up call for us was punishment enough.

I'm so glad he's not here. Harper hands me a raspberry soda and heads back into the kitchen. The scents of spicy jalapeños and sweet-and-salty peanut butter cookies are almost too much to handle. I walk to the window and plop down into the chaise in the living room, which has been my favorite chair in the house since we were kids. I look out the huge bay window, where I can see the deep black water of Lake Washington, and the tiny headlights of cars crossing 520 like little marching ants, miles farther down the lake. Mount Rainier has faded behind the evening fog and clouds, but if we still had daylight, I'd be able to see the snowy peaks. In the summer, the view from this window looks like something out of a postcard. This chaise is so soft and fluffy even though it looks stiff, like one of those fancy ones out of an Ethan Allen catalog, and with how long it's held up in this house with two kids who have grown up into teenagers with it, I wouldn't be surprised if it cost as much as my parents' SUV. In any case, I know it's too expensive for me to go leaning my shea-buttered curls against it. If I leave oil stains on this chaise, I'd never forgive myself.

"Want one?" asks Harper. I look back in her direction just as I hear the oven door shut, and she pops up from the other side of the huge kitchen island with a baking sheet full of big, round golden-brown disks of ecstasy, and I jump up and run to the kitchen.

The cookies and jalapeño popcorn smell delicious, and I wonder why in the world I've waited so long before coming back over here.

"Wanna eat in the study?" asks Harper around a mouthful of popcorn. Before I can reply, she's got the giant stainless-steel bowl in her arms and is stepping down into the living room and around the corner through a pair of glass french doors.

I've always known Wyatt and Harper's parents are filthy rich—they both work at Gutenberg Enterprises, the same company where my dad works, except my dad gets paid to analyze things, and her parents must get paid to decide what's worth analyzing. But we never let that come between us. Harper has a trust fund. I have scholarship applications. Harper has silver Yeezys. I have white Keds. But she never talks about money, she doesn't make me feel weird while we're out for pizza by offering to foot the whole bill, and we both take our shoes off at the front door and put them on the same shelf.

But as we sink down into the antique brown leather chairs in the study next to the pool table, which smells like cigar smoke even though nobody in the household smokes, I sink my teeth into a still-warm peanut butter cookie and listen to Harper bring up our conversation from earlier.

"Hey," she says, leaning over and resting her hand on my knee and looking me in the eyes, "I'm sorry for what Wyatt said to you earlier. I'm sorry for even asking that question about my hair. It was ignorant. I knew it would make you and Steph uncomfortable if I even posed the question, so I should've kept it to myself. Or fucking googled it, for God's sake."

I have to smile. As much as I know Harper will never fully understand what *SLAY* means to me, she does try to understand me. Things were different when we were little. We actually met at Seafair, the biggest annual festival in all of Puget Sound, at the funnel-cake food truck. I used my allowance money to buy her the first funnel cake she ever had, and it was best friendship at first sight. We've lasted through so many different wedges that could've easily forced us apart—her parents have always gone to church and Wednesday night prayer. I wouldn't suspect my parents have been inside a church since their wedding day. She was sent off to Sweden for a summer for bassoon camp— which I didn't even know was a thing—while I spent middle school summers cutting the neighbors' blackberry bushes for extra cash. She went to private school. I went to Belmont. But by the time we both ended up at Jefferson together, we'd somehow managed to stay close enough to greet each other with *Hey, girl, heyyy.* Close enough to invite each other over for raspberry sodas and peanut butter cookies.

"Did you end up googling it?" I grin, taking another bite of cookie.

"Yeah, and I found just as many different answers as you told me there would be," she says, then tosses a few more jalapeño kernels into her mouth and pulls her legs up underneath her in the chair. She looks extra comfy in her pink pajama bottoms and gray Hello Kitty tank top, and I'm glad I wore my sweats and a loose T-shirt, otherwise I'd be asking to borrow some of her pj's. That's how you know you have a *best* friend on your hands. Regular friends invite you over and ask if you'd like water or coffee or something. *Best* friends offer you their favorite raspberry soda and their comfiest clean pajamas. *Best* friends can meet up after not speaking for a while, as if nothing happened.

But are we really best friends if I can't tell her my biggest secret? Are we really best friends if she doesn't get my experiences, or at least believe me when I tell her about them?

"I don't think I'll get dreads," she says finally, passing me the bowl of popcorn. I take it gratefully and pick up a handful of kernels. I can't lie. I'm shocked. Harper doesn't just "change her mind" for any old reason.

"Really?" I ask. "Why?"

She stares at the floor for a long moment, and for a while, I think she'll leave the question unanswered. But then she shrugs.

"I don't know how to explain, really," she says. "I don't want it to make you . . . uncomfortable."

Something about the way she says the word "uncomfortable" hurts. Her ice-blue eyes are fixed on the floor, and she shakes her head absentmindedly. She looks lost.

I set the bowl of popcorn on the floor and hold my hand out to her. She forces a smile and takes my hand, when I realize all our fingers are covered in butter.

"Oh God, ew," I say, as we both wipe our fingers on our sweats. "What a way to kill a moment." She busts out laughing, and I try to finish my thought through a fit of giggles.

"I know I've been distant lately," I say. "And I know you want to avoid questions that make me feel uncomfortable, but you can still talk to me about anything. I'm still your friend. It's just, lately *all* we talk about is politics and cultural appropriation. That's not *all* I ever want to talk about, Harper. Can I be your Black friend *and* just your friend?"

Harper runs her fingers through her short blond hair and shoves her bangs to one side.

"All right," she says. "I get it. I really do. And as for the dreadlocks thing, I don't know if they're technically appropriating a culture, and neither does Google, but if I do get them, a significant number of Black people are going to be insulted. Like, a *significant* portion. It's not worth a hairstyle. It's just not worth it."

Well, that's . . . not exactly the reasoning I would've gone through to get to that conclusion. You can't go around living your life doing *only* what won't offend people. But I can't say I'm not relieved to hear that we won't have to talk about dreads for a long while.

"You have to decide this for yourself, Harper. I can't just *give* you an answer, or tell you you've come to the right answer. Just like Google doesn't know, neither do I."

"I know," she says. "And I realize it was unfair of me to expect you to know. You shouldn't have to answer for all Black people, as if you *all* have the same opinion about it."

She's right. She's finally got it. I smile at her, reach over, and squeeze her hand.

"Thanks, Harper. I really appreciate that."

"Just do me a favor," she says. "Let me know if I ever do that again. You don't even need to be nice about it. Just 'Harper, I'm not answering that shit' will work."

I laugh so hard, I feel a shell of a kernel of popcorn fly up and stick to the roof of my mouth so far back that I'm relieved it didn't get lodged in my nose.

I'm thankful, relieved, and glad I came over, all at the same time. The energy in the room has changed. It feels like Harper has changed. Maybe now we can have some hope of keeping our friendship alive after I move to Atlanta.

The front door slams shut. The alarm system announces overhead *"Welcome home,"* indicating that someone with a passcode is here.

"Dad?" asks Harper. When there's no reply except the sound of a heavy bag being slammed down on the kitchen counter, Harper looks at me in confusion, as if *I'm* supposed to know what's going on.

"Wyatt?" she hollers.

"Yeah?" calls his unmistakably squeaky voice from the other room. Then, just as I'm halfway through reasoning out a plan of escape, his freckly face appears in the doorway to the study, his hair dark with rainwater and stuck to his forehead. His face is flushed red, and his mouth is curved into a grin.

"*Hey*, Kiers!" he exclaims, *way* too happy to see me.

"I'm not answering any interview questions," I say. I didn't come over here to play games. I came over here to relax.

"What are you doing home, anyway?" asks Harper, catching my drift.

"Jeez, a man can't come home to his own house without being interrogated?" he asks with a roll of his eyes. He folds his arms and steps down into the study in his blue-and-white Jefferson Eagles practice jersey, soaked with rain, still wearing his cleats.

"We got rained out. They canceled halfway through practice. Which I'm cool with."

He plops down into the third brown leather chair in this room, filling the room with the scent of grass and mud, grabs the remote, and switches on the TV.

"Wyatt, really? We were talking in here. And take your

shoes off and go shower before you get the carpet and the chair dirty."

Wyatt glares at Harper with a look so sour, for a minute I think he's about to launch into a full-on rant about how she can't tell him what to do. But instead, he kicks off his cleats, sending tiny clumps of mud across the carpet, swings his feet up onto the edge of the pool table, and clicks the volume-up button until the newscasters could be heard through the rest of the house if anyone else were home.

"Come on, Kix," says Harper, scooping up the bowl of popcorn and the plate of cookies and making her way to the door. "Let's go hang out in the piano room instead."

I barely hear what she says. My eyes are glued to the TV where two newscasters sit staring back at me. The reporter named Jan speaks first.

"And Dr. Cannon, what is it about *SLAY* in particular that caused this incident in Kansas City? We've reported on several violent video games like this before, but few that have resulted in cold-blooded *murder*."

The camera pans to a white man in his early thirties with huge red glasses, almost exactly like Steph's big round ones, except his are rectangular and wire-thin. He has a narrow nose and dark, beady eyes, but when he speaks, he speaks with the authority of someone who, oh I don't know, actually programmed the game.

"Well, you have to look at something like this from multiple angles, Jan," he begins. A banner appears below his face: *Dr. Brandon Cannon, associate professor of civil rights law, Sutton University.*

Sutton University.

I swallow a lump in my throat. That's the school that gave Jamal the scholarship. He might have gone to this school if given the chance. He might have actually *met* this man. He might have shaken his hand onstage at his own graduation ceremony. I have to take a deep breath and focus to keep the burning in my cheeks at bay. Harper is silent behind me. Wyatt has sat up a little higher in his chair and is watching on curiously.

"We have to consider the demographic this game is targeting."

Targeting? I never targeted anyone with my game.

"The game is free, and it features exclusively characters with dark skin tones, meaning the kids most likely to identify with it are underprivileged kids from low-income families in impoverished areas. As long as they have the virtual reality gear—headset, gloves, and socks—these 'SLAYers,' as they like to call themselves, can access the game whenever they want."

None of that is true. You can pick characters who are as light or dark as you want! And I can't believe this guy is really on national TV telling people *SLAY* is targeting underprivileged kids. Yeah, sure, kids play it. But those kids who approached me in the grocery store asking me if I eat meat were wearing private school uniforms. Cicada goes to one of the best schools in Paris, for God's sake.

She said they only take two hundred students a year! Even Annette Coleman, CEO of her own law firm, *SLAY*s. This Brandon Cannon really wants the world to think we're a gang of potential criminals just *waiting* for something to incense us.

Brandon—I'm *not* calling him "Dr."—glances down at the reference materials on his desk before continuing.

"This game is absolutely dangerous," he says. "It *prompts* users to initiate these 'duels' in which two players fight to the death using powers wielded from Black icons, including law-abiding American citizens who would *never* approve of this kind of simulated violence—Maxine Waters, Oprah, Angela Bassett, and Dr. King himself. This game is a slap in the face to everything Dr. King stood for, everything he said."

What, I think as I feel my throat close up with rage, *that riots are the voice of the unheard?* For a professor of civil rights law, he knows jack shit about the Dr. King you *don't* find in a high school textbook, the Dr. King that Steph had to school Holly about, the one who would be first in line to create a *SLAY* account today if he were here.

"If we are ever to have equality in this country," continues Brandon, "we must eradicate every exclusionary group, including this online Blacks-only gang." His face is turning a bit pink now as he lifts an accusing index finger to the camera. "Emerald is a dangerous character, and he should—no, *must*—be held responsible for perpetuating racism and inciting violence."

"I've never seen a video game that's specifically designed to target low-income youth of color," says Jan, stoking the flames. "It sounds like it feeds off their anger at racial inequality in this country—"

Brandon interrupts her.

"And breeds further divisiveness at a time when we need unity."

Wyatt's voice echoes his.

"Further divisiveness at a time when we need unity," he says, raising his hands in the air and turning to me. "What was I saying the other day?"

I want to dive over this pool table and punch him so hard he forgets what he was saying earlier. But Harper interrupts my thoughts.

"Speaking of what you said the other day, Wyatt," she says, setting the popcorn on the seat cushion beside her and folding her arms across her chest. "You owe Kix an apology."

"I'm not about to apologize for having an opinion," he says.

"And I'm not about to ask you again," snaps Harper.

My eyebrows fly up. Harper may have the blondest hair and the whitest skin and the bluest eyes, but she has the resolve of a Baptist church deacon who just discovered a tiny servant of the Lord stealing extra Communion crackers after Sunday service.

"Then don't," says Wyatt. "I don't even know why I'm entertaining this conversation with either of you. Like you two know anything about game programming."

I *almost* bust out laughing. He plays hours of *Legacy* on the weekends, but I'd bet a hundred bucks he doesn't know vectors from vertices. Ooh, I *wish* I could wave it in his face that while he's been screaming at his computer and losing campaigns, I've been *designing* campaigns.

Jan is talking again.

"I mean, something like this can't continue indefinitely, Dr. Cannon. There *has* to be a party working to stop this . . . this . . . well, most accurately, this *gang*."

"I haven't heard reports of anything yet, Jan, but in my professional opinion as a man who's spent the greater part of twelve years studying American civil rights, I can tell you it's only a matter of time before someone rises up and brings litigation against this Emerald character on discrimination charges."

"Hell yeah!" exclaims Wyatt. "What was I saying on Friday? Harp, I talked to Dad and Duncan on FaceTime last night, and they said it's *totally* a valid case."

Okay, now I have to ask.

"Who's Duncan?"

Wyatt rolls his eyes as if I've asked something asinine.

"Our family's lawyer."

Harper and Wyatt's parents have a personal chef, a driver, and a maid. Would it be that much of a stretch for them to have a family lawyer? I think of the CEO of NoonMoon, who could buy the services of whatever lawyer he wanted, and I wonder, if he knew he might get caught, might he have had an attorney at the ready beforehand? Would it be that outrageous for a rich father to let his son borrow that attorney over a video game dispute?

"This *SLAY* thing will be gone in a few months tops," he continues.

"Oh yeah?" I ask. *Now* he's gone and pissed me off. "And *Legacy* won't?"

"Uh, no," he chuckles. "See, the only thing that makes *SLAY* different from *Legacy* is that it's apparently *no whites allowed*. This Emerald guy thinks he's so exclusive, so elusive. Untouchable. But it's soooo easy to get a *SLAY* passcode, seriously. I have one."

It feels like someone has just punched me square in the gut.

He . . . *has* one?

I glance at Harper, who's looking at me apologetically, probably since she couldn't get him to apologize to me. But an apology from Wyatt is the furthest thing from my mind right now. How the hell did *this* boy, who's made it very clear that his only Black friends are me, Steph, and Malcolm, get a passcode to my game? Who the hell gave him access?

"No, you don't," I say. He has to be bluffing.

"Uh, yeah I do. Sixteen digits. Always starts with a one. Got it from some guy in a *Legacy* chat room."

I feel like I can't breathe.

Wyatt looks up at me and shrugs.

"As long as I live in a free country, I can play whatever game I want. All I need is a passcode."

Why does that sound familiar? Where have I heard that before?

It hits me when I remember Dred's words: *As long as I live in a free country, I can inbox whoever I want. . . . All you need is a passcode.*

My heart is pounding. It all makes sense. Dred, after Dred Scott, and after the dreadlocks debate. Dred, who clearly has experience playing MMORPGs, like *Legacy of Planets.* I feel dizzy as the full realization sinks in.

Wyatt is Dred.

Wyatt, whom Harper and I used to babysit. Wyatt, who used to beg to come to the movies with us and then threaten to tattle if we didn't buy him popcorn. He's now kicked it up a notch and infiltrated my greatest accomplishment, harassed me online, for not letting him play a video game.

I give Harper a half-assed excuse as to why I have to go home that minute. I don't even remember putting on my Keds or walking out the front door to my parents' SUV in the rain. All I remember about the drive home is feeling myself transitioning from shocked to angry. He's put the whole game in jeopardy. He's put my friendship with Harper in jeopardy. I want to tell Steph so bad, but if I do, she could never look at Wyatt the same way, which would put strain on her and Harper's relationship, so her sorority would suffer, which would mean her scholarships could suffer, which could mean her college prospects would suffer. I absolutely can't tell Steph, but maybe if I take her advice and battle Wyatt—I mean *Dred*—he'll go home and lick his wounds and forget that he ever tried to challenge Emerald. Maybe he'll be so miserable and embarrassed after losing that he'll go away on his own. I can go back to playing my game in peace, and nobody will have to hate anybody.

The minute I'm home, I sneak down the hall to my room and shut the door carefully before booting up my computer.

I open my *SLAY* inbox and find Dred's message and begin typing: *You want control? You want attention? You want to be included? I've got a proposition for you.*

But I don't send it. This isn't the way to do this. If I send a private message, he'll be able to archive this conversation and use it against me. I can't sound threatening just because I know Dred's identity. He still doesn't know it's me. I could *tell* Wyatt it's me, and he might drop the charges, or he might tell the whole world my identity.

Think, Kiera, think.

Then I remember Spade's words.

You are a queen, and this is your game.

I know what to do.

I unlock my bottom drawer, pull out my headset, my gloves, and my socks, and take my place in the middle of my room. I click the announcement bell in the top right corner of my screen—the bell I use to direct everyone to City Hall in the Central Plaza, where I make all my important announcements. Usually I reserve City Hall for game-changing news, like when I release a new update, or do a giveaway of new weapons to beta testers, or change the game rules or something. But today I'm saving the integrity of the game itself. Today I'm going to address what I should have addressed last week. Today I'm going to salvage what Jamal's killer almost destroyed.

I pull my trigger finger, sending Emerald sailing through the air. The northern lights are still aglow on the horizon, sending red and purple flames in ribbons across the sky. I fly over the snow and ice, watching the characters below make their way through their villages and huts. Some carry firewood, some carry swords, some carry staffs and shields or baskets of rice. I think about how much time each of them must be spending each week to build a virtual life for themselves, building up their characters and buying them clothes, forging weapons and textiles and other tradable goods, carefully managing their inventories and dueling other players to earn coins. Here, we all get to be the same. We all get to be "normal" in our own fabulous uniqueness.

Whatever happens between me and Wyatt, I'm proud of what I've created. I'm proud to know that I've given my people a space where we can be ourselves without limitations, regardless of shade or financial ability. Nobody has to worry about real-life problems here. The police don't profile us, people don't gentrify our neighborhoods, and we don't have to remind people not to touch our hair. And if experiencing that here in my game, just for a moment, makes even one *SLAY*er rethink their role in the world as a Black person, if it gives them the power to face whatever they have to in the real world, that's enough to make all of this worth it.

Just as I reach the Central Plaza, which is made entirely of marble and has been lovingly nicknamed King Jaffe's Palace after the king from *Coming to America*, my door creaks open.

I rip off my headset so fast it takes a couple of hairs with it.

"Whoa, whoa, it's just me," says Steph.

I breathe a sigh of relief, but I also want to kill her. "What are you doing just walking into my room like that?"

She shrugs and produces a headset of her own from behind her back.

"My *SLAY* sister Q.Diamond sent me a Discord message that you're about to make an announcement. I'm guessing it's about how you're going to drag that asshole so hard it'll give his children road rash?"

Discord is the communication app, mostly used by gamers, that Cicada and I *would* be using if we didn't have secret identities to maintain.

"You're on Discord too? Since when?"

"Since I found out about *SLAY* a couple of months ago." She's smiling proudly and shaking her head. "I still can't believe you're Emerald. Does this mean I'm kind of a princess? Sort of?"

"You know there's no official hierarchy in *SLAY*, but if you stay on your best behavior, I might just make you a mod."

She squeals so loud I have to remind her that our parents are just a few rooms away in the dining room, and they know Steph and I don't have enough in common to be in the same room squealing about anything. She nods and pulls a pair of hot-pink gloves and socks from the back pocket of her jeans and slips them on. Then she situates her matching pink headset over her hair and pulls the goggles down over her eyes. I smile at the wise allowance investment. She's got the 3500 series—the two-hundred-dollar set that launched two months ago.

"Don't you need to be near your computer to interact?"

"Oh, yeah!" She pulls off her headset again and swings the door open. "I was so excited I forgot!"

She slams the door and I hear her footsteps fly down the hallway. If Mom and Dad don't ask her what she's doing making all that noise this late at night on a school night, I'm going to wonder if they've fallen asleep at the dining table.

I pull my headset down over my eyes again and look out over the plaza steps. It's sunrise in *SLAY*, and the sky has turned purple, fading into orange. I check the Central Plaza chat, and it reads fifty thousand. My hands are getting clammier as that number ticks up to sixty thousand, but I tell myself that if MLK can improvise a speech in front of two hundred fifty thousand people, I can certainly type out some text in front of sixty thousand in a world where no one knows my name. I tell myself this, but it doesn't make me any less nervous.

I begin typing.

"I will make the announcement in two minutes."

The crowd roars to life as if I'm announcing a duel. Text

bubbles appear in a rainbow of colors above their heads, hurling questions at me, with some characters jumping up and down to catch my attention. I read a few to get a feel for the general sentiment.

"LONG LIVE JAMAL! LONG LIVE ANUBIS!"

"New mod?"

"CAN I BE MOD?"

"ANUBIS!!!!!!!!!"

"Will we have an Anubis memorial?"

I hadn't thought of an Anubis memorial. That'll be first on my to-do list as soon as I save this world from total destruction. A bright pink message catches my eye because it belongs to a character that hasn't stopped jumping up and down since I announced the two-minute countdown.

"EMERALD, IT'S ME, HYACINTH!"

It's so strange to see my sister in the game! Her character suits her, though. She's wearing a hot-pink catsuit, long thick hair tied up into a huge braid interwoven with flowers, over-the-knee diamond boots, and a black top hat. Why so extra with it, though? I wonder if she's ever been to Cicada's house. I have a feeling they'd get along just perfectly.

It's been two minutes, and I step forward and raise my arm for silence. Characters stop jumping. The ones who have their headset mics enabled go mostly silent. Some sit down. I take a deep breath and begin typing, hoping I don't say something that'll make this lawsuit worse.

"Welcome, kings and queens!"

The audience bursts into applause and I keep typing.

"Today I have a special announcement to make. You're all aware of our fallen brother Anubis. Many of you in the Desert region hailed him as your leader. While I never dueled him personally, I know he was a valiant fighter and a humble soul who was widely revered throughout the *SLAY* universe. He will be missed."

My jaw is aching from holding back tears, and I didn't even know this boy. Then, in a stroke of sheer impulse, I open Google and search "Jamal Rice." I see all those identical pictures of him, holding up a peace sign in front of that Ping-Pong table, probably at an after-school club in Kansas City, where he thought he'd get to grow up. I wonder who is across the table from him about to spar, and I wonder if they're a *SLAY*er too, and if they're watching me—Emerald—right now.

I reach my arm out and grab the photo, dragging it into my *SLAY* photo album that I keep on my desktop and broadcasting it on the blank wall above the City Hall steps. Jamal now stands two hundred feet tall behind me, and the audience roars to life again. Some are bumping up against the first steps at the bottom of the staircase, and I'm glad I wrote in code that allows only me and mods to come up here. I resume typing.

"Jamal's photo will remain here at City Hall until I determine a permanent way to commemorate his beautiful life."

Now for the hard part.

"You may have also heard about *SLAY* in the news," I type. "The media has called us thugs. They've called us criminals. They've called us racists for wanting a space where we can be ourselves."

Murmuring erupts through the clusters of people. Some resume jumping up and down. Text bubbles start flying again.

"WTF? Hell no!"

"TEAR THEM APART!"

"WHAT ABOUT DRED?"

So he *has* been in other people's inboxes, trolling, making people's lives miserable.

"A troll has been making his rounds here in our world. He claims that this place is discriminatory, and that we are racist against white people," I type. My pulse is pounding in my throat now. I'm mad. I can't stop being mad. My family has never had anyone break into our house, into my room, and take something important to me, but if they had, I can't imagine being any madder than I am right now.

"What he fails to realize about white people is that not everything is about them."

My people love it. They're all jumping now, text bubbles paragraphs long are cropping up, people are screaming and throwing things. I feel a swell in my chest, and my nervousness fizzles away into pure adrenaline. I take a deep breath and I keep typing.

"I cannot legally reveal his username, but many of you may have met him. He has an account. I cannot ban or block him because that's exactly what he wants. But what I *can* do . . ." I pause for dramatic effect, and my eyes find my sister again. She is standing there silently watching, and

I take a deep breath before typing my announcement. "Is make him a deal. YOU! USURPER! INVADER! If you can hear me, I challenge you to a duel!"

The crowds cheer so loud I have to turn my headset down. I draw a broadsword from my inventory and raise it high above my head, then lower it in front of my face.

"If I win"—I duck down low and jump back, slashing the sword through the air—"then you concede to having your account deleted, leaving the *SLAY* universe forever, and forgetting about whatever legal shit you were planning on dragging me into."

"And if I win?" appears a message in the top right corner of my screen. He's inboxing me. My eyes search the crowd. Where is he?

Come out, coward.

I can't find him. There are people everywhere. You'd think it'd be easy to find a Charles Manson–looking, swastika-tattoo-having white guy among scores of Nubian royalty, but no. I navigate to my map, open up my developer command console, and type in *D-R-E-D*, and I find him sitting alone on a mountain peak in the highest part of the Tundra. Without even asking, I tap the "hook" tool on my developer console, reach my hand out, snatch his ass right up into the air, and literally drag him to the Central Plaza. He falls to the ground in a heap, and every member of the audience is bumping up against that invisible barrier at the bottom of the steps. Swords are drawn, whips emerge and start snapping. One guy who's wielding two snakes begins hovering menacingly. A woman with a lion's mane wrapped around her head is growling with huge saber teeth bared and ready.

Dred pushes himself to his combat-booted feet and turns to face me. His character is as muscular as a gorilla, with huge bulging shoulders and flashing red eyes. That doesn't scare me. But knowing that a skinny sixteen-year-old white boy whose father has a family attorney at his right hand makes me terrified.

He holds up his hand for silence, but the crowd erupts in booing and spitting. I have to admit, I knew they'd reject him, but I didn't anticipate this much enthusiasm. I can't explain what it means to know I have over sixty thousand people rallying behind me. I observe them all now and casually hold up my hand for silence. The multitudes seem to begrudgingly quiet down while he types, and text appears above his head.

"And if I win?"

"What do you want?" I ask.

"Control."

Of course he wants control. Of course Wyatt wants to make the rules. Everyone in here can see what we're typing to each other, and I'm too deep to backtrack now. I have to wager something. Something that'll get him to agree to duel me so I can kick his ass and be rid of him for good. Something that Wyatt, spoiled brat that he is, won't be able to resist.

I take a deep breath and hope I'm doing the right thing.

"If you win," I write, knowing the next thing I type might result in mutiny, and that it will *definitely* result in my inbox being toast, "I concede all developer rights, access to all code, and my character, Emerald, to you."

I shut my eyes behind my headset. I can't look. I can hear the audience rumble into silence, but I'm afraid that if I read what they're typing, I'll completely lose it. To forfeit everything, my game, my world, my character, to this man, scares me in a way that nothing else ever has. But it's not enough for him.

"Are you serious?" he types. "Duel in your world, by your rules, with your cards? You could have the whole system rigged against me and I wouldn't know it until I lose. Do you think I'm just gonna walk right into that one?"

The crowd hollers their disgust at his insolence, but unfortunately, he's right. As painful as it is for me to wager three years of hard work—whole nights spent coding and crafting weapons, scheduling duels, naming and designing new regions, making announcements, and launching updates—it's still not a fair arrangement. I know every arena, and I know every card. I sweeten the deal even more.

"Fair enough. You can draw your six cards now and study them until the duel."

"And how will I compete against your cards?" he asks. "I'll never have seen them, but you'll know my cards' capabilities as soon as you hear their names. I want to see them all."

My throat twists into a knot, and I reread his demand to make sure he said what I think he said. The crowd is roaring their disapproval, but Dred is staring at me like he knows my hands are tied. If I say no, Dred gets to terrorize everyone in the game unchecked, and Wyatt gets to keep up this self-victimization-fueled discrimination lawsuit against me. I'm in no position to bargain.

I raise my arm for silence.

"Request granted. We duel tomorrow night at three a.m. Central European Time."

The less you know about Emerald, the better, Wyatt, I whisper quietly in my room.

"What time is that Pacific Standard?"

I can't believe Wyatt's just giving away his location at this point.

"You want to take over managing an MMORPG universe, but you don't know how to google shit? Six o'clock p.m."

Laughter rips through the audience amid cheers and screams. I'm not usually a sarcastic person, even when I'm hiding behind a virtual character, but I'm done letting Dred think he has the upper hand. Nice Kiera is gone. Tomorrow night we're going to battle, and I'm going to win my game back.

"Which region?" says the text above his head.

"I'll beat you wherever you want," I say. "Rain Forest? Tundra? Desert?"

"Swamp," he says. "Fitting, right?"

I'm assuming he's referring to the days of slavery, when my ancestors ran from his ancestors and their dogs and whips in the swampy southernmost regions of the United

States. I squint my eyes. It's hard for me to imagine that Wyatt might be an actual white supremacist, but everything from the faux swastika, to the name Dred, to his chosen biome, smacks less of intimidation and more of all-out terrorization.

I'm Kiera during the day, and I turn into Emerald online, but I don't want to believe the Wyatt I know at school comes home and turns into Dred when he thinks no one's looking.

"Swamp," I announce. "Beyoncé Bayou. Tomorrow at three a.m. CET, seven p.m. PST. I, Emerald, will duel against Dred with a standard six-card stack. He will have until tomorrow at the start of the duel to study the entire deck."

I go to my inventory, find my golden cards, and click the duplicate button on my developer panel, just as a message appears in my inbox.

Cicada: Please tell me you're not actually giving him a copy of every card.

Me: I don't have a choice.

She's typing as I'm clicking and dragging the deck copy into Emerald's hands.

Cicada: You're just going to give him all our secrets? Everything we've worked for? Just like that?

I hold out the cards to Dred before I have time to change my mind, and he swipes them from my hand and shoves them into his black leather jacket pocket.

Cicada: I hope you know what you're doing.

"Tomorrow, snowflake. I'll see you in the Swamp," says Dred's text bubble. "We meet at dawn."

I log out without replying and take off my headset, gloves, and socks and shove them in the drawer. Then I bury my face in my hands. What in the world have I done? I'm supposed to be leading these people—all half a million of them. And now it looks like I've just given away all our secrets, all our cards. I know I didn't really have a choice, but . . . what do I do now? What *can* I do?

My door flings open and Steph explodes into the room.

"Are you out of your fucking mind?" she shrieks.

"Shhhh," I urge, jumping up and shutting the door behind her. "Do you even *care* that Mom and Dad are out there? What if they hear you?"

"What if you *lose?*" she screams. "I'm not putting Hyacinth under the control of *that* guy! How could you do this?"

"You think I wanted to do this? You're the one who suggested I duel him! Why are you upset?"

"I didn't mean put the entire game on the line, and I *definitely* didn't mean you should let him study all the cards. I haven't even seen them all! Expert duelers haven't seen them all! How could you just give him the whole deck?"

How dare she? Does she think this is easy for me? Does she think I don't feel this like she does? The threat of losing *SLAY?* I created it, for God's sake. It's been a hobby for her, a way to pass time after school. But it's been my entire *life* for the last three years. It's everything to me. Something dark and agitating seeps into my veins, and I explode.

"Get out!" I scream. I don't care that I'm screaming now.

I don't care if Mom and Dad hear this part, just as long as they keep Steph out of my room for the rest of the night. "Get out of my room!"

I slam the door shut behind her, climb up my ladder, and curl up under my covers with the light off. It's eleven at night, but I still can't fall asleep. I check my texts to find just one message from Malcolm that says **You up?** and one from Cicada. I open that one instead.

Cicada: You know if he knows all the cards, he'll have a permanent advantage over every other SLAYer in this game, right?

Me: Knowing all the cards won't do him any good once I win.

I stare at the ceiling all evening. Cicada says nothing. Harper says nothing. Steph says nothing. I ignore Malcolm.

I'm alone with my thoughts until a knock sounds at my door. Mom asks if I'm okay.

"I heard the door slam, Kiera," she says. "If you want to talk about it, I'm right here."

Tears prick my eyes, and I nestle more snugly under the covers. I don't know when I'll be able to tell her or Dad what I really do every evening, but I don't think I can physically take it tonight. I need to first worry about this duel tomorrow, school Wyatt's ass in the Swamp, reclaim what's mine, and then I can think about bringing the rest of my family along. I'll be lucky if Steph doesn't tell them all about it tonight after I forced her out of my room like that.

"I'm fine, Mom, thanks," I holler. I'm too far away from the door to hear her footsteps leave. My phone lights up again.

Cicada: Whatever happens tomorrow, you should know that building SLAY with you has been the best thing I've ever done.

I smile and press my palms against my eyes, wipe my tears, and take a deep breath, remembering our conversation from earlier that went unfinished. I pull my comforter up cozily around my shoulders and hold my phone with both hands as I type at lightning speed.

Me: You do know that you're Black enough, right? I don't know how you got the idea that I would think less of you if I knew you were mixed, but I don't care. You don't get to be who you are at school either. You need SLAY as much as I do.

Cicada: I really, really do. I need SLAY, and I need you.

A lump forms in my throat, and my face suddenly feels hot. I've never even met Cicada, never even heard her voice, but we're close somehow, and I realize how much I need her, too. And how much I need her to know me.

Me: I'm an Aries.

I keep typing, fast, before I can convince myself this is a bad idea.

Me: I've only dated one person.

Me: I've never been outside the US.

Me: I have one sister.

I smile, dry the last of my tears, and pull my comforter closer around me before typing the last one.

Me: I never liked Candy Crush, but Gangnam Style was my jam. If we ever meet in person, I'm teaching it to you.

My heart is racing at what I've just sent. Those three dots of hers flicker to life, and I watch them closely as they die and reappear. Who knows what she'll say? Maybe it was reckless of me, presumptuous even, to suggest that we might meet in person one day. I'm suddenly regretting having sent anything, until I see her next message.

Cicada: Promise?

My heart rate jumps, and heat seeps into my cheeks. Promise what? That we'll meet in person? That I'll teach her Gangnam Style if we do? I'd love to promise both, so I answer:

Me: I'd be honored.

I'd be honored to meet her, if fate allows. And I'd be honored to teach her Gangnam Style.

Me: ♥ Wish me luck tomorrow.

Cicada: ♥ I wish you luck, pride, and all the power of our ancestors tomorrow.

Our ancestors. I shut my eyes and put my phone away with the warmth of that thought in my head, and finally, I drift off to sleep.

12. A GAME WORTH THE CANDLE

PARIS, FRANCE

I'm taking Biocomputing and Computational Learning this summer. I should probably be in my room getting a jump start on the reading, but instead I'm getting real-world experience in the basement of the research building, doing server maintenance.

I'll be here all afternoon. Maybe into the night. I should've packed something to eat.

But I'm lucky to have this space. The École normale supérieure spares no expense for its computer science students. We can rent servers for our own personal use. Very few questions asked.

When I filled out the application, I only had to give a title for my project and the number of servers I needed, and check a box saying I wouldn't use university property to conduct illegal activities. I called the project "MEET" after the code phrase "We meet at dawn," and I requested the maximum number of servers allowed—six.

I adjust my seat on the floor and move down to the next item in my server maintenance checklist—updating our operating system. We're two updates behind where we should be, and it's totally my fault. I've been busy with school, but that's no excuse for neglecting the servers. I could've been doing this instead of collecting all that ore in the Desert region last week. But the new iron headpiece I was able to craft from it is pretty dope.

I smile, click the update button, and lean my back against the wall. This might take a while.

I pull out my phone and navigate to WhatsApp, hoping for a new message from Emerald. I texted her yesterday asking if she ever found that lawyer for herself, but she never actually answered that. I hope whatever happens after this Dred duel, she's okay. I walk through the halls of my university every day overhearing Black students ask each other if they "eat meat" too, but I'm not in any real danger. Everyone in the game knows me as a mod, but it's Emerald's name that's been plastered all over the American news. It's Emerald who's being blamed for Jamal's death. It's Emerald they're after.

Every time I close my eyes, I imagine Jamal's smiling face. His eyes stare into the camera like he can see right through me. His right hand is holding the Ping-Pong paddle, and his left hand is holding up a peace sign. He deserved peace. He deserved safety.

SLAY was supposed to have given him both, and we failed him. I failed him.

The server closest to me blinks, prompting another response from me. I enter my passcode and set it on to the next update.

If Jamal was so savvy in the game, I wonder if he would've grown up to study computers one day like me. I wonder if he would've been doing server updates like this one in college. I wonder if he might have visited France, and if I could've met him one day. I wonder way too many pointless things about what could have been.

"You using this?" comes a voice in French.

The voice makes me jump so hard, I bump my head against the wall behind me. I wince and raise my hand to my head, and when I open my eyes again, a boy about my height is standing over me, pointing at the antistatic vacuum cleaner in the corner. I shake my head and pull my knees to my chest.

"No, it's all yours," I say, also in French. He reaches over my head to grab the vacuum, and as I clean another button on the server, I hear a second voice from the doorway on the far side of the room call over to him in French, "Our server utilization is fine, but we can add more RAM if you want."

"Yes. I'd rather be proactive," says the first boy.

I grab the brush in the corner of my server room, which is really more like a small closet at the far end of the common room, and begin sweeping the dust off the floor of my server closet out into the hallway. They've lowered their conversation to hushed tones behind me, and they don't raise them again until they switch languages to Italian. They couldn't have known that my mother is Italian, or that my father taught me a bit of Portuguese, or that I learned English in school, and Spanish on my own. They wouldn't have said what they say next if they knew.

"That's the African girl."

I freeze, resolving not to turn around. The African girl? Really?

I flip another switch and check our server utilization. Sixty-six percent isn't bad. Not enough to buy more RAM over.

"What's her name?" comes the next question, also in Italian.

I take a deep breath and begin checking out our system security, moving down my checklist to my list of the Ten Immutable Laws of Security Administration. But the boys are still talking, and now they're discussing blockchain security.

"Do you think she would know? She's in our class, right?"

"The hell would she know about blockchain?"

All right, I've had enough. I give up on finishing my list, push myself to my feet, shut and lock the server room door, and turn to face them.

"I'm happy to help," I say in my sweetest Italian. "Would you prefer that I explain in Italian, English, or French?"

The first boy, the one with the dark hair and blue eyes, is looking at me like I just did a forward flip over their heads and somersaulted out the door. I close the distance between us and step between the two of them in silence and down the hall, hands trembling around my bag strap. My head is throbbing, and I feel dizzy. With our operating systems updated, and the whole server room taken care of for the week, I decide I can finish my list tomorrow when those two aren't here. For now, I plan to go straight back to my flat.

I step through the front doors of the research building and feel the fresh air on my face, and suddenly my cheeks begin to burn. The clouds are out, bringing with them a cool, welcome change from yesterday. I pull my sleeve over my knuckles and wipe my eyes dry. It's ridiculous to be crying right now, I know, but "the African girl"? I know those two boys. I saw them in my Cryptographic System Security course last semester. They always sat at the back of the class and asked a million questions, and I always knew the answers to at least a third but never spoke up in class. I just assumed they were doing what all of us do— ask questions you already know the answers to, in order to get class participation.

Maybe I should start answering their questions directly in class from now on, just to remind them what I know. Maybe I'll even answer in Italian.

I walk down the steps into the western university garden just as my phone buzzes in my pocket. I pull it out and read the name and my chest tightens. I stop walking. The world around me feels like it's been sucked into a vacuum. I can't answer fast enough.

"Ciao, Dottore Ricci? Come sta? Come sta mia mamma?"
Hello, Doctor Ricci? How are you? How is my mamma?

I'm prepared for the answer, and I'm not. He doesn't even give me official news, really. He just asks, "Would you like to speak to her?" and I know what that means.

This is the phone call. The phone call I knew was coming eventually, but you can never really prepare for. I find a quiet spot on a concrete bench by a wall with a trellis of roses leaning against it, out of the way of anyone who might have nothing better to do than hang out in the western garden on a Monday. Dr. Ricci finally hands the phone to my mamma. Her voice is soft. Softer than usual.

"Mia luce," she says. She sounds absolutely drained of energy, but I can hear her smile through the phone.

"Ciao, mamma," I manage. I hope she keeps talking so I don't have to keep hiding the fact that I'm crying. *"Come ti senti?"*

She proceeds to tell me that she's doing just fine, but she's sleepy all the time now, and no matter how many times she tries to play it cool and act like nothing's out of the ordinary, the doctor won't forget to make her take her pills.

"There are blue ones," she says in Italian, "that are the size of euros! Big blue oval euros. And they taste like rotten eggs. It's not natural."

It gets me to smile, even as I wipe my tears.

"Mamma, I'm coming home to see you," I say, although I have no idea where I'm going to get the money. My scholarship covers only room and board, and meager food. I have exactly thirty-seven euros in my bank account.

"No, no," she insists, prompting a fit of coughing through the phone, which grows muffled, I'm sure from her coughing into her arm instead of into the speaker. "Stay and study. Too expensive for you to come home. Don't waste your money."

I would spend every last dime I have to be back in my mother's house in Florence right now, making spinach-and-sausage pizza in the wood-burning stove and sneaking sips of *limoncello* when she's not looking. I would spend all my money to go back to a time when her mind was well enough to notice me sipping anyway, and her body was well enough to chase me around the house for it.

"Mamma," I say, "I want to see you."

Nothing.

"Mamma?" I ask, panic suddenly gripping my chest. Maybe she fell asleep? Maybe she dropped the phone?

"Mamma?" I ask again.

"Hmm?" comes the answer. I breathe in relief that she must have dozed off. That's it. I'm going to see her.

"Mamma, I'm coming to see you. I don't care how much it is."

"*Mia luce*," she says with a yawn, "study hard, okay? Call your father sometimes."

I haven't spoken to my Afro-Portuguese father in over a year, and he lives in Avignon, right here in France. In his mind, I was never supposed to learn computer science

beyond how to refresh a browser, because it's "too dangerous." Too dangerous for *him*, maybe. Too dangerous if you
dabble in layers of the Internet no one should dabble in.
Too dangerous if you gamble with your nest egg on sites
no responsible adult has any business visiting. Too dangerous if you blame the Internet for the consequences of
your actions instead of your own hubris. If I spoke one
word of computer-related anything to him, the conversation would be over, and since coding has become my life, I
have nothing to say to him. I won't call him. But I can't tell
my mother this.

"*Va bene,*" I assure her. Her breathing has changed. She
must have fallen asleep with the phone closer to her mouth
this time. She and I used to run two miles a day together
in the summer every morning. She was a warrior—still is
a warrior. My jaw aches terribly as I hold back more tears.

"I'm so proud of you, *mia luce,*" she whispers.

If I could show her what Emerald and I have built
together, and the hundreds of thousands of people who log
in every day to watch us, she'd be exponentially prouder.

But, my mother is white.

I knew I was sworn to secrecy the day I volunteered to
be a *SLAY* mod. I knew from the beginning that it meant
I couldn't tell certain members of my family what I do.
Not ever. But now, holding this phone to my ear, hearing
my mother say she's proud of me, something nauseating
settles in the pit of my stomach, like I'm lying to her in the
silence. There's a lump in my throat I can't swallow.

"I love you, Mamma," I finally say.

But I don't hear her voice anymore. There's a rustling sound that echoes through the phone, startling me, before Dr. Ricci comes back on the line.

"Claire, are you able to come visit this week?" he asks.

I know what he's asking, what he's telling me. My mother, the only one I can call when I'm lonely, the woman who taught me never to be ashamed of who I am, and to seize what I want in life, is about to leave this earth. There's a high-speed train that runs from Paris to Milan, and a two-hour train that runs from Milan to Florence, and then I have to hope I have enough money left to buy a half-hour taxi ride to my mother's house.

I nod and reply, "Absolutely."

I have to make it out there. I have to kiss her face one more time. I have to tell her how I couldn't have done any of this without her support.

"*Bene,*" he says. "I look forward to seeing you."

Dr. Ricci has been around since before I can remember. He was my grandmother's doctor when she was sick, and I'm sure my mother once got a call just like this one about her. My stomach knots up at the realization that the only one whose hugs can help me get through the pain of loss without my mother . . . is my mother.

"*Anche tu,*" I say.

I hang up the phone and navigate to the TGV train ticket website, where I find a discounted student ticket for sixteen euros, which means I can travel to Milan, and I'll figure out how to get to Florence from there, somehow. I buy the ticket so fast, I'm physically exhausted from the stress of it. I lie on the concrete garden bench and stare up at the blue sky, and at some point, I drift off to sleep and dream of running down a dirt road in Florence in shorts and a tank top under an even brighter blue sky, with my mother running next to me.

The next morning I walk into Jefferson looking a hot mess. I threw my hair in a puff, didn't even have time to shower or smooth down my edges, and I'm wearing brow pencil only. No lipstick, no eyeliner, no mascara, nothing. I'm actually hoping I don't see Malcolm today, not so I don't have to explain to my boyfriend why I'm not wearing makeup, but because if he's particularly attentive, he might ask me if I'm sick, or ask me to explain what's wrong, and I don't have the energy or the brainpower to think up convincing lies on the spot today. He'll see right through me.

But other students notice. Harper notices. She brings it up at lunch. It's chicken tenders day, and the lunch lady gives me an extra honey mustard sauce without protest, which never happens. Those workers guard sauce packets like Smaug guards gold. Harper has found us a spot at the far end of the room before Malcolm can find me. I haven't seen him all morning, and I'm starting to wonder if he skipped.

"So," says Harper, leaning forward and smiling cheerfully at me, "I told the lunch ladies that I wanted a cookie instead of a granola bar, because today they have peanut butter cookies."

She takes the peanut butter cookie off her tray and slides it onto the edge of my plate next to the cookie I already have. I'm already halfway through my fries and a quarter of the way through my chicken tenders. My stomach is begging for food like I haven't eaten all weekend.

"Thanks," I say between bites.

"Anything for my Kix," she says.

I smile.

"Did I ever tell you why I call you Kix, by the way?" she asks, leaning in closer until I'm forced to look up at her. I shake my head. I never really knew there *was* a meaning behind it.

"'Kix' was a slip of the tongue when we first met that day at the funnel-cake truck. I didn't mean to say it. I meant to say 'Kiera, this cake is amazing,' but I said 'Kix, this cake is amazing,' and I didn't want you to think I was an ass for saying your name wrong, so I played it off like I meant to do that. Even back then, I couldn't admit when I was wrong. But now, I'm admitting it. I was wrong. And, listen, I'm sorry for what Wyatt said to you last night. I know I technically didn't say I agree with him, but it took me way too long to say *anything* to him, which is almost as bad."

I'm impressed with Harper for saying that. I think of

that Elie Wiesel quote again: *Silence encourages the tormentor, never the tormented.* "Lucky for you," she says as she puts a forkful of salad into her mouth, "Wyatt faked sick this morning. Guess he's just not into Mondays now?"

Of course he faked sick, I think. *He has to study over a thousand flash cards about Black culture so he can fight me tonight in an online virtual reality arena in a game that I invented but can never tell you about.*

"Thanks," I say finally. "And thanks for the cookie."

It's salty and sweet and delicious, and I'm genuinely grateful to have two now, and equally grateful not to have to face Wyatt all day. My phone buzzes just as I spot Steph walking across the lunchroom with Holly and Gretchen, who are both Beta Beta Psi, and a third girl I don't recognize. She's short, skinny, and very light, Rihanna's shade, and she has long chocolate-brown hair that falls down her back in tight little coils, and bright gray eyes. She's too far away for me to tell if they're contacts. Must be the new Beta, Jazmin. She looks like a *SLAY* character, maybe someone from the Tundra like Cicada. I wonder if she plays and if they've dueled before.

"Hey, what's up with you and Malcolm lately?" asks Harper. "Like, I don't want to be nosy or anything, but I am curious, did you break up with him?"

"No, why would you think that?"

"He says you've been ignoring him. *Look.*"

She hands me her phone and I read the messages one by one.

[Saturday, 9:02 p.m.]

Malcolm: Ay you talked to Kiera lately?

Harper: Who is this?

Malcolm: Malcolm.

Harper: Hi, Malcolm.

Malcolm: You seen Kiera?

Harper: I haven't talked to her since last night. I think she's avoiding me. Maybe she's mad at me?

Malcolm: Yeah, she been blowing me off today too. Tell her I don't like it.

Harper: Don't you have her number?

Malcolm: Yeah, but I ain't seen her. She's definitely avoiding me. Won't talk to me, won't let me over. Mad disrespectful.

Harper: Sorry.

[Sunday, 4:38 p.m.]

Malcolm: You heard from Kiera today?

Harper: Yeah, she texted me.

Malcolm: Cool.

[Sunday, 9:04 p.m.]

Malcolm: What did she say?

Harper: Why don't you text her?

Malcolm: I did. She won't answer.

Harper: Maybe she doesn't want to talk to you.

Malcolm: Fuck you then.

[Sunday, 11:40 p.m.]

Malcolm: Hey I'm sorry for wat I sed earlier. I been drinking. Was Kiera in keyboarding today?

Harper: No, Malcolm. It's Sunday.

Malcolm: Right. I'm going back to bed.

[Monday, 8:01 a.m.]

Malcolm: Kiera's definitely ignoring me and I need you to tell her that I don't like it. Have you told her yet?

Malcolm: Harper? Tell Kiera I don't like being ignored.

I look at Harper now. She looks a little confused and a little nervous.

"You didn't text him back?" I ask.

"Not after that! I hate to say this, Kix, but your boyfriend is kinda scary, and I don't mean because he's Black, I mean because he's just scary."

Harper gets all my side-eye at this moment, and she quickly realizes her mistake.

"I didn't mean that your boyfriend is scary because he's the only Black guy here. Sorry—that was silly—I didn't need to bring race into this at all. Ugh. I just meant that he's scary because he's sounding more and more threatening, and his texts are bordering closer and closer to harassment. I don't know what's going on between you two, but you'd better work it out before this gets out of hand—"

"Queen!" booms a voice from the middle of the cafeteria. I look up, startled, to see Malcolm walking toward us. He's got on that black-and-yellow Honey Lemon jacket I bought him for Christmas last year, and jeans and fresh white kicks. He could use a lineup, but otherwise, he looks fine as ever. I haven't texted him in over twenty-four hours, and I know he wants answers. Despite my exhaustion, and my lack of makeup, and my shaking fingers and racing heart, I leave my tray at the table and step around to meet him.

"Hey, boo," I say as sweetly as I can manage. I take his hand and begin to lead him back to my and Harper's table, when he yanks his arm away from me and bellows, "You ignoring me altogether now?"

People are glancing over their shoulders at us now as we stare at each other in the middle of the lunchroom. I'm glancing around and silently begging him not to embarrass me. I've been going through enough lately. I just need him to stay calm so we can talk this out like adults. I just need him to come over and hold me after I win this duel against Dred, which I really wish I could tell him about. *If I win.* Panic comes over me again, when I remember that I have to basically fight to the death tonight for everything I've worked for the past three years. I don't need this stress right now.

"Babe, please," I say in the smoothest voice I have. I move my arm down his and interlace our fingers, guiding his hand to my hip as I lean in close. "I'm sorry I've been away. Come over tonight?"

He's so close to me now, but his eyes are flashing wildly. I don't recognize him.

"Are you okay?" I finally ask.

"Am I okay?" he asks, his nostrils flaring. "You got the nerve to brush me off for almost two days and then ask me if I'm okay? I thought you were my queen. You're supposed to have my back. What happened? Where the *hell have you been?*"

I want to tell him everything right then and there—

about Emerald, about *SLAY*. I want to believe he'd understand that my game is different from all the ones he says
are a distraction for Black men. That I fell in love with video
games before we even met, and that VR has to be my first
priority right now because I'm the sole guardian of a safe
space for hundreds of thousands of Black people. That *has*
to be important to him, right? I look up into his deep brown
eyes, searching for a hint of softness, some confirmation
that he'd be open to hearing an explanation. But all I see is
rage, and I'm petrified.

"Malcolm—"

"You don't owe him an explanation," comes a familiar voice behind me. Steph loops one arm through mine
and stares him down. In the other hand, she's holding a
cup of black coffee without a lid, even though she exclusively drinks hot cocoa with extra marshmallows. I can see
the steam rising off it, and I already know she went and
grabbed it from the coffee machine for one purpose.

"Steph, what are you doing?"

"Allowed in your room or not, I'm still your sister. And
this Negro is about to be reminded of that."

"Steph, are you crazy?" I ask.

"Crazy? What? No," she giggles. Then she directs the
sourest glare she can muster in Malcolm's direction. "I just
suddenly felt like grabbing a nice big ol' cup of hot coffee."

I have to defuse this. If this gets out of hand, Steph might
actually throw that cup at Malcolm, in which case my boyfriend would be in the burn unit at the hospital, and Steph

would be in jail and possibly forfeiting any chance she has at a scholarship and maybe getting kicked out of Beta Beta Psi.

"Steph, that's not necessary—" I begin.

"Oh, it looks pretty necessary to me," she hisses, although she hasn't taken her eyes off him. Her voice has gotten louder and it's getting louder still. "In fact, while we're sitting here discussing what it *looks* like—it *looks* like this boy is bullying you, which is strictly prohibited at Jefferson. It *looks* like this boy is asking too many questions. And it *looks* like this boy is asking for a reason to leave."

She holds up the coffee cup menacingly. The whole cafeteria is watching now, and I want to crawl under the nearest table and become invisible. I know what everyone in this room is thinking, and I know what they're going to go home and tell their parents if something goes down.

Mom! Dad! The Black kids at Jefferson fought today!

When Malcolm's mom transferred him out here, she did so thinking this place would soften him up and allow him time to focus on his studies. But although trouble doesn't always follow Malcolm, Malcolm seems to always find trouble. He's staring at me now with his chin high in the air, and I realize his eyes are glistening. He may be angry, but right now all I see is a wounded animal. I see the little boy who was curled up in a beanbag chair, controller in hand, sleeping off the loneliness.

"What are we, Queen? Huh? What am I to you? Am

I your king? Make your choice. I'll be here when you get your shit together and come back home."

He lifts his hands up in surrender and turns to leave the cafeteria.

I get through the rest of the school day, but not without Malcolm, Steph, Harper, and Dred lingering in my mind all day long.

Three hours till the duel, and I'm a mess. I can't stop shaking even though it was sixty degrees outside on the walk home—warm for Seattle—and I'm sitting on the living room couch wearing sweatpants, one of my dad's sweatshirts, and my fuzzy socks. With shoe toothbrush in hand, I'm cleaning the gunk out from the bottoms of my white Keds onto a paper plate in my lap. It's amazing how much dirt and how many rocks can accumulate in the grooves on the two-block walk home. It's therapeutic, actually—something I can do without having to think. Normally my de-stressing activity is coding, or dueling, or designing Emerald's outfits, or talking to Cicada about what new weapons or cards we'll create next. We talk about Hexes and Battles and Defenses, and new regions we want to build—or we *did* until Wyatt discovered us. Lately, he's all we have time to talk about anymore. Now I can't stop glancing at my phone for notifications, not that I'm expecting any. I catch myself biting my nails mindlessly, even though my fingers were *just* picking rocks out of my shoes. Gross. My phone buzzes on the cushion next to me, startling me, and I'm frustrated at how jumpy I am.

Steph: Can I watch in your room when I get home, or are you going to throw me out again?

That's just what I need. An audience.

If I text her back, I'm afraid I'll say something I'll regret. I already have to apologize to her for yelling her out of my room last night. I don't want to add to the list of things to feel guilty about. And I have to apologize to Harper, too, for all of those texts Malcolm sent her asking where I am. Just hearing his name in my head sets my blood boiling. He's such an asshole sometimes. Steph insists he's antifeminist, and he insists he's antifeminist, but I don't think he is. I think Malcolm wants equality for all people—Black and white—but he thinks Black people are owed more to make up for what's been done to us, like affirmative action and reparations. I don't know how I feel about reparations. I mean, I'm not going to turn down a check in the mail from the US government apologizing for what was done to my ancestors. If they want to buy me a brand-new car, they can go for it. But I doubt it would solve any of our systemic problems. I want to talk to Steph, but not about the duel. I text Cicada instead.

Me: Do you believe in reparations?

Cicada: Do I believe in them? Like I believe in the Easter Bunny?

I roll my eyes, set my shoes on the floor, and lean back against the sofa.

Me: No. Do you believe in them, as in, do you believe we should get them?

Cicada: I'm not American, and I'm only half-Black, so I'm not really quali-fied to answer that, "Black enough" or not.

It stings, the phrase "not really qualified," but I guess since she's not American, that's fair. She's typing again.

Cicada: I didn't mean for that to hurt. Sorry. I just meant that since I'm not American, I don't know if my opinion on reparations matters.

Something's different about what she's typing. Some-thing's grayer, duller. Sadder. I ask her something that I think will cheer her up. She always perks up when we talk about each other.

Me: What do you like to do? I mean besides SLAY. I feel like we don't know enough about each other to convince people we met three years ago.

Cicada: I don't have time to do anything but study and SLAY.

I don't believe that, and I'm not giving up that easily.

Me: Well, I like to shop. I like to cook and read. I like to clean my shoes, which sounds neurotic when I type it out like this.

Cicada: I like to shop sometimes. Sorry, I don't feel like talking.

Me: Are you okay?

She takes a while to text back, but when she responds, I understand why.

Cicada: I didn't know how or when to tell you, but my mom died last night.

I don't know what to say. It's weird, but Cicada has always been this invisible force on the other side of the world, like an android that I check in with that helps me keep *SLAY* run-ning, so it hits me hard when she tells me this.

Cicada: I was on my way to the train station to see her when her doctor called me and told me the news.

I don't know what to say. I start typing and then delete, type, and then delete.

I hear the front door unlock, and my own mom's voice echoes through the foyer.

"Hey, girls, I'm home," she says. I hear her handbag as she sets it on the console table, and she begins her afternoon ritual of sorting the mail.

"It's just me, Mom," I say loud enough for her to hear me but not loud enough to be a classified holler. "Steph is at chapter meeting."

"On a Monday?" she asks as she slides out of her slip-proof shoes and steps into the living room. "Since when does she have chapter meetings on Mondays?"

I shrug and glance at her as I text Cicada back.

Me: I'm sorry, Cicada.

Cicada: My name is Claire.

Something swells in my chest, and I feel strangely lighter.

Claire.

Not sure why, but Cicada never really sounded like a Claire to me. A Victoria maybe, or a Trixie, or a Jacqueline. Something sharp. Claire sounds so sweet, so gentle, so . . . something.

Me: Claire is a nice name.

Do I tell her mine? Before I have a chance to think, Mom is sinking into her favorite armchair across the room from me and letting out a loud sigh that demands my attention, signaling she's about to talk to me about her day, and my day, and I'm going to have to find something to talk about that'll convince her nothing is wrong.

I can feel her staring at me.

"You okay, sweetheart?" she asks. I feel bad for her. If I had a daughter who suddenly checked out for days, stopped eating her favorite foods, started neglecting her appearance, and stayed in her room all the time, I'd suspect drugs.

"Yeah, I'm okay," I say. "Just tired. Math exam today."

"How'd it go?"

Same as it always goes. "Aced it. Harper did too, actually."

"Guess that girl finally found a way to study without you." There's a smile in her voice, but I'm not convinced she's not thinking quietly to herself, *It's about time that girl stopped taking my baby's help for granted.*

But I've never felt like Harper takes me for granted. Harper's just one of those people who doesn't know when to stop asking people for things, and I don't mean to say that she's selfish. She's one of the nicest girls I know. She just doesn't know where the line is. I've had to bail her out of situations more times than I can remember. I remember the day she discovered the Harlem Shake—not the *real* Harlem Shake, but the meme-ified one where you grab a dozen of your closest friends and get one of them to do something weird like hump the wall while the rest of you freeze, and then when the music drops, you all act like you ain't got no sense. A bunch of sophomores, including the girls of Beta Beta, roped me into filming a Harlem Shake video with them in the east wing, which we all forgot was dangerously close to the library. The superintendent leaned his head out the door, and while the rest of us scrambled to stop whatever weird dance moves we were doing, Harper was all by herself with her legs up the wall, twerking with a beach ball strapped to her butt for a solid ten seconds. Harper asked me to accompany her to the administration building myself just to talk the superintendent out of giving her a week of detention. I talked him down to two days. Harper later told me she couldn't hear us over the music, but I still say she should've been paying attention.

Cicada—I mean Claire—texts me again.

Cicada: You don't have to tell me yours if you don't want to.

I type, *Sorry, I was just talking to my* . . . and then I remember what she just said about her own mother, and I abbreviate my message to:

Me: Sorry.

And then I tell her.

Me: My name is Kiera Johnson.

Cicada: Kiera is a pretty name. Nicer than Claire. And I'm jealous of your last name. Mine is Chappelle. Imagine having to explain to everyone you meet that you're not related to the only Black Chappelle they know. You'd be surprised how many French people love Dave Chappelle.

I smile as I text back.

Me: I never realized Chappelle was a French name. Guess that makes sense.

"What did Malcolm say when you told him about Spelman?" my mom asks with a grin. My smile disappears as quickly as it came.

"We're not talking."

"Oh," she says. "Everything all right?"

"Yeah," I say, hoping she'll take the hint. "I just don't have time for him right now."

It's only half-true. I have time for Claire, for Steph, and for Harper, and for hundreds of thousands of people I've never met, but not for my own boyfriend. Or whatever he is to me now. Maybe he'll forgive me for neglecting him. We used to spend every other evening together. I rarely saw Steph. I rarely saw my parents. It was just me and Malcolm, or me and SLAY. They'd never competed before, but they certainly do now—now that a real-life boy in Kansas City is dead because of my virtual world, and now that that virtual world is putting real-life me in the crosshairs of a choice— no, an undeniable *responsibility*—to be un-silent about the real-life consequences of it.

It was easier to balance real life and SLAY when SLAY wasn't so big. When it wasn't so heavy. I just need to beat Dred—Wyatt—so things can go back to normal. I look up at the ceiling fan, watching it spin and spin, and I run through the cards in my head. Do I know them all? All 1,245 of them? How can I be sure unless I study them? If I can just look at their names before the duel, I'll feel a lot better.

"Hey, Mom, I'm going to lie down for a bit. Not feeling well."

Mom has been quiet for a while, and I didn't notice. She's staring down at a small white envelope with burgundy letters in her lap, and I run through the list of schools I've applied to with red in their school colors. Harvard. Stanford. University of South Dakota. University of Georgia. Illinois State. Boston University. I've been accepted to every single one of those, all acceptance letters except the one from Harvard. Which one am I forgetting?

Then a thought crosses my mind. Holy shit. Is that a letter from Wyatt's attorney? My heart starts pounding and I begin to feel dizzy as Mom pries the top open and tears the envelope with her finger. Then she notices me staring.

"What?" she asks. "Honey, are you okay? You look sick. What's going on? Talk to me."

"What's that?" I ask, trying to sound as relaxed as possible.

"It's your father's bonus check," she chuckles, but I can tell it's because she's shocked that I would be so freaked out over an envelope. She slips out a single sheet of paper with a check attached at the bottom, and I blink a few times in disbelief. What's wrong with me? Normal Kiera wouldn't be this panicked, this jumpy, and normal Kiera would've probably realized immediately that it's impossible for Wyatt's attorney to send me a summons when (1) he'd be suing Emerald, not me, and (2) he would have to know that I'm Emerald to know to send it to my house.

"I'm going to go lie down," I say again before retrieving my shoes from the couch and tossing them into the foyer.

"Honey," she calls after me just before I can disappear down the hallway. I look over my shoulder as she asks me, "You know you can tell me anything, right?"

I shut my eyes and take a long, deep breath. I want so badly to be able to tell her. *SLAY* is the best and hardest thing I've ever done, my best accomplishment. I want my mom to know about it, to see it, to experience it one day. I want her to be proud of me. I want to show her all that I've had to teach myself just to program a game like this, to create a virtual world for over half a million people. But if she doesn't want me saying "ain't," if she thinks glasses with tape on them are *tacky*, if she has to consciously focus on avoiding the word "ghetto," I don't know if she's ready to see the range of Blackness that *SLAY* covers. I'm already getting used to the fact that Steph *SLAY*s. I'm not ready for my mom to know too.

"Yeah, Mom. I know."

When I get to my room, I lock the door immediately and go straight for my bottom drawer. I realize that I haven't texted Steph back that no, she absolutely *cannot* come into my room and watch me duel. She'll inevitably start talking to me, and I need absolute silence to concentrate. What if Wyatt was able to study all 1,245 cards today? He would have had twelve hours to study the deck if he woke up at six and studies till the duel. That would be about a hundred cards per hour. A card every forty seconds. That's long enough to read all of them, and if he stayed up all last night with them too . . .

He could know them as well as I do.

I log in and see my logo—*SLAY*—appear on the screen inside my goggles. I slip my gloves on as I step back into the center of my room. I wonder for a minute if this is the last time I'll get to put these on. I wonder if this is the last time I'll get to play my own game. But I can't let myself wonder that or I'll start psyching myself out. I bounce my feet over the carpet nimbly like a boxer, taking a deep breath in and blowing the air between my lips until they flap. It loosens me up a bit, until I notice the chat count.

In total, 500,637 people are online right now, waiting for the duel to begin. That's almost every single person with a *SLAY* account, even the inactive ones who haven't logged in for months. Instantly, the nerves are back.

My fingers fly to chat, and I type in *D-R-E-D*. He's grayed out, indicating he's offline, and somehow that brings me some comfort. I search *C-I-C-A-D-A*, and she appears green, which brings me even more comfort.

Me: Hey.

Cicada: Hey.

Me: I just thought of something. If he wins, we'll still talk on WhatsApp, right? You won't hate me for losing?

Cicada: Of course. You're the sister I always wished I had. ♥

It occurs to me that I've thought of Cicada as a kindred goddess and fellow developer all this time, but never as a sister. I guess I'm as close to a sister as Cicada's probably ever had. Correction: as close to a sister as Claire Chappelle has ever had. I raise my hand in the air and pull my trigger finger, sending me sailing through the air. I'm in the Rain Forest, where I was surveying a new kind of miniature chimpanzee we released into the jungle, and I'm flying over the canopy now, which I probably made a little too close to lime green. I'll correct the color later, if there is a later. If Wyatt wins, who knows? I descend and my feet meet the ground. I move forward and keep typing.

Me: My favorite color is green, but you probably knew that.

Cicada: Would never have guessed. ;) Yellow for me. Have you always loved green?

I think hard about her question. Have I always loved green? I think so.

Me: I think it started with the first time I saw The Wiz.

Cicada: Never seen it. I wish I had a story that interesting, though. I think I've liked yellow best since the first time I saw the sun.

I smile, and I imagine what it would be like to be in the same room with her, side by side, watching *The Wiz* together, her for the first time, me reliving the wonder of the Emerald City all over again. And then that, thinking of the future, makes me wonder something else.

Me: Will you still SLAY if he wins?

Cicada: Hell no.

I laugh, basking in the satisfaction. Wyatt can have it all—the servers, the domain, the designs, the ideas, and even the cards—but he can't force the players to stay. I find myself hoping that if he wins, every player on this server deletes their character and boycotts *SLAY* until he's dethroned. That thought brings comfort over me like cool medicine. Even if it all goes to Dred, even if we lose everything today, he can't take *everything*. He can't have this community. He can't have our experiences here. He can't have Claire. He can Columbus the game, but he can't Columbus *us*.

I arrive at the edge of the Swamp to find scores of characters clustered around a single blank patch of gray cobblestone arranged in a swirly pattern I spent way too many hours designing. The arenas in each region were carefully crafted. Cicada and I designed this one together in the deepest part of the Swamp. This arena isn't made of diamond, and it doesn't project the northern lights across the skybox, and it doesn't even look like an arena from an aerial view. The building itself is actually camouflaged until one of us gives the word.

I lower myself to the cobblestone patch—another developer-only spot on the map that started as a design zone so I could actually build the brick pattern without characters walking through here. It's sunset now, and the sky through the trees is a brilliant orange-and-pink watercolor piece that I bought from an indie Black artist on DevelopArt. It turned out gorgeous from this angle, and I decide it was worth the twenty bucks. I'm realizing now how much allowance and tutoring money I've put into this place. The Swamp trees—the roots that protrude from the water—are actually duplicates of a commissioned piece from the same artist. They were forty dollars—Claire's forty dollars. We've both wagered so much tonight. So much depends on me winning, and thinking about it is just making it worse, but I can't stop thinking about it because there are only ten minutes left until the duel.

Me: What if he wins?

Cicada: Turn around.

For a minute, I fully expect Claire to be standing behind me in my room, but I glance over my shoulder, and there's her character, Cicada, standing in the middle of what will soon transform into Congo Square Arena. It's a name we agreed on together, after a section of Louis Armstrong Park in New Orleans, Louisiana, which used to be the only safe place for enslaved Black people to gather while they were under the rule of the French. They would sing, dance, set up booths where they could sell goods to raise money to buy their freedom. And they would make music that I would give anything to be able to hear today. It was Pike Place Market before Pike Place Market was cool. Fitting that she and I should be here, together, American and French, in the middle of Louis Armstrong Park.

Cicada and I almost match, with our long robes trailing behind us, mine green, hers white. She and I have dueled here before many times through the years, and I'm wishing so badly to be able to send everyone else home, lay out my six cards, and her six, and duel under the rising moon without anything to lose. But I know that can't happen, and the reminder comes as a slap across the face as Dred's message appears in the corner of my screen in a private chat window.

Dred: You ready to duel, chocolate puddin'?

My nose wrinkles reflexively, but I tell myself that nobody who feels prepared for an exam has to resort to mind games to get an advantage, and I write him back.

Me: Only if you are, stale sourdough bread.

I open Cicada's chat box again and write:

Me: Here we go. 2 minutes till showtime.

Cicada: Even if we lose, I'll rebuild it from scratch with you if I have to.

Me: Hopefully we won't have to.

Cicada runs forward and throws her arms around my shoulders, and I squeeze her back. I shut my eyes and pretend she's standing here in my room with me, and we're hugging, just the two of us without a care in the world, and when all of this is over, we're going to laugh about that guy Dred and how he almost ruined the whole game.

But first, I have to win.

When the hug is finally over—although neither of us wants it to be—Cicada raises her arm and whooshes up into the sky, and I activate the arena. I lift my arms high into the air and yank my fists down to my carpet as hard and fast as I can. The carpet doesn't respond, but the cobblestones arranged in the middle of the Swamp begin to slide against each other and swirl around faster and faster. The trees are rising up on all sides, their roots still in the water, which I've programmed to stay completely still and not pool in the middle of the arena. Characters are standing in the water, ascending into the night sky, and I watch as the ground itself lifts up into a bowl so high that I can barely see the top without the moonlight blinding my eyes. I can see the stars now, but only if I look directly above me. The circle is getting smaller and smaller as the bowl grows into a vase as high as a skyscraper, and all at once, light explodes through the arena.

My eyes take a moment to adjust, but once they do, I look up to see Cicada floating down through the center like a bald Beyoncé with a million angel wings flying out from all sides of her dress. I roll my eyes. Classic, extra, Cicada. If I ever meet Claire in real life and get a chance to introduce her to Steph, I know humanity will never see the end of their conversation.

"Kings and queens," she bellows through the arena. Her voice is clear and crisp. Wait. Her voice? Her *voice*?

My fingers fly to my inbox.

Me: What are you doing? Why is your mic on?

She doesn't text back. Instead she speaks!

"Emerald, if this is going to be my last duel, I'm not going to spend it typing at a keyboard."

It's so strange to actually *hear* her! Her voice is light and airy, soft, with a faint hint of a French accent whenever an *R* or a *T* comes up. It makes her real. It makes her human. It makes her Claire. I watch her fly up to the stands again, the spotlight following her as she reaches out toward one screaming fan. I'm glad we created that invisible guard around this thing so he can't actually fall into the arena, because he's reaching so far out with his arm just inches from Cicada's that I would be scared if I were him.

"Sorry, sweetheart," she says as she drifts away and back toward the middle of the arena. "Don't let this French accent fool you."

I can't help it. The laughter bubbles out of me. What in the world is this girl doing? I suddenly regret not having her mic on all the time. She's a better announcer than I am! The crowds are loving her. I can hear farther up in the rafters the soulful howls of Zama's followers. It's a full moon against a cobalt sky. Too perfect.

Dred: Gorgeous night for a lynching.

I shut my eyes and try so hard to ignore it, but it's like the words are burned into my mind. Black gamers go through this shit every day, I remind myself. It's just part of gaming while Black. In pretty much any online game besides *SLAY*, Ms. Coleman's kids would have to hear it when they come home from school. Dr. Abbott hears it in the presence of his nephews while they're playing *Legacy of Planets*. This racism crops up in so many places, I should be used to it by now. But I shouldn't have to be. Not here. Not in *SLAY*. I tell myself I'm here to defend that right to safety, to defend this space. *I am a queen, and this is my game.*

I close out of his message with such fury that I'm glad it's a virtual screen so it doesn't crack in front of my face. Cicada is standing before me now with her arms raised to the multitudes—the five hundred thousand or more who came to see if they'll get to log in tomorrow.

I take a deep breath as Claire begins to speak again in that subtle accent of hers.

"Welcome, kings and queens, gods and goddesses, artists and warriors, pharaohs one and all."

Damn, she's good. If Emerald survives this duel, I relinquish all announcing privileges to her. I'll stick to fixing bugs.

"We are all here tonight to witness the duel of our lives. Our queen!"

Cicada extends her hand in my direction, and the whole arena erupts with shrieks of praise. I can barely see any individual characters—not because of the lights or the height of the arena, but because of text bubbles. I read a few of their messages lit up in colors across the rainbow.

"We love you, Emerald!"

"Thank you, Emerald!!!!! ♥♥♥♥♥♥"

"Emerald, you have to make more games like this!"

"You can take him, Emerald—drag his ass!"

"LONG LIVE EMERALD! LONG LIVE CICADA!"

"LONG LIVE OUR QUEENS!"

"LONG LIVE SLAY!"

I look up at the hundreds of thousands of characters flailing their arms and waving their flags and robes, thumping their spears against the ground beneath the water, and their noise blooms into chanting.

"Emerald! Emerald! Emerald! Emerald!"

Whatever I said before about never getting tired of being able to raise my hand for silence, I'd take this instead any day.

"Our queen," says Cicada again over the roar of the crowd, "against a usurper."

The crowd's tone sours, and a low rumbling symphony of boos and growls and barking from farther up in the rafters cries out their disgust.

"A thief and a terrorist," hisses Cicada. "Merely someone who wants attention, power, and control."

More enraged howling from the crowd. A group of kings in the front row across the arena are whooping and hollering like a pack of hyenas, painted in gorgeous white body paint and red and orange masks with big black eyes.

"Dred Scott, the slave who was told by the Supreme Court of the United States that he was not human enough to buy his own freedom," Cicada continues. "This usurper, Dred, has named himself such because he knows no weapons but intimidation. But today, he is in *our* world! *Our* Swamp! *Our* game! And we *will not have it!*"

Cicada's voice has begun to falter, and I have to tell myself not to cry. My throat is closing up, and my chest is pounding as she announces finally, "Kings and queens, meet Dred."

She points toward the only entrance to the arena—the one right behind us on the south side of the ring—and the door drops to reveal that huge silhouette of a man I met before on the plaza steps. He doesn't know how lucky he is that I programmed that net in, otherwise he would have weapons, produce, baskets, animals, and whatever else people have in their inventory hurled straight at him right now.

He should be humble, being a guest in my house. But he steps through the gateway and down the steps wearing a red robe as thick as a shag carpet, which dusts the floor behind him. I swear he's used a hack to grow another three feet, until I notice his boots, which have a platform under them that's more than a few inches tall. He steps into the light, and the crowd roars into outrage at what they see. I want to scream with them. I ball my fists in the middle of my room and want to kill him right where he stands. He's exchanged the faux swastika for face paint, which is jet black, from widow's peak to chin. To walk into *my* game and try to take over is one thing, but to show up in Blackface? *Now* I'm pissed.

Cicada is silent for a moment, and she looks at me pleadingly, like she's asking if there's anything I can do. But I can't. The face-paint option is available to all, and I included all colors, since Blackface was never a concern among a community of Black people.

A bright red block of text appears above his head that says, "Ready to dance?"

It'll take an act of Black Jesus for me to wake up tomorrow, go to school, and walk past Wyatt in the hallway without carrying out an attempt on his life. My trembling hands open the keyboard, and I type so furiously that I have to backspace through multiple typos.

"I'm ready to duel. By the power of my ancestors, let's get this over with."

The audience roars their approval, and Cicada raises her arms again.

"These two warriors will duel for the throne. This mutineer against our queen, who has guided us through glitches and patches, who has forged weapons for us, who has heeded our cries for new clothes, new cards, new terrains, and new regions."

She turns and looks down at me now.

"With whom I have stayed up so many nights designing these sacred cards, one by one by one." She holds out her hand, and the deck scatters, sending individual cards drifting down through the arena. The gold pieces glint in the yellow arena lights, and I realize just how many there are. If fifty-two-card pickup feels like a spill, a thousand feels like a waterfall.

I smile as I watch her suck them all back up into one bell-shaped white sleeve and send them zooming out through the other.

"The rules of the duel are simple," she recites. "Each dueler will draw six cards, two cards in each category: Hex, Battle, and Defense. Because this is a very special match, each dueler will pull a card from the top of the deck to decide who gets to play five seconds before the other. Defense cards beat Battle cards. Battle cards beat Hex cards. Duelers will play two cards each in three rounds. The scores will appear on the Megaboard as the game progresses."

I glance up at the Megaboard to see those double zeros staring back at me, and I shut my eyes and pray—to whom, I'm not sure, my ancestors maybe, if they can hear me—to give me cards I can work with.

"Please," I say aloud.

A knock at my door startles me back into reality. Oh God, of all the times for my mom to come knocking.

"Yes?" I ask as inconspicuously as I possibly can.

"Hey, Kiera, Mom and I are going to pick up Dad from work and go to dinner. Want us to bring you back anything?"

The first question that runs through my mind is *why would Steph come knocking at my door in the middle of a duel?* And then the realization sinks in. She's keeping Mom and Dad out of the house for me! I can duel in peace! I can turn on my mic if I want! But on second thought, I don't want Wyatt recognizing my voice. But whatever! I have the house to myself!

I don't know how I'll ever pay her back, but for now, I yell back, "No thanks!" and hope she hears the gratitude in my voice. I knew I could trust her to keep this secret, even if it means she's going to miss most of the match.

I lower the headset back over my eyes, and I find Dred staring at me with a text box above his head that says, "Glitch?"

I mouth a swear word in the privacy of my room. The front door slams, and I type furiously.

"I was giving you a minute to breathe. Ready, Cicada."

She nods. "Duelers, draw your initial card from the deck to determine who goes first."

He draws one of my favorite cards—the McDonald's Money card.

Every American Black child knows the term "McDonald's money," even if their parents never used it. It's not from the McDonald's Monopoly game (as Harper, who clearly hasn't played it, asked me once). It's the go-to response when you ask for McDonald's. "You got McDonald's money?"

And the conversation usually ends there, which is why it's a Battle card.

Even if Wyatt now "knows" this card after studying it last night, he'll never truly *know* it.

I draw my card and laugh. It's perfect enough to make me want to dance where I stand in my room, and I might if I didn't have five hundred thousand people watching me. But then I figure that it might be my last duel, and I'll regret it if I don't have a little fun. So I hold up the card, waving my right arm and sinking into a perfect nay-nay, tongue out and everything. The whole room shrieks with laughter and applause as I celebrate with a Michael Jackson spin and smoothly transition into the Running Man.

It's the Shea Butter card. Smooth, creamy nectar of the motherland saving my twist-out *and* my virtual reality Nubian universe. "Thank you," I whisper.

I can hear Cicada's smile as she announces, "We have Dred with the McDonald's Money card, and our queen with the Shea Butter card, come through. Defense card beats Battle card. Our queen goes first! Kings and queens, you know the drill."

My chest is pounding as she holds up her hand and recites the next part.

"We are here first and foremost to celebrate Black excellence in all its forms, from all parts of the globe. We are different ages, genders, tribes, tongues, and traditions. But tonight, we are all Black—most of us. And tonight, we all SLAY."

The audience erupts again, but I tune them out and keep my eyes on Dred.

"In-game betting on opponents," recites Cicada, "hacking, lag mechanisms, and unapproved mods to characters, skills, and environments are strictly prohibited. And even under the given circumstances, no—"

The multitude of Black kings and queens finish the sentence with her, as do I, while staring right into the eyes of Dred.

"Tomfoolery!"

Dred doesn't say it along with us, because how would he know to say it? Even now, he's probably oblivious to the fact that he *is* the tomfoolery. He shrugs one shoulder and cracks his neck, bouncing up and down like we're about to start a boxing match.

"Duelers, select your cards!"

I shut my eyes as I draw blindly from the purple deck of Hex cards, the red deck of Battle cards, and the blue deck of Defense cards.

Come on, ancestors.

I look down at the six cards as Cicada bellows from above us, "The duelers will have ten seconds to arrange and study their six randomly selected cards in three . . . two . . . one. Go!"

All six of my cards fly up onto my screen in three rows of two, and I read the titles as fast as I can.

Hex 1: Black Love
Hex 2: Innovation
Defense 1: Hell Naw

Defense 2: Representation
Battle 1: That One Auntie's Potato Salad

I look at my second Battle card, and I almost can't believe it. The J's card? Really? I grin and throw a silent *thank you* to my ancestors, or karma, or whatever made this happen. I'll save that one for round two. For now, I have to figure out which combination to use in round one. Wyatt is a trickster in real life. He's played countless pranks on me and Harper, although I've learned to watch for them and dodge them. He'll save his Battle cards for later, which is when I'll need at least one Defense card, in round three. That leaves three cards to choose from— Innovation, Black Love, and That One Auntie's Potato Salad. The Innovation card is a 25 percent point boost, and since I have no points on the board, that leaves Black Love and Potato Salad.

I move both of those to the first-round slots, loving the passive-aggressiveness of it. My first duel with a white guy and I'm going to whip out the Black Love card in round one. And what does Wyatt know of the fear that comes with peeling back the Saran Wrap on a huge tinfoil pan of flavorless white potato mash? He'll learn today.

I pair the Representation card with the J's card for round two. Representation will triplicate me, creating three Emeralds, and the J's card will summon the power of the ultimate sneaker and let me jump all over the ring. With three of me flying all over the place, Wyatt won't know which one to hit first. By combining a Battle card and a Defense card, I've created a very Hex-like maneuver.

That leaves Innovation and Hell Naw for the last round—a point boost, and an impact reversal card. That'll work against whatever Battle cards he's planning on holding on to. I'm ready. I look up at Cicada and nod. Then I turn back to face Dred.

"Duelers, have you chosen your cards?"

I raise my Black power fist in the air, and he lifts both hands to the sky, never taking his eyes off me. He thinks he's got a strategy, but I have an advantage. I know him— the *real* him—Wyatt. He has no idea Emerald is actually the quiet nerdy Black girl in his class with the big hair who helps his sister with math homework, or that despite my nonconformance to his perceptions of Blackness, I'm Black enough to crush him in a *SLAY* duel.

"Duelers, on your mark!"

I lower myself to the floor, one knee on the ground, knuckles sinking into my carpet, eyes on Wyatt. He's got his feet spread way too far apart in a weird anime-like pose that's probably supposed to look intimidating. To me, he just looks easy to topple.

"Get set," says Cicada.

I can hear my pulse in my ears, and the auditorium dissipates into almost dead silence.

"Go!"

I race for my first card, and I tap mine just before he taps his.

"Okay!" cries Cicada. "Come through, Queen, with the Black Love card. Yaaaaas."

I lose it laughing at Cicada's attempt at the very American "yaaaaas," which ends up sounding exaggerated from her accent. Then I watch my card take effect. Dred grips his head and falls to his knees. He's wobbling, a golden twinkling haze floating around his head like fireflies. The Black Love card is so named for its ability to mesmerize and daze your opponent, because love, marriage, and romance in the Black community are ultimately symbols of intangible strength. It's kings and queens building each other up emotionally, praising and prioritizing each other. I think of myself and Malcolm and all the nights we've shared in each other's arms, not necessarily having sex—just talking, lying out in the backyard, looking at the stars and dreaming about Atlanta. I think of all the times he's called me Queen. I think of all the times he's shared an excerpt with me of something he's read about the experiences of Black women, and confirmed with me if it's true. He *believes* me. He believes my experiences. He loves me in his actions. And when he makes love to me, he calls it worship. I glance up at the card on the Megaboard, at the artwork of two crowns side by side, undazzled by jewels, just plain gold. Genderless. Equal. I'm grateful to actually have the opportunity to enjoy this, until Dred, lying helpless on his side, holds up his next card.

"It's," continues Cicada, "the Shuffle card? Dred has used a Shuffle card in round one—what a dirty trick!"

Shit. I had so much fun creating that card too—it's a double entendre. Shuffles are done at Black weddings, birthday parties, and other events all over the world, and the Shuffle card, named after them, shuffles all six of your opponent's cards—in this case, mine.

I watch as all six of my cards, now facedown in the corner of my screen, slide around to different slots and light up gold. Before I can assess my next move, Dred's fingers are on his second card, his eyes are glowing blue and pink, and I take off sprinting in the other direction. I already know the card before Cicada makes the announcement.

"Dred chooses the Black Jesus card!"

I can hear the first laser charging up, and I dart left and sprint as fast as I can around the ring. He's watching me, both of his arms glowing, one pink and one blue. The Black Jesus card was a ludicrous invention of Cicada's one day when she was feeling especially mad scientist. It's literally an amalgamation of everything epic she could think of mashed into one big ball of godlike awesomeness—or horror, from my perspective.

I know a few of Dred's powers—the laser eyes and arms, and the flying, which he's doing now. But I forget about the telekinesis until a glowing blue dagger flies out from under his robe and sails straight toward my face. I forget for a moment that I'm a warrior and yelp as I dodge it just in time, and I'm glad I decided to leave my mic off. And then I freeze, remembering my Black Love card is still at work, making him dizzy. I'm hard for him to see. And if I stay *perfectly* quiet . . .

I slink across the floor like a cat and touch my second round one card, hoping it's still That One Auntie's Potato Salad.

But it's not.

It's the Innovation card. Dammit! His Shuffle card scrambled my point boost card into the first round, which means I just boosted my zero points by 25 percent. Useless!

Cicada breaks character and gasps from somewhere above me. The audience rumbles into booing and rattling of chains and swords and jewelry. I'm out of round one cards, and he's still got a solid thirty seconds of lasers, flying, and telepathy, and he knows it. His arms emit searing light in all directions, like one of those strobe lights you see outside strip malls, except these are flying as fast as a ceiling fan, which makes them impossible to dodge. I jump over one and duck under another. I even have to roll to dodge another, and I worry that I'm getting too close to my bunk bed. This arena may be the size of my backyard, but my combat space is still only as big as my room.

I've been to Wyatt's house. His room is the size of my living room. He can flip and jump and swing his laser arms wherever he wants.

One of the lasers hits me and pink sparks explode across my screen, blinding me. I shriek, startled as Emerald goes careening backward, landing on her back with her green gown flying up over the screen in a green haze. I scramble to brush the sheer green fabric away from my face so I can dodge the next laser, just as the drums begin.

"*Yes!*" I holler in the privacy of my room. Finally we can move on from this bullshit and I'll get some cards I can actually use! Bring on round two!

"All right, everyone, that marks the end of round one. We have Dred on the board with three hundred points and our queen at zero, but that's okay! That's okay! We've got two more rounds, people. Here we go. Round two on my count. Duelers, are you ready?"

I pry Emerald off the ground and raise my fist in the air. Dred has descended back to the ground, and the hex has worn off. Since he forced me to use both Hex cards in round one, I either get a Battle card or a Defense card. No more funny business. Just offense or defense.

"Three . . . two . . . one . . . Go!"

I'm not messing around this time. I slap both cards, ready for whichever two of mine are next, curse that Shuffle card. So does he, and I dart left, knowing anything could come flying out from under that huge red cloak of his. His inky black face is zooming toward me as quick as the Flash, and I spot the blur of his now giant feet encased in the whitest of sneakers just before he picks me up under my shoulders and slams me to the ground.

The Michael Jordan card. It gives players increased agility.

I look around, wondering what in the world my cards are doing. Are they working? I don't look any different. I don't feel any different. He's still standing over me, about to pick me up again, and I dart between his legs, under his robe, watching the fabric wash over me. And then I think up an idea, and I pray to whatever that Cicada—Claire— actually got around to that update.

I grab two huge fistfuls of the fabric and yank as hard as I can, sending him flying backward. The sound of his body hitting the floor of the ring rattles the whole arena, and I can hear the audience roaring from under this cloak of his.

Yes! I wish I had time to open my keyboard panel and thank Claire. The fabric isn't immaterial anymore! It's interactive now, and very, very grabbable.

He's rolling around out there somewhere, but I keep playing games while I'm waiting for my cards to kick in. Then I notice the fabric is moving differently around me. I kick and it seems to catch on my feet. I start kicking and crawling my way out from under the cloak and realize I'm wearing J's! The J's card is one of my round two's! My jumping ability is increased by 70 percent.

"Excellent use of the Michael Jordan card by Dred. His agility is up by 50 percent, but that's a masterful execution of the J's card by our queen. Dred also has an activated Swerve card, canceling 80 percent of that throw to the ground."

Shoot. Why, though? He's getting way too lucky with these cards. I decide to put those J's to good use and roll out from under the cloak and spring up on him from behind, leaping thirty feet through the air and wrapping my legs around his waist. My arms are clamped around his neck and I'm gritting my teeth.

Go home, Wyatt! Go home!

But he can't hear me. I'm channeling my anger now, though. I just want to kill him. I clamp harder, and his hands fly up to try to pry my arms from around his neck. I watch the Megaboard as my points tick up and up. It's 300–150, since my Hell Naw card reversed the points from that body slam I took earlier. I'm clamping as hard as I can. 300–250. 300–275. The drums rattle the arena, and I release him grudgingly. If I had just had ten more seconds, we could be tied!

"We end round two with a twenty-five-point lead by the usurper, kings and queens!"

The stadium is hollering, and I hear them take up chanting, "Emerald! Emerald! Emerald!" high up in the stands, some howling in my honor. It's admirable, and it's meant to give me hope, but I know what each of us has left in our decks—a Battle and a Defense. No tricks left up his sleeve. No tricks left up mine. It's all brawn vs. bob and weave now, and if he's been keeping track, he knows it too.

"Duelers, are you ready for round three?" hollers Cicada.

I raise my fist into the air one final time as I take one more look around the stadium—at all the characters standing in the swamp water in all their splendor. So many colors, so many shades, so many gorgeous faces, and then I spot those red deer antlers and that rainbow face with the piercing blue eyes.

Q.Diamond is watching me, unmoving. Just staring. A chat bubble appears above their head in white.

"Finish him," it says.

Hell yeah I will.

Cicada yells, "And go!"

I tap my last two cards, Dred taps his, and two Emeralds appear on either side of me, courtesy of the Representation card. They operate on their own, racing around the ring until we're encircling the man in Blackface with the huge red cape who was invincible just a few moments ago. Now we have him. The other two Emeralds will mimic my every move, which can be a benefit or a drawback.

I summon the power of That One Auntie's Potato Salad and conjure up a potato from my right hand, then hurl it straight at Dred's head. An arm, long and bony and pale sickly green, bursts out of the floor in front of him and I reel back.

What kind of noob gets lucky enough to draw the Michael Jordan card *and* the Michael Jackson card in a single duel? My Emeralds and I hurl potatoes from our hands like softball pitching machines, but Dred's Thriller zombies are faster, catching potatoes and launching them back at all three of us. One Emerald is hit square in the head and lands in a heap on the floor, and I decide to change up my strategy, lifting my hand, pulling a mountain of mashed potatoes from the ground underneath me and pushing it across the ring while I swing my arms as fast and hard as I can, showering Dred and his undead horde in a torrent of french fries.

It was fun explaining to Cicada about the horrors of

That One Auntie's Potato Salad—you know, that auntie who's not allowed to bring food to the cookout unless it has a price tag on it. The thing about that one auntie's potato salad is that you never know what's going to be in it. I've seen all kinds of things in Auntie Tina's—raisins, almonds, grapes, pickles, peas, and avocado chunks.

Dred is lucky I only have potatoes in my arsenal.

But he's *unlucky* I know all the things you can do with potatoes.

I rain down a ring of razor-sharp french fries around him, encasing his zombies in a potato jail while I circle on my wave of mashed potatoes, but his zombies get creative and yank them out of the ground, wielding them like swords. But before they get too many of them, I go straight for Dred. I take a leap from the crest of my mashed mountain, flip, snatch a potato sword from the ground, raise it over my head, and thrust it through his eye with every ounce of strength in my arms just as the drums begin to rattle the arena.

He picks Emerald up and throws her to the ground, and, with my vision blurry, I look around at the sea of zombie limbs and tattered clothing disappearing into the ground. One skull that doesn't feel like being a good sport twitches and clicks its jaw open and closed before dissolving into dust.

"Well, well, well!" sings Cicada's voice from the rafters. My eyes dart to the scoreboard and my heart sinks.

Dred's score reads 700, and my score reads 700.

"For the first time I've seen in person, kings and queens, we have a perfect round three tie!"

Dred is staring at me and pacing the floor like a raging bull, but I'm smirking. After all this fighting and running and throwing potatoes and shooting lasers, this game will come down to luck. Karma. The ancestors. Whatever.

"Please," I say again.

Cicada descends to the ring until she's standing between us.

"In the event of a tie, duelers will each draw a single card from the master deck and duel. The first warrior to score a point wins."

I look up at the crowds from where I stand in the middle of the ring, and that's when I notice all the text bubbles.

"New York, New York."

"Jakarta, Indonesia."

"Abidjan, Ivory Coast."

"Berlin."

"Los Angeles."

"Paris."

"Oslo, Norway."

"Nairobi."

"Cloghan, Offaly, Ireland."

"London."

"Corvallis, Oregon."

"Lahore, Pakistan."

What did I miss in chat? I keep reading, and Cicada must notice my distractedness.

"Queen Emerald, look at these kings and queens, look at where they're from. Look how far and wide our support goes!"

"Paris" appears over Cicada's head, and I start typing in a private chat as the crowd roars and shakes their spears and stomps their feet at the revelation that their beloved Cicada is from France.

Me: What are you doing?!

Cicada: I don't care anymore. Let them know. Let everyone know. You should announce where you're from!

Me: We are at risk of being sued! You think it's a good idea to announce to everyone where we're from?

I hate to be so cut-and-dried about it, but it's a fool-hardy thing to do. Cicada thinks with her emotions a little too much sometimes, and in this case, it might actually get us thrown in jail.

Cicada: Good point. Good thing Paris is a big place.

I look up and around at the arena again, reading locations I've never even heard of before, across all continents. I guess I shouldn't be surprised to find out there are Black people in some of these places, but I am. I read *Amsterdam, Beijing, Reykjavik,* and a place in Sweden called *Gothenburg.* We really are everywhere.

We really *SLAY* everywhere.

But Bellevue, Washington, isn't big enough. If I announce my city, Wyatt might put it together. There are only so many of us here anyway. He'd figure it out, or at least ask me about it at school, and I can't lie for anything.

Me: I can't, Claire.

It still feels amazing to know her real name. Even if I can't declare to the masses where I'm from, I can at least tell my most trusted friend.

Me: But I can tell you. I'm from Bellevue, Washington. Just across the water from Seattle.

Cicada: No wonder you're so good with programming.

I have to laugh. She knows her geography. Puget Sound is home to so many tech giants, it's a wonder I wasn't born knowing how to code.

Cicada: Ready for me to deal these last two cards?

Me: Hell yeah.

A long pause lingers as she continues typing.

Cicada: I wish my mom could've met you.

My heart sinks, and the guilt overwhelms me. I've been so focused on kicking Wyatt out of *SLAY* and back to the land of the white normal that I've forgotten about Claire's mom entirely.

Me: I wish I could've met her too.

Me: I'm so sorry, Claire. I'm so, so sorry. For you and your family.

She's typing again.

Claire: It's okay, Kiera. She would've loved to see all of this. You, these people, everyone in this arena, you ARE my family now.

By the time I start typing again, her voice is exploding through the arena.

"Duelers, are you ready?" she screams. All five hundred thousand characters are jumping up and down and splashing the swamp water all the way up the walls of the auditorium, and I look up at the night sky and take a deep breath.

"Let's go," I whisper into the silence of my room.

"On my count, you will draw your next card and fight! Let the best warrior win."

I look up at Cicada, who's looking at me as she counts, "Three . . . two . . . one . . . Go!"

I lunge for my deck, pick up the first one, read the word "Unbothered," and throw my body across the ring, across my carpet, as hard as I can. Emerald slides and raises her arm above her head to create a crystal clear diamond shield over her body as Dred goes wild with the blows outside her shell. I, Kiera, slide across my carpet, feeling the heat intensify up my arm as the rug burn sets in, and I hear a loud, sharp *crack!* like the snapping of a pencil in my left ear.

Pain explodes through my shoulder, and I shriek and grip my arm as the bright red boxing gloves deal deadly blows to the glassy bubble over me. I've never dislocated a shoulder before, but if this is what it feels like, I understand that scene from *Lethal Weapon 2* with the straitjacket, where Mel Gibson was screaming his head off. I'm still shrieking. I can't help it. My whole left arm is pins and needles, and it feels like a knife has been wedged between my shoulder and my neck. The thunder of the boxing gloves continues, and I wonder if Dred thought the Muhammad Ali card would be the end-all card to win him the game—*my* game.

I just lie still on my carpet. I'm too scared to move. Every breath sends knives deeper into my shoulder, my arm, and all the way down to my fingers. My tears are fogging up my headset, and sweat is escaping from under my twist-out and running down my face. Whatever that Megaboard says, I gave this fight my all. Whatever happens, there was nothing more I could do.

"Please," I whisper, shutting my eyes and letting my tears absorb into the carpet.

The thing Dred doesn't know about the word "unbothered" is that although the literal definition is "showing or feeling a lack of concern about or interest in something," it has another implication that Cicada—Claire—brought up while we were sitting in our respective rooms, chatting across the world well past both of our bedtimes.

Claire: Wouldn't it also have an adverse effect on the person dealing blows?

Me: The Unbothered card? Seems like it should just be a total immunity card.

Claire: Yeah, but the thing about being unbothered is, when someone is unbothered by another person, they're literally not absorbing their energy, right?

Me: I guess?

Claire: So then, if that energy's not going anywhere . . .

Me: Science isn't my thing, math is. Help me out here.

Claire: That energy has to go somewhere.

I take a deep breath and brace for impact as the diamond shell around me explodes into shards and light fragments, and I see Dred's red robe and black face go flying. The sound is deafening, but I ease my eyes open. The drums are pounding somewhere that sounds far away. I look up and around at the audience, which looks like dancing ants from this angle, extending way up into the heavens, and then I hear in my headset Cicada's voice.

"Nine hundred to seven hundred! Emerald wins! Emerald wins!" There are tears in her voice as she screams, and the world joins with her—my world, *our* world.

"Em-rald! Em-rald Em-rald! Em-rald!"

I shut my eyes for a moment and bask in the sound, but another one quickly yanks me back into reality—the sound of the doorbell. At first I think it's my parents returning home from dinner with Steph, and then I wonder why any of them would ring their own doorbell, and then I hear the voice, muffled all the way from the other side of the front door. But I can just barely make out what it says.

"Kix? You home? I know we're unannounced, but this math homework is kicking my ass, and if we don't do it together, I'm kinda doomed."

I roll my eyes and sigh, waiting for Harper to go away after hearing silence in reply. I feel awful leaving her hanging the night before the homework is due, but I'm right in the middle of literally saving the world, and I might have a dislocated shoulder. And then, just when I think she might have gone, I hear another voice, the last voice on the planet that I expect to hear at my front door right now.

"And you have to let me in because I owe you an apology."

Wyatt?

Panic floods my body like a river through my veins, and I try to think clearly. Why would Wyatt be at my front door?

How *could* he be at my front door if he's got his VR headset on? What the hell? What the *hell*?! If Wyatt is at my house, then who is Dred?

I turn my head, sending bolts of pain exploding through my neck, and I stifle a shriek of pain so they can't hear me at the door. Dred is kneeling across the ring, still facing me, and as if he can hear my thoughts, I see a private message pop up in the corner of my headset.

Dred: You win, chocolate puddin'.

Rage takes the place of panic, and I roll to my good side and push myself up with my right arm slowly, painfully. I clutch my left arm to keep it from hanging, because it sends shooting pain across my chest. What have I done to myself?

I walk gingerly to my keyboard and pull my headset off, because the sweat is beginning to fog up my screen. The cool air in my room is refreshing on my eyes, like a tall glass of water after running a marathon, and I stare at the message and begin typing with one hand now that I can rest my arm across my leg.

Me: Who are you?

Dred: That wasn't part of our deal.

He's right, it wasn't, but I have to know. If I don't have a name, a face, an identity, there goes my leverage should he decide not to uphold his half of the deal. Sure, I have the chat logs, but I can't prove that Dred is connected to any real person. If the human behind Dred does decide to sue me, I need to be able to prove he's been harassing me all this time. I have to squeeze it out of him. I have to know.

Me: What's your name?

Dred: I'm more concerned with YOUR name.

My heart is pounding.

Dred: This whole time you actually thought there was a lawsuit. There's no lawsuit, at least not from me.

I'm confused. I'm angry. I'm frustrated. My eyes are brimming with tears. I don't trust him.

Me: What the hell do you want?

Dred: I want you to know why Black women should stay focused on being Black women.

Me: The hell are you talking about?

Dred: You know why Black people suffer the way they do? You know why they're always on the bottom? Always getting kicked to the curb? Know why they keep getting beaten down by the white establishment? Know why slavery's been abolished since 1865, but we STILL can't get our shit together?

Did he say "we"? My stomach tightens into a knot, and I can feel my heart racing.

I start typing, but not before he sends another message.

Dred: You ever read Robert Greene?

Robert Greene. Where have I heard that name? I've heard it recently. I watch as Dred keeps typing.

Dred: "Never be distracted by people's glamorous portraits of themselves and their lives; search and dig for what really imprisons them." My nigga Robert Greene said that. Black kings always wanna be distracted by GLAMOROUS SHIT—cars, clothes, jewels, movies, video games. Distractions, all of them. And instead of helping us build an empire and protect Black PEOPLE, you want to build this! It's another nail in the coffin for OUR PEOPLE. ANOTHER DISTRACTION TO KEEP US FROM BECOMING GREAT.

I search my mind for the name—Robert Greene—and then it hits me. The book! *The 48 Laws of Power*. I say the name out loud, hoping it'll sound less ridiculous if I do.

"Malcolm."

Dred: I can see you now.

Shit! Did my IP address fail to scramble? I jump out of my chair, sending an explosion of pain through my shoulder, and I clutch my arm as my eyes dart around my room. My computer monitor is casting a bluish-green light all over my walls, but otherwise, the room is empty. I walk to the door and double-check to make sure it's locked. Then I look under my desk, and around the side of my bunk bed. My blinds are closed. There's absolutely nobody here in my room, and nobody can see me from outside. Then I read the next message.

Dred: I like you in pink.

I look down at my pink Henley and a chill goes up my spine. How the hell can he actually see me?

And then I notice the tiny red light just above my computer screen. My camera. The one that's built into my monitor. Reflexively, I reel my right hand back and deliver a slap so hard, the monitor slams against the wall and the screen goes dark.

I stand there staring at it with my mouth hanging open. Malcolm. It was Malcolm. And now Malcolm knows. He knows about everything—*SLAY* and why I've really been ignoring him lately. I glance at my door, hoping Steph and my mom and dad come home soon. I'm cursing myself for not letting Harper and Wyatt in while they were here. What if Malcolm just decides to come over and . . . I don't know, *confront* me? I'm sure Claire is freaking out about where I went and if I'm okay. I have to tell her what's going on.

I pick up my phone with my good hand and sit on my sofa so I can lean back against something and support my bad arm. Texting with one hand is slow, but I get halfway through the message I'm okay, but my boyfriend—before a new message with a picture interrupts me.

Malcolm: I suspected you played, but I never thought you were the one who STARTED this shit until I traced your IP address and saw your face. I only got a passcode so I could go after the developer. I couldn't watch that li'l king die and do nothing when there could be more victims. I had to end this game. Emerald owes the world answers. You owe the world answers. You thought you was just gon lie to me, to all of us, without consequences?

And then that blue-tinted webcam photo of my face—twist-out a mess, pink Henley, no glasses, no makeup, no jewelry. Like a mug shot.

I take a deep breath and open my conversation with Claire again, staring at my unfinished text. I'm okay, but my boyfriend . . . My boyfriend *what*? How do I even begin to explain this to her? There's certainly no way to tell her the whole story like this, in this tiny text box. Where would I even start? I send off a quick I'm okay and lean my head back against my sofa and try not to cry as I wait for Claire to text me back. I close my eyes just for a moment.

I realize I've fallen asleep, or passed out, or something, when I flutter my eyes open to the pitch blackness of my room, and panic grips me as I remember Malcolm. My first impulse is to jump off the sofa and turn on the light, but the minute I sit up, pain explodes through my shoulder, and I let out an involuntary scream.

Steph and my parents must be home by now. I don't know what else to do but text her. Something is horribly wrong with my arm—something I can't fix by sleeping it off. This is a pain like I've been shot. I can barely move my fingers. I pick up my phone with my right hand to find thirty-six new messages from Cicada in WhatsApp. I hate to make her wait, since I'm sure she thinks I'm dead, but I need painkillers, and *fast*. I find two messages from Steph.

Steph: Hey, you alive in there?

Steph: I logged in as soon as I got home, but Cicada announced that she has no idea where you are, and your door is locked. Don't tell me you got into the wine while we were out and passed out drunk. I swear, I leave you alone for two hours . . .

Me: Steph, come here plz. Don't tell m or d.

I breathe a sigh of relief that she's home and I don't have to worry about Malcolm sneaking up behind me and murdering me, although I do glance over my shoulder just to make sure, and then I navigate back to WhatsApp.

Cicada: OMG THAT WAS FLAWLESS!

Cicada: GAME SET MATCH! SLAY IS OURS! And you SLAYYYYYED him, girl. I've already booted him off the server.

Cicada: Hey—u there?

Cicada: Emerald?

Cicada: Kiera?

Cicada: Do u even Wi-Fi?

Cicada: Hello?

Cicada: Holy shit, have u seen twitter recently?

Cicada: GIRL OPEN TWITTER YOUR PIC IS EVERYWHERE

Before I can open Twitter, a soft *tap tap tap* echoes through my door, and I take a deep breath to calm my nerves. I jumped when it happened, and my arm is throbbing with pain. I wince as I hold my forearm and rock my way up off the couch.

"Steph?" I ask.

"Yeah," she whispers from the other side.

I swing open the door, and she throws herself into the room, squealing uncontrollably in nothing but a white bathrobe and a hot-pink bonnet. God, how long was I asleep?

"Oh my *God*, tell me all about it. I want to hear *everything*—"

"Steph, listen," I interrupt. "I know you just got your permit, but I need you to drive me somewhere. Please."

Her smile falls and so do her eyebrows.

"Do you see this bonnet? Do you see this robe? Do you see that my bra is off? My night is *over*. For God's sake, it's—" She pulls her phone out of her robe pocket to glance at it. "It's two in the morning! On a Tuesday!"

"I need you to drive me to the hospital."

Her eyes get huge and then drift from my face down to my shoulder, and her eyes narrow when she notices I'm clutching my arm.

"You better explain every last detail on the way."

I do.

We manage to sneak out of the house and into the garage, get into the car, and drive off without waking up Mom and Dad, or they did wake up and didn't care because they figure Steph and I are responsible kids. They've done that before when I've driven her to Taco Bell in the middle of the night. As long as our grades are up, they don't ask questions. The hospital is fifteen minutes from our place, and Steph asks questions the entire way. I tell her about every move of the duel, right down to the boxing gloves pounding the outside of the diamond shell and having the energy from them explode and knock Dred's points down. I don't mention Malcolm, or that Malcolm is Dred. If Steph was about to throw a hot cup of coffee on him for hassling me in the lunchroom, I don't want to know how she'll handle learning that he hacked my webcam. I'll just let her find out that Malcolm and I have broken up and be obliviously happy. She finally slows down the questions when we step through the emergency room sliding doors. The hospital waiting room is stuffy and smells like rubber and hand sanitizer, and the chairs are stiff and uncomfortable. I watch as Steph talks to the attendant for a while, pulling two ID cards from her wallet in the process. I don't know how she managed to avoid suspicion and get us checked in without them notifying our parents, but I hurt too much to ask questions. My arm is still throbbing, and Steph mercilessly starts with the questions again.

"I can't believe you broke your arm playing a video game. This is too good! You're like those people who throw the game remote at the TV, forgetting it's not real."

I ignore her and text Cicada back.

Me: I'm ok.

Cicada: OMFG!!!!!! WHERE HAVE YOU BEEN IVE BEEN DYING OF WORRY WHAT HAPPENED

Me: Sry. I hurt my arm. At hospital. Im happy we still have SLAY.

Cicada: ME GODDAMN TOO BUT IM JUST HAPPY YOURE ALIVE.

Cicada: HAVE YOU SEEN YOUR PIC ALL OVER TWITTER?

Me: I heard. U can turn off caps now.

Cicada: [photo attachment]

It's that same blue photo of me with no glasses, no makeup, and a dusty-as-hell nine-day twist-out. I reach up with my good arm to make sure the back of my head doesn't look like a pancake from sitting against the sofa, but even that motion aggravates my bad arm.

"Will you stop trying to move?" asks Steph, reaching up and fluffing out my hair for me, and I smile my thanks. She looks so grown-up. Sometimes I think she's more mature than I am.

"Thanks."

I can't believe I ever doubted her. Now that she's kept my biggest secret safe, for as long as it stayed a secret anyway, kept Mom and Dad out of the house while I fought to protect the thing most precious to me in the world, and driven me to the hospital before getting an explanation, I can't believe I ever thought she'd let me down if I told her about the game.

"And I'm sorry for yelling you out of my room last night." She shrugs and smiles.

"Eh, I was kind of being pushy. You can handle trolls like Dred however you want. It's your game."

You are a queen, and this is your game.

"Thanks, Steph. Really. For everything."

"Don't thank me yet. I need to know why your picture is all over Twitter and why you're not telling me about it. You had to know I'd see it eventually."

Sometimes she's like my grown-up little sister, and sometimes she's more like a second mom. Just as I open my mouth to tell her, the doctor comes in and calls my name.

"Kiera Johnson?"

Steph raises her arm and jumps to her feet.

"I'm Stephanie Johnson. This is my sister, Kiera. She broke her arm."

"We don't know it's broken yet. I fell off my bunk bed and it's been hurting ever since," I lie. I still can't form my mouth to say the words *I was playing a video game* out loud yet.

As we're walking down the hall to the X-ray room, where Steph knows she won't be allowed to go with me, she peppers me with questions to make up for the eventual lost time.

"So who hacked your webcam?" she asks. "I know it's a webcam picture. Have you been filming yourself on weird amateur cam girl sites for spare cash? Why didn't you tell me you were struggling like that?"

I would nudge her *so* hard if my entire arm wasn't pounding with pain.

"We'll talk after the X-rays."

Steph rolls her eyes.

"That's when you'll tell me we'll talk after you get your cast, and finally, we'll talk when we get home, and then you'll never tell me."

"Not true," I whisper, hoping Steph will follow suit and lower her voice too. "And I won't be getting a cast, because it's not broken. It can't be broken. I just dove across the floor. I didn't *actually* fall off the top bunk."

"Whatever. If you can't move your fingers, it's broken."

The X-ray tech confirms that Steph is right. My arm is

broken. To be technical, my clavicle is broken, so we were both wrong, but whatever. I don't get a cast. They strap me into this harness thing that's a cross between a corset and a straitjacket for just one arm. I thank my lucky stars I'm right-handed. After they've strapped me in, and we're back in the waiting room, waiting for them to bring us our papers and prescriptions, I check my phone and realize I have twelve notifications from friends and family, including texts and DMs from Auntie Tina, Harper, and Wyatt. I'm sure they've seen my picture. It's everywhere.

Auntie Tina: Hey, baby, I heard your photo is going viral over a video game? Everything okay?

Harper: OH. MY. GOD. You DO SLAY! We need to talk ASAP. Call me. R u ok?

Wyatt: You could've just told me, Kiers. This would've all made a lot more sense. I wouldn't have said some of the stuff I said.

That one catches me off guard. Would Wyatt really have said anything different to me if he'd known I was the creator? Even though he's not quite *Dred*-level problematic like I thought, his words still light up in my mind, burning me like hot coals: *We can't exclude them, and they can't exclude us.*

Us. Them. He said both of those words so casually, as if Steph and I weren't standing right in front of him, talking about us like we weren't even there. I don't know if I believe he'll be different. I just know it's going to take me a long time to trust him with anything.

I bypass all those and open the convo from the person who deserves an explanation more than anybody.

Me: I've seen the pic. I have a confession.

Cicada: ?

Me: I know who Dred is. I thought it was this kid at my school, but it turned out to be my boyfriend. He hacked my webcam and the pic is all over.

The one time my IP address shuffle command fails. I could kick a wall. The hell did I do to deserve such god-awful luck? Steph leans over to me and asks, "Does it hurt?"

"Does what hurt?"

Steph is looking at me with pursed lips like I've missed something, and then I remember she's talking about my arm. Duh. I shrug my other arm, which I didn't think would hurt, but it does, and I wince.

"Peachy, huh?" she asks.

I shake my head.

"Not now, Steph."

"So how'd they figure out it was you?" she asks. "And who is 'they'? I hope you realize the longer you wait to tell me what's going on, the more I find out from Twitter. And you *don't* want me to find out this way. There's some nasty shit about you on here."

I can't keep it from her forever.

"I thought Dred was Wyatt."

I can feel her looking at me, and she chuckles.

"What? Seriously?"

"He talked about wanting to sue Emerald, so is it really that far-fetched an idea?"

"You really haven't talked to Harper about this, have you? She said her parents won't let Wyatt sue over something so arbitrary, and since he's still a minor, he legally can't on his own."

Thank God. There's no lawsuit from Wyatt, and there's no lawsuit from Malcolm. Hopefully the news was blowing everything way out of proportion for clicks and views, and no actual lawsuit comes out of this. Then I can start sleeping at night again. I check my messenger app again and find no texts from Malcolm. What's wrong with me? Why am I still checking for texts from him? He's taken everything I've worked for—nullified all the effort I've put into keeping my identity a secret. He took every word of criticism, every bitter assessment of this virtual world, the opinions of all the Brandon Cannons and Jans and Dereks of the world, and funneled them straight to my front door. Everyone knows I'm Emerald. Everyone knows my face. I'll probably be on the news tomorrow. People could easily track down my address. I could get doxxed. Mom and Dad will see and find out their daughter is responsible for developing a video game that got a boy killed.

"So how'd you figure out Dred wasn't Wyatt?"

I take a deep breath and brace for the inevitable I-told-you-so. There's no avoiding it now.

"Dred is Malcolm."

Steph puts her phone down and stares at me for a solid minute. I finally look at her and nod. Her eyes are huge and unblinking.

"You can't be serious."

I nod again and notice a new message from Cicada.

Cicada: Dred is your boyfriend?? You gave your white boyfriend a SLAY passcode?! 😲

Me: No, my bf is Black. He disguised himself as a white supremacist.

Cicada: Why?

It hurts as I text her back, but I know I can't avoid the truth, and I know it means admitting that Malcolm isn't the man I thought he was.

Me: Because he doesn't recognize Black excellence when he sees it.

According to Malcolm, if Black people are to progress, we need absolute focus, relentless drive, and undying ambition, and that looks like something very specific to him. Unless we're starting our own businesses, building a nuclear family, and avoiding "white propaganda," we're not progressing. But the nuclear family doesn't work for everyone. Not every Black man has to be an entrepreneur. We don't all have to go to college. And not every piece of information and every social construct is a trick of the "white man." He's wrong. He's been so wrong about everything. He acts like Harper and Wyatt are the enemy, and I hate it. I've always hated it. Harper and Wyatt may be clueless about a lot of things, often willfully. They may ask unfair questions and misunderstand me and make me feel like I'm some kind of alien from a distant planet. And yeah, there are white people out there who are full-blown bigots, racist white supremacist assholes, many who literally hope we die off. But Malcolm made me realize another threat to my people, one that's less obvious, one that creeps in slowly like a disease. The threat of self-hatred. The idea that Black people who don't live up to whatever standards society has are somehow less deserving of love and support. And if all of Malcolm's behavior so far hasn't convinced me of this, *this* thing with Dred certainly has. *Fuck* respectability politics.

Tears are streaming down my face as I look up at Steph.

"He hacked my webcam after the duel. He said there's no lawsuit. He just wants the game to end."

"Why the hell would he want that?!" She's whisper-screaming at me in this waiting room now, and I look up and around at all the old people sitting in here with us on their phones and magazines, and I hope none of them recognize my face if they're reading the news.

Steph's eyes narrow.

"Is this part of his 'video games are evil' thing? He hates them so much that he tried to destroy the one you *made*? Hates them so much that he outed you online and just *invited* the trolls to eat you alive? Is he *trying* to die today? Because I will find him."

She's talking louder now, and people are looking at us.

"Steph, shh," I say. She rolls her eyes and lets out a frustrated sigh.

The minute the nurse comes back and hands me some papers that explain what to do with a freshly broken clavicle, and a prescription for enough ibuprofen to knock out a horse, Steph snatches up her handbag.

"Come get in this car so I can tell *you* what I really think and not all these people."

By the time we get to the car, Steph has finished explaining to me that I'll need to make up a story for Mom and Dad that explains why my face is all over the Internet, why I'm in a harness with a broken clavicle, why I didn't tell them about any of it, and why they don't need to insist I stop playing *SLAY* because it poses a threat to my health. Now she's back to talking about Malcolm, speeding down the street—she always speeds when she's angry—and I'm sitting in the front seat watching the road, hoping we don't die on the way home.

"I just can't believe a human being would actually do that to someone they claim to love. I don't understand. I hope your breakup text to him was iconic. I want to read it later."

There's no breakup text. There won't be from me. Despite everything, I can't let him go, and I can't sit here and think about it because I'll completely lose it. I choose not to reply, and instead I direct my attention to Cicada's text.

Cicada: So your boyfriend turned out to be a psychopath. I'm so sorry, Kiera. ♥

Despite all that's going on, I take a minute to notice how good it feels to see Cicada call me by my real name. To see *Claire* call me by my real name. But her words also sting. The word "psychopath" stings.

Me: Yeah.

I say "yeah," but I don't mean it. Malcolm's not a psychopath, necessarily. He's extremely passionate and extremely confused. And he hates me for going behind his back.

"You *did* break up with him, right?" asks Steph.

I stay quiet, hoping she'll drop it, but it's Steph, and she doesn't drop anything this important.

"Kiera!"

"What, Steph?"

"If you don't cut that Negro out of your life, I'll do it for you."

I get another text.

Cicada: I mean ex-boyfriend. I should fly you out here to Paris so we can be super single together. Lots of cute Spaniards out here. None have noticed me yet.

Yup. She and Steph would get along great.

"Not now, Steph."

"Yes, Kiera, *now*."

The horizon is melting into a warm brown, hinting at the impending orange glow of sunrise, and we drive past Jefferson, where there's not a car in the parking lot. I imagine waking up in a few hours and going to school in a sling with my face all over the Internet. Everyone is going to recognize me now. Everyone will be asking questions. There might even be a news crew here waiting for me later this morning. We drive past a streetlight in our neighborhood that's just shut itself off for the morning and pull into the driveway of our little gray house at the corner. We sit there in the car for a while in silence. I stare out the window at the shrubs in the front yard, feeling Steph's eyes on me.

"I know you really like Malcolm, okay? Maybe you even love him. But nobody treats people they love the way Malcolm treats you. And nobody treats their own people the way Malcolm does. He's manipulative, he's a liar, and he's dangerous."

I rub my good hand against my leg to scrunch my sleeve over my knuckles so I can have something to wipe my tears with. I'm crying because I know she's right. I'm crying because I want the old Malcolm back—the Malcolm only I get to see. The Malcolm who would hold me and stare at the sky with me. We had so many dreams for Atlanta. Now I don't know how I can go to Spelman knowing he's across the street.

"What's Malcolm's Twitter handle?" she asks.

"@xxPeaceMongerFOOxx," I say absentmindedly. I don't know why she's asking. If she plans to send him a message, he's never on Twitter. Better to text him.

"Thought so," she says. She tosses her phone into my lap, startling me, and I wince from the pain and give her the sourest glare I can.

"Sorry," she says. Then she nods at her phone. "Is this enough to convince you to dump his ass?"

I look down at the phone to see another copy of my picture in a tweet from @xxPeaceMongerFOOxx with a caption that puts a lump in my throat.

Meet #Emerald, the SLAY developer. Jamal Rice's blood is on her hands. If u see her, avenge him. I kno I will. #AvengeJamal #LongLiveKingJamal

I reread that one part. *I kno I will.*

Malcolm wouldn't. Steph snatches her phone back, as if she knows what I'm thinking, and clicks a few buttons.

"That's a death threat, Kiera. I'm calling the police," she says.

"What?!" I scream, jerking my head a little too fast. I groan as stabbing pain begins to fade and the ache sets in, and I can't wait to get in the house and find some painkillers. But I have to stop Steph from calling the cops.

"You can't do that, Steph," I say. "I'm serious. This isn't even about me and Malcolm. It's about a Black man and the cops. Do you know what might happen if they show up at his house and arrest him? You can get him expelled, get him kicked out of the city, get a restraining order, but you will *not* make my boyfriend the next police brutality hashtag."

"*Ex*-boyfriend!" hollers Steph. "And I'll make him the next hashtag before he makes *you* a hashtag. Believe me, after Tamir Rice was shot in the back by that cop in Cleveland, I swore on my life that I'd never call the cops on a Black man, because yes, we have to protect our own, and yes, we queens have to support our kings. But I'll be dead before I let a Black man abuse my sister because I'm not allowed to call the cops on him."

"Steph, listen. Malcolm isn't abusive. He's confused—"

"Nah, he's bitter. And entitled. He's so wrapped up in fighting 'the white man's agenda' that he threatened your life on Twitter and tried to take over *SLAY*. That's ironically the most white-boy troll shit I've ever seen!"

"You still don't get it," I say, wincing against the sudden shooting pain in my shoulder. "If they show up and arrest him, if he's lucky to live through getting arrested, and I press charges, he's going to prison. White boys have committed literal murder and gotten community service. Black boys have been killed on sight for selling loose cigarettes. If Malcolm goes to jail, he might never come out."

"Kiera, I get it. But if you don't press charges, he gets to walk around threatening you and whoever else as he pleases. I know it's unfair, and I know he's bound to get a raw deal, but there must be consequences, even in an unfair system."

"Steph," I say. But what else can I say?

She's staring at me with tears in her eyes. I can't look at her. My eyes are burning too. What am I so afraid of? Loneliness? Isolation? Pushing away the last remaining sliver of the person I was at Belmont? Why is this so hard?

"He's not unfixable."

"It's not your job to fix him," she says without hesitation.

"You don't know him like I know him."

"You *thought* you knew him," she says. "The Malcolm you know doesn't exist, Kiera."

I shut my eyes and breathe gingerly to avoid setting off my clavicle pain again. I downloaded a development engine, I created a character, a card game, a forum, an entire universe for people worldwide to communicate in secret and engage each other in epic duels, but I can't tell one man that I'm sick of his games. I imagine Malcolm's face. I can see him lying next to me on the trampoline in the backyard, smiling. His eyes are alight with something—hope? I think

of a much smaller boy, curled up alone, nestled in a beanbag chair, controller in hand, three CPUs on the TV screen
patiently waiting for their human companion to wake up
from his nap. Lying next to him on the trampoline, looking into his eyes, all I saw was littler Malcolm, grateful for
a friend.

"I can't do it, Steph," I sob. I wipe away more tears
and feel Steph's hand on my knee, which makes me cry
harder. Eventually I'm ugly crying right there in the car—
not because I don't want to leave Malcolm, but because I
know that if I'm going to have any hope for a future, I *have*
to. That future in Atlanta won't happen. It was never meant
to happen. Malcolm—the real Malcolm—is too bitter to
allow a future like that to bloom into a forever love. He's
confused. He's angry. And Steph's right—he's dangerous.
After I spend the next twenty minutes staring at the bushes
in the front yard, and blinking makes my eyes burn, and the
tears have dried on my face, Steph moves her hand over my
knee and says softly, "I'm going to make the call now."

And I let her.

Once I explain everything to Mom and Dad, they agree to let me stay home from school for the next week. The police process Steph's report with screenshots of his threatening tweets and arrest Malcolm without incident, and even after everything he did to me, I'm glad he's one of the lucky ones—he lives long enough to make it to jail. They issue a restraining order against him in my name, I block Malcolm's number from all my apps, and I try to forget he ever existed, which, despite everything, is damn hard. I don't think I'll ever forget him. I think of him when I think of Spelman, or Morehouse, or Atlanta, and I realize I can't go to any of those places if I'm going to ever truly let go of what I was so sure my future would look like. I don't know where I'm going anymore, and that's scary and freeing all at the same time.

My mailbox has blown up. Not my inbox, although that maxed out last week at sixty-five thousand messages. My *physical* mailbox. The one at the end of our driveway. Packages, padded envelopes, cards, and letters, most of them from fellow *SLAY*ers, have been flooding in. Mom freaked out. At first she only let me open the envelopes. Too many package bombs on the news lately, I guess. But after a while she came around, and now I have a stack of *SLAY*-related items in the corner of my room—bobbleheads of me and Cicada, and a few of Hyacinth, scarves, buttons, patches, a jacket with SLAY written across the back in huge green letters with green LEDs underneath that twinkle like emeralds. And fan art. *Endless* fan art. The wall behind my bunk bed is almost full, and it'll be time to move on to the wall behind my computer desk soon. Every night I get to go to bed with drawn, painted, and airbrushed images of Emerald, Cicada, and Hyacinth slinging cards. One girl from Kansas City—Jamal's hometown—sent me a photo of her cosplaying as Zama, with dreadlocks, wolf cloak, bracelets, and all. Behind her, with a Guy Fawkes mask lifted off his face so I can see his features, is a boy who's cosplaying as PrestoBox. In his letter, he told me his real name.

Damar Rice.

SLAY name: Osiris.

Jamal's brother.

In his letter, he told me *thank you*, of all things.

His exact words were: *Jamal was always happiest when he was playing SLAY. I'd never seen him so proud of who he was, as he was in his last few months. Thank you, Emerald. From Osiris. Orisha Tribe forever.*

I keep that picture on the wall right next to my face, so I can look at it as I fall asleep.

Since my picture went viral, Claire's been sending me news clips of Dr. Abbott, Jan, and Derek from Channel 5 debating whether *SLAY* is a racist game, and over the course of several videos, they seem to reach a verdict. Since I'm only seventeen and still a child in their eyes, the American media seems to collectively decide that—although I'm perfectly capable of speaking up for myself—I can't be self-aware enough yet to speak for my entire race, although in every video they consult Dr. Abbott like they expect him to. If Derek and Jan really want "the Black opinion" on something, they're going to have to interview all one and a half million *SLAY*ers—up a whole million in the last six weeks—one by one to get an aggregate answer. There's no such thing as being "old enough" to know all of that.

Claire and I have disabled *SLAY* coins for now. All items must be bartered until we can figure out how to prevent more Jeremiah Marshalls in the future.

It takes six weeks for my collarbone to heal enough for me to function without the sling, and two weeks beyond that for Mom to let me even think of going near "that game" again, which is when Steph and I can finally stop playing in secret from our rooms and let her and Dad watch a match. Steph moved her desk, monitors, CPU, and all her hot-pink VR equipment into my room just for the day so we can duel side by side. Dad helped her rotate my bunk bed so he and Mom can both sit on the couch and watch the match on the computer screen. I tried to show them how to use my VR headset so they can get their own and experience the game from the stands like true *SLAY*ers, but Mom couldn't wear it for more than ten minutes without getting dizzy, and I don't think they make a headset in the world big enough to fit Dad's head.

Maybe one day we'll get to see Mom and Dad in the stands smiling down at us. I imagine Mom wearing something from the seventies—with a giant Afro and gold hoop earrings and roller skates, and Dad wearing something space-age, like Major Lazer. Steph and I stand staring at each other in the middle of Fairbanks Arena with the spotlight beaming down on us, Mom and Dad watching behind us in the real world. That feeling that I thought I'd feel after opening that letter from Spelman? That blessed assurance that I'm doing exactly what I was always meant to do? That relief I was so sure I'd get? I get it now, with my whole family right here in my room, watching this duel, both halves of my world converging. Hyacinth is dressed in a ridiculously over-the-top leopard-print catsuit, complete with tail and hot-pink claws, because why not? Claire designed it just for her. Now Steph talks to Claire more than she talks to her own sister. I smile, knowing I was right. They get along just fine.

"So, what happens now?" asks my mom, her muffled voice competing with the roar of the audience in my headset. Steph answers, since she's keeping one of her headphones slightly off her ear to hear them better.

"Round three is about to start," she says. "We'll tap our last two cards, and then I'll lay Kiera out."

"Don't forget who designed these cards," I say, wiggling my fingers at my hips like I'm in a scene from *The Good, the Bad and the Ugly*.

"Some of mine are in there too now," she says.

"Exactly two," I say to Mom. "But who knows? Maybe she'll get lucky today."

Steph convinced Claire to let her add the Yaaas card, which cracks me up because I don't even know what it does. Steph said she wants me to be surprised, but knowing her, it'll be extra AF. Cicada's voice echoes somewhere above us.

"Duelers, ready! Round three starts in three . . . two . . . one . . . Go!"

I, Emerald, tap my next two cards, and Hyacinth lunges for hers. Mine flip over and I prepare to battle as Cicada announces giddily, "Ooh, we've got Queen Hyacinth with Reclaimed Time and Yaaas, and Queen Emerald with Fufu and Canceled! This is gonna be a fierce one, kings and queens!"

"What in the world is the Yaaas card?!" I squeal as Hyacinth sprints at me with her super speed from the Reclaimed Time card. I hold up my hands, she bounces off my force field from the Canceled card, and we both go flying.

"Whoa!" we scream in unison, each of us watching our characters peel themselves off the floor and prepare for the next confrontation. Her pink eyes are flashing from across the ring, and she extends her hot-pink claws to intimidate me. I like battling Steph. She likes to play tricks just to mess with me, but they don't work.

"Just battle, Queen," I say to her. Mom chimes in again with another question.

"What is 'Reclaimed Time'? What is that?"

Steph jumps in before I can.

"That's Auntie Maxine coming through, Mamma!" she cries as she lunges at me again. I plant my feet firmly on the carpet and produce another force field, knocking her back a few feet.

"You know," says Mom, "if you knew those vocab words like you know these cards, you'd spend less time agonizing over homework."

"Not true," whines Steph, sucking her teeth. "That's different."

I direct the conversation back to this game.

"You gonna show me what this Yaaas card is all about?" I ask. She's holding it back, waiting for the perfect moment, maybe? I'm a little nervous. Is a whole team of Missy Elliott background dancers going to pop out the ground like Michael Jackson's zombies? What does *yaaas* even mean, except an enthusiastic "yes"? What would a "yes" card even look like?

"She's going to turn into Beyoncé," chuckles Dad.

I roll my eyes and smile at how funny he thinks he is. I can almost feel Mom rolling her eyes behind me.

"Wanna see?" asks Steph as I hear her lower herself to the carpet. Hyacinth begins prowling around the ring.

"Wow, look at that, Charles!" cries Mom. I don't think

she'll ever get over the novelty of watching Emerald and Hyacinth mimic on-screen what Steph and I are doing in real life. I'm still holding up my force-field hands, ready to whip out my Fufu card if the Yaaas card happens to be something it'll counter. Hyacinth raises her catlike hindquarters, making her tail wiggle like she's about to pounce.

"Really?" I ask. Again, extra.

"YAAAAAAS!" yells Steph.

A black cube the size of a vehicle zooms toward me, and I lower the force fields and dodge to my left. I feel my foot catch Steph—the real Steph—in the ankle, and Mom gasps.

"Careful," she calls as I regain my balance. "Space yourselves out a bit."

Steph calls out again, "YAAAS!" and I watch a second black block fly past me so I can get a good look at it. It's not a block. It's the word "YAAAS" in capitalized Arial letters, twice my height and three times my width, flying past me like a freight train.

"Isn't it beautiful?" she asks, circling the ring again.

"Gorgeous," I say flatly. I clap my hands together and when I separate them again, a small ball of dough hovers between them.

"What the hell is that?" demands Steph.

"Whoa, whoa," thunders Dad as I reel back and haul it straight at her. "Watch your language in this house. We aren't your li'l online friends."

"Sorry," she says, diving out of the way. I hear her land in a heap on the floor next to me and I laugh and stretch my arms out as wide as they'll go until the dough grows to the size of a house, hovering twenty feet over Hyacinth's head.

"What is that?!" she shrieks. "Is that the Fufu card? What even is fufu?"

I bring my hands down hard and flatten Hyacinth with the dough. My points on the Megaboard jump from 1800 to 2300, and the whole arena goes wild with cheers and whoops and hollers.

"It's a staple food in so many African countries! How have you never heard of it?"

I raise my fists in the air to lift the dough ball off poor Hyacinth, who's lying on the floor, trying to get up.

"Come on, come on," hisses Steph. "Get *up*, you useless—"

I slam the ball down a second time and say, "It's popular in Ghana and Nigeria."

And a third time.

"It's made of cassava and green plantain flour."

The round three drums rumble through the arena, and I hear Steph take off her headset, so I lift my goggles up to my forehead, grin smugly at her, and finish with, "Often served with peanut soup."

And then I take off both gloves and toss them on the floor.

"Did you just win, Kiera?" asks Mom.

"Yes I did! *Boom!*" I holler before sticking out my tongue and dropping into a flawless nay-nay.

"Yeah, yeah," groans Steph. "All right, all right, student hasn't surpassed the developer *yet*. I'll get there."

She smiles and throws her arms around me as I hear

Cicada's voice from my headset announcing, "Queen Emerald wins! Queen Emerald wins!"

But I listen closely to the arena's cheering. Half are chanting, "Long live Emerald," and the other half, mixed in, are chanting for my sister.

"Long live Hyacinth!"

"Long live the queens!"

"Long live the queens!"

"Long live the queens!"

I hold my sister tighter, even after she pulls her arms down to indicate she's done hugging me.

"Thanks, Steph," I say.

"For going easy on you? Don't get used to it."

"For talking some sense into me about Malcolm. For having my back. For *SLAY*ing with me. For everything."

I feel her nod, and the audience fades and I hear the chat menu sound in my ears. Cicada's voice comes through loud and clear.

"Well done, queens! Excellent duel! What do you think of the Yaaas card, Kiera?"

"She thinks it's *ridiculous*," says Steph, pushing away from me and unplugging the USB on my CPU so Cicada's voice resounds through the room instead.

"But it's a fun one," I add. "And it's definitely something we say. Hey, Claire, you're on speaker now. My parents are here."

"*Bonjour*, Mr. and Mrs. Johnson!" she cries. "It's nice to finally meet both of you!"

Steph and I look back at our parents. Dad is still sitting, but Mom is pushing herself off the sofa and grinning.

"*Bonjour*, Claire! It's good to hear your voice. We've heard so much about you! Heard you're in school."

"Yes, going to university. Math is difficult right now."

"Kiera can help you with that," chimes in Steph, grinning at me smugly, "as soon as our plane lands."

It hits me in slow waves.

"What plane?" I ask. Mom and Dad are both standing now. Mom's hands are clasped and her eyebrows are both raised high. This time they're saying, *you heard her*. My eyes get huge.

"Claire?"

Her giggling starts softly, like she's trying to contain it, but it grows and grows, and Steph joins in, and eventually so do Mom and Dad.

"Are you all serious?" I scream. I'm really going to fly to Paris? I'm really going to meet Claire in person? I scream and jump up and down, and Steph jumps with me, throwing her arms around me.

"Oh my God!" I cry, "Thank you, thank you, thank you!"

I don't even know where to begin. My hands are shaking. My heart is racing.

"When do we leave?" I ask. "Mom, who's paying for this?"

Mom and Dad look at each other with a grin, and Dad says, "I think we'd better let Claire explain this one."

"Story time!" squeals Claire's voice through the speakers.

I wish she used her webcam so I could see her face right now. My heart is thundering. I can't believe I'm really going to get to see her!

"Can you all hear me? Kiera, can you hear me?"

"I can hear you, Claire," I say. "Just hurry up before I die of anticipation."

"I got a message in my inbox," says Claire with a smile in her voice, "a few weeks after your picture went viral and the local Paris news began reporting the story. My inbox blew up, but one message caught my eye. It was called 'CEO of IDC wants partnership.'"

I look at Steph, and her smile indicates she knows what in the world Claire is talking about, so I fold my arms and listen.

"IDC stands for Île de Cerveau. That's 'Brain Island' in English. It's a virtual reality technology start-up that's scheduled for an IPO at the end of this year. The CEO's name is Maurice Belrose, also known in *SLAY* as Spade. Yes, *that* Spade."

My eyes grow huge. Spade? The same Spade who gave me the mantra I've been putting on my cover photos and screensavers and even my phone background for the last couple of months? The *You are a queen, and this is your game* guy?

I can barely speak. It comes out as a croak. "Yeah, I know him."

"He and I have been talking. I met him in person in a café, and I didn't tell you because I knew you'd talk me out of meeting strange men in person that I met online."

She's absolutely right. And nuts.

"He said that he's seen the news, and he thinks we could partner forces and pair SLAY with Brain Island's devices and existing games. Lawsuits may be a very real reality for us as long as we're making games just for our people, but under the umbrella of a Black-owned company with other games available to all, we could fly protected. We could lead a whole team of developers to make updates, we could have time to translate the in-game text into more languages than just English, adapt the game so it's compatible with accessibility-friendly devices, and take SLAY from great to awesome. And he wants to fly you and Steph out here so you can meet him *this weekend!*"

Steph squeals and practically tackles me where I stand, and I have to shift my weight to keep from falling over. My chest is pounding, and my eyes are brimming with tears as I hold my sister. Mom comes and joins the hug, and Dad completes it.

"I'm going to pack literally everything I own," says Steph, her voice muffled under the layers of bodies in this hug. We all laugh until my sides begin to hurt, and Claire, who I've forgotten can't see a thing that's going on, asks meekly, "What do you say, Kiera? You in?"

"That's a yaaas from us!" yells Steph. I roll my eyes and play-slap her shoulder.

"That's a definitely and a half," I say.

"Better get packing, then!" says Claire. "I'll be there to pick you up from the airport on Saturday morning."

My heart skips. Claire's going to be there? She's going to be the first face I see in Paris? I don't even know what she looks like. Oh God, she has no idea what *I* look like. I mean, not for real. Just a picture from Twitter. A *bad* one. I really do need to start packing, strategically.

Steph darts out of the room to commence the process, and I begin to follow her, when I hear my mom's voice behind me.

"Baby?" she asks. I turn to see her standing there, glancing at my dad and then smiling at me with those pursed lips and outstretched arms. It feels so good to be able to hug people again now that I don't have to wear that sling anymore. I wrap my arms around my mom and let her hold me without fear of pain.

"Thanks for letting me go. To Paris. I can't tell you what this means to me."

I don't know what else to say. Meeting Claire, meeting Maurice, it's everything I could've ever dreamed of for my role as developer of this game. Now we get to take *SLAY* to the next level, and I get to be at the helm.

"Of course, baby. We love you. *So* much. I didn't want to pressure you right away to tell us—we wanted to give you time to recover from . . . all this. But why did you keep all this to yourself? Why didn't you tell me you made all this?"

It stings. The words sound accusatory, but I can tell by the tone of my mother's voice that she's hurt.

"I thought," I begin, choosing my words carefully, "I . . . didn't think you'd understand."

"What wouldn't we understand?" comes my dad's voice from the sofa.

I sigh, realizing I have to get to the heart of what the problem has been this whole time.

"Mom, remember when you told Steph to swap her red Rihanna glasses for something less 'tacky'?"

I feel her nod, and she kisses the top of my head.

"And how you don't want us saying 'ain't'?" I continue. "And how up until recently you've used the word 'ghetto'?"

"Now, wait a minute, some things *are* just . . . scrappy, Kiera. Just . . ."

"Ghetto," says Dad, pushing himself to his feet and stepping forward. "Scrappy. Tacky. Ghetto. They all mean the same thing, Lorette."

Dad doesn't call Mom by her first name unless we're talking about something serious.

Mom loosens her hold on me and I look up at Dad.

"I love you both," I say, "but there are things about being Black that you don't embrace. Things about *my* Blackness that you don't embrace. I slip into Ebonics, or AAVE, or whatever, when I'm around people I'm comfortable with. People who I know will accept me. This pressure to conform to a standard that's not mine, I . . ."

I don't even know how to continue that. I what? I . . . *what?*

"I think I get it." Dad smiles down at me through his huge glasses. "This game—*SLAY*—it's not just a game to you. It's not just a hobby. It's not just something to add to your résumé. It's *you*. Steph brings home heaps of opinions on Dr. King and 'AAVE,' but for you, we've missed it. We've missed out on yours. We haven't asked. We haven't given you space to tell us, or fostered the kind of environment that would encourage you to. And we—I," he says, resting a hand over his chest and glancing at Mom, "am sorry."

Mom's face has softened, and she looks at me and nods, her eyes full of tears, one streaming down her cheek.

"Your father's absolutely right," she says. "I've always wanted to show my girls what it means to be a strong Black woman, and I thought I knew what that meant. I had very *specific* opinions on what that meant. I . . . I just don't know if I know anymore. I don't know what you believe about your role in this world as you blossom into a young woman, Kiera, but I'm so *proud* of you for exploring it. *So. Proud.* And I'm going to put you on that plane knowing my baby is going to lead millions to do the same."

She pulls me close, into another hug, and I smell that coconut oil wafting from her hair as she says, "You be whoever you are. Be whoever you are as a strong, beautiful, Black woman, and I'll be right here. Always. I love you. *We* love you."

I'm a blubbering mess right now, pressing both my sleeves into my eyes, and my parents hold me right there in the middle of my room until I finally stop. I don't know what to say to them. *Thank you* doesn't seem to cover it. Not even close. So I just nod at each of them in turn, and follow Steph so we can start packing.

Just a few months ago, I was sure Malcolm and I would graduate, move to Atlanta, have three gorgeous melanated babies, and live out the rest of our days together among people who look like us. But here I am on a ten-hour flight halfway around the world to Paris with my little sister, courtesy of a Black French CEO and his wife, Sylvie, who called us this morning to make sure we made our flight on time.

The pilot announces that we're beginning our descent and that we should be landing at the Charles de Gaulle Airport in twenty minutes. Steph is sitting next to me in the window seat with the sun beaming down on her face. I don't know how she can sleep when it's so damn bright outside, but I figure I'll give her another ten minutes before I wake her up. On our family trip to Orlando last summer, turbulence woke me up during the landing, and I'll never forget the terror that went through my mind. I thought I was falling *out* of the plane. I look out the window and smile, thinking about how silly it seems now. We're still above the clouds, and the skies are the clearest blue. The ride is smooth.

I quickly ran out of programs I liked on the in-flight TV, so I slipped my phone into a ziplock bag and hung it from the tray table mechanism in case I want to watch some video game walk-through videos on it without holding it in my lap, although right now I'm just playing some Kendrick Lamar and thinking.

Claire and I had a long talk Thursday night while I did laundry and finished packing for the trip. She reminded me that Jamal had someone in his life who was willing to murder him for something as arbitrary as unredeemable video game currency, so whether or not *SLAY* existed, he was in danger of getting killed. If it hadn't been *SLAY* coins, it would've been something else.

I remember the boy in the photo—the one holding the Ping-Pong paddle. He should have had a chance to grow up. He should have had a chance to be excellent, whatever that would've looked like for him. He should at least be remembered as a *SLAY* hero, but I can't think of what to do to remember him—a statue seems so . . . ordinary. Eventually, statues fade in with the rest of the scenery, and as people forget the circumstances of the tragedy, statues become occupiers of real estate that should be torn down to make way for more important, more relevant things.

What can I make for him that will live on and on for as long as the game exists?

Then it hits me. A card! A card would never fade. It would never get old, and it would pop up every once in a while and remind everyone in the arena of the tragedy that befell one of our own. The Anubis card. Anubis, the Egyptian god known for embalming the dead, the god of mummification. The Anubis card could tie the opponent up in a mummy wrap, rendering them immobile for a given time, maybe five seconds.

It's perfect. I can't wait to talk to Claire about it in just a few minutes.

Steph yawns loud enough for me to hear her over Kendrick, and I pull out my earbuds and shush her.

"Act like you've flown before," I scold.

"You should talk," she says with a smile, pointing to my phone hanging in front of me. "Most ridiculous thing I ever did see."

I consider her choice of word: "ridiculous."

"You mean innovative," I say, "or do you mean 'ridiculous' as in 'ghetto'?"

"Why do you sound like a more awake version of me?" she asks. "You know I didn't mean 'ridiculous' in a bad way. It's just . . . creative."

"Uh-huh."

I know Steph didn't mean it, but other Black people do all the time. Making do with what you have and finding creative solutions to problems big and small are marks of the Black community, and we can't only celebrate Black excellence when we succeed in "acceptable" ways. Malcolm was about that respectability politics—that BS about some Black people being worthier of respect than others based on education, occupation, or intellectualism. I say it's Black elitism. In history class I once read an essay by Du Bois in a book called *The Negro Problem* in which he uses the term "the talented tenth" to describe the likelihood that only one in ten Black men—he doesn't mention women—will be equipped to lead the Black community to social progress, and that he will be equipped to do so through pursuing a classical education, reading and writing books, and engaging in politics.

But Du Bois lived before the age of the Internet. He lived before the age of worldwide social media platforms, YouTube, video games, Etsy, and viral photos, and I say we let go of this idea that only a tenth of us can "lead" or be "successful." If we in the Black community are thriving, surviving, learning, and living our best lives, we are *all* in the talented tenth. For all of Du Bois's education, he couldn't see our potential—not like I can. If he could have seen the majesty I see in *SLAY* every day, he might have thought differently.

Ding! The seatbelt sign lights up above me, and I look at Steph and smile. She's already checking her phone to see if the data is back on. She'll do great things one day. Hell, she's already doing great things with me on this game! I don't know if either of us will go to college right away, and for the first time ever, I'm okay with that. All I know right now is that she and I wrote twenty new cards together last week, and I've got ideas for dozens more. And I know that I want to figure out this in-game currency situation with Claire. And that I want to add more regions—maybe a sky region, or even one in space. Maybe an underground arena?

Guess I know more than I thought I did about what I want.

The plane lands without incident, and I pull my backpack out of the overhead bin. Steph struggles with her handbag and backpack, and we head to the baggage claim to find her two suitcases. *Two*. Who brings two suitcases on a weekend trip to Paris?

"I can't just fly to the City of Love without taking everything I love with me," she'd said.

So I help her pull the bags off the conveyor belt. I'm looking around for Claire, and there's a nervous lump in my throat I'm having trouble swallowing. Why am I so nervous? My phone lights up.

Cicada: I see you!

I look up and around, but I don't see her. There's a mix of people everywhere, since everyone likes to fly on the weekend. A man grazes my arm and some of his coffee splashes out of his to-go cup, and he glances over his shoulder that's not occupied by a cell phone and yells, *"Excusez-moi!"* in my direction, which I know means "sorry."

Steph knows some French, since she's known about this trip for weeks, and she yells back in the most American accent ever, *"Ça va!"*

I hope she and Claire don't mind helping me out with

the translation issues we're bound to encounter. I was shocked when Claire told me that she was actually born right here in Paris and has lived here her whole life. When you think of Paris, you think of skinny white women casually sipping tea and eating croissants in a cafe. You don't think of bald Black girls in Converse, ripped jeans, a Dave Chappelle shirt, and round glasses, but that's exactly what I see walking toward me and Steph.

While Steph is fumbling with her bag, I nudge her and she sees what I see. Claire is even more beautiful than I imagined. Her eyes are huge, her lips are bright red, and her smile lights up the whole terminal. Steph and I forget where we are—or rather, we just don't care. We run to her, pulling her into a hug so huge and loud and full of laughter, I'm sure people are looking at us. We're all squealing, and soon, we're all jumping up and down in a big ball of Black girl magic.

When I shared Emerald with the world that day I opened up the forum on that slow-ass server, I never imagined I'd end up here, in Paris, with two like-minded women who SLAY. And there, in the middle of the Charles de Gaulle Airport, I sink into a flawless nay-nay and offer a silent thank you up to my ancestors, or karma, or whatever.

ACKNOWLEDGMENTS

For me, *SLAY* has been a journey of self-discovery. In creating Kiera, I was forced to reconcile my experiences as a Black girl, now a woman, with what the world tells me Blackness is. Everyone has an opinion about how we as Black people should act and which of our accomplishments deserve respect. Writing *SLAY* taught me that the magic of Blackness is what *we* make it, that *we* define our future, and that we as a people deserve all the greatness our ancestors imagined for us.

I have to start my thank-yous with the man whose undying love and support got me through so many moments when I doubted everything: my husband, (the handsomest man in Seattle) Steven Morris. Thank you for having kind words for me even when I have none for myself. I love you more every day.

To my agents, Quressa Robinson and Kristin Nelson, I can't thank you enough for believing in me, and in *SLAY*. You've made my wildest dreams come true. And to my editor, Jen Ung, whose literary genius (and copious doggo pictures) helped me polish *SLAY* into exactly what it was meant to be. Thank you for constantly building me up and making me a better writer with each draft (and for making it fun along the way!).

To my beta readers, Jackie Mak, Monica Gribouski, Becca Baker, and Alexandra Keister, thank you for reading my words at their rawest, and for giving the most honest, constructive criticism I could imagine. You da real MVPs.

Thank you to my grandma Vivian "Rappin' Granny" Smallwood, my great-grandmother Edith Lewis, and my great-great-grandmother Katie Thompson, the original queens, who truly exemplified what it means to be royalty. To my mom and dad, who, despite the ups and downs, always believed in me. Thank you for buying me and Jerome our first gaming console and letting me explore being the master of my own character. (I still play that GameCube today.) And to my siblings, John, Derrick, Tiffany, and Jerome, and their families, thank you for your endless love, support, and encouragement.

To my friends, whose unconditional love got me through various stages of life: Becca Baker, Chris Mikkelson, Aaron Oaks, James Stoner, Grayson Toliver, Almendra Lopez, Dreeny Paine, Sydney Clark, Ari Bloom, Amber Inoue, Artemis Finch, Tiana Sherman, Caitlin Gunn, Casey Higgins, Brett Huggins, Chelsea Williams, Sauni Govere, Alex Govere, Alex Snell, Matthias Kriegel, Annastasia Nuñez, Brittany Nuñez, Ari Nuñez, Tara Krishnan, Alise Fleming, and Vaidyanathan Seshan.

To my fourth-grade teacher, Mrs. Jasperson, who read chapter one of my first attempt at a novel aloud to the class as proudly as if it were a classic, and sparked in me a love of connecting with readers. Thank you.

To the girls in STEM, don't let anybody tell you what you can't do, where you can't go, or who you can't be. To the Black gamers out there hungry for more heroes who look like us, I wrote this for you. #SLAY

Don't miss Brittney Morris's
next explosive novel:

The
COST
of
KNOWING

Turn the page for a sneak peek!

SCOOP'S

I pick up the ice cream scoop, and the vision begins.

I see a familiar light-skinned hand with knobby knuckles and dirt under the nails, passing the scoop I'm holding into a new, unfamiliar hand as dark as mine. This new hand is amply lotioned—no ashiness in the crease between the index finger and thumb. The nails are clipped short. A glittering, diamond-encrusted ring indicates this man must have more money in his wallet than I'll make in my entire life. But the most telling detail, the revelation that might affect *my* future, lies in the background. Behind the two hands, sitting on the grass, is the sign that hangs over the front door of this place—the one that says SCOOP'S. In my vision, someone's leaned it carelessly against the white siding, which is coated in a thin layer of green and black grime, the kind that builds up over months of neglect.

Scoop, the owner of this place, is going to sell the business.

I blink, directing all my focus into darkness, the abstract, *nothing*. I breathe. I think the word *stop*, and silently, I command the vision to end. When I open my eyes again, I'm looking down at the scoop in my hand. I'm back to the present day, turning the scoop over in my fingers. Only a second has gone by in the real world, even though I just watched a twenty-second vision. They always last only a moment.

I briefly consider telling Scoop. But what would it change? What good would it do?

"When *you* own the shop, *you* can make the rules," he'd say.

He's never listened to my ideas before—not when I suggested we invest in a shelving unit so we can finally organize the supply boxes obstructing the hallway, not when I suggested we buy blackout curtains for the front lobby so the afternoon sunlight doesn't turn this place into an oven, since we're a damn *ice cream* shop and we can't operate at ninety-five degrees without jacking up our refrigeration costs. Nah, he won't listen to me, and even on the off chance that he does, Scoop doesn't do anything without asking a million questions first. And my only answer to the inevitable question, "How do you know for sure?" will be "I can see the future," an idea so ridiculous that *I* didn't even believe it until it started interfering with my daily life. I can't touch anything with the palms of my hands without seeing what will happen to it in the next few moments. The longer I touch it, the further into the future I can see.

With most things, I can make the vision stop a split second after it begins, so it's more like a photograph flashing in my head, but if I *want* to see further, which is rare these days, I can let it keep going for as long as I'm touching it.

I've picked up this scoop so many times working here. I've seen myself holding it while I'm wearing a tank top and my arm is glistening with sweat. I've seen myself holding it with my long sleeves tucked over my knuckles as the front door swings open and gusts of snow flurries fly in behind a customer who has no business buying ice cream in that kind of weather. Then it changes hands—a white hand is scooping ice cream as customers enter in tank tops. More kids staring from the other side of the counter in bathing suits and sunglasses. Then gradually, people coming in with red-gloved hands curled around hot coffee cups, ordering through the scarves pulled up over their faces. Two summers. Two winters. I'd say Scoop has about two years left before this place goes under. Two. I'll have graduated and gone off to college by then. And even if this place closed tomorrow, there'd *still* be no point in trying to warn him.

I've tried to alter the future too many times to think it'll work anymore.

I remember a vision I had during a camping trip three years ago—a vision I'll never forget. Me, Aunt Mackie, my little brother Isaiah, my best friend Shaun, and his little sister, who's now my girlfriend—Talia—spent a weekend at Starved Rock State Park out in Oglesby. Aunt Mackie was grilling hot dogs, and she asked me to put the bag of buns on the picnic table. I picked them up and caught a vision of Isaiah slipping on the bag, falling, and breaking his arm. So, despite the risk of flies and flying charcoal pieces landing on them, I took all the buns out of the bag, left them open on a plate, and tossed the bag in the garbage.

Crisis averted, I thought.

But then Aunt Mackie asked Isaiah to run the trash to the dumpster. The crumpled-up little bun bag rolled out at some point while he walked, and on his way back, his foot found the slippery plastic.

Another time, while walking past a construction site, I tried to prevent a beam from falling and bursting a fire hydrant, which I'd touched, by yelling up at the foreman to *watch out!* If he hadn't been distracted, he might have caught it.

And then there's what happened at the funeral. The funeral I never talk about.

No matter what I do, it doesn't help. The mess happens anyway, and I just end up embarrassed, often because it looks like I caused whatever I had been trying to prevent. So I've stopped trying. Better, and less humiliating, to just lie low and let fate happen.

That's the real reason I don't tell Scoop what I saw. Whatever I say, whatever I do to stop it, this place is doomed.

"Alex!" snaps that commanding voice from the kitchen door. I jump, dropping the scoop into the dirty sink water, sending an explosion of suds in all directions, soaking the front of my apron and dousing my face.

God, ew, a little got in my mouth.

"Sorry, didn't mean to scare you," he apologizes. Before I can say I'm okay, he's moved on. "Ross is going on break soon, so I need you up front."

I drag my dry forearm across my face and remove my glasses. The vision flashes. One of me wiping my lenses off on a shirt I'm not wearing. One I don't even own yet. I've touched my own glasses so many times that I'm at a few months into the future with visions of them. I make the vision end, and I do exactly what I just saw myself do—wipe them off. It's become routine for me. Touch item. See vision of item that's either so far into the future I don't have to care yet, or if it's a new item, see vision of exactly what I'm about to do with the item. Do exactly what I saw myself do in the vision.

"Daydreaming again?" asks Scoop. His voice is quieter and kinder this time.

Sure. Daydreaming. That's the closest thing to it that he'll understand, so I nod. I grab the hand towel hanging above the sink and wipe my hands before removing my soaked dishwashing apron. I hang it up by the sink to dry and take a long, deep breath as the full weight of Scoop's words sinks in, heavy like an anvil on my chest. *I need you up front.*

I *hate* working up front. Not because I don't like talking to customers—I'm actually pretty good at that part, and the customers are usually nice. They're mostly young parents with kids under ten, who are in and out in a few minutes. And the kids are almost always well behaved and happy while they're here because, hey, they're getting ice cream.

Nah, I hate working up front because it means touching a million items with my bare hands.

It's an anxiety minefield out there.

Visions fly through my head with everything I touch, like one of those old-school slide projector things—every tap of the register screen, every dollar I count, every spoon I pick up, every hand I brush while giving out samples, every cup, every cone, every scoop. I can't focus on all of that *and* do my job. I can't constantly be thinking of what's *going* to happen and stay focused on what *is* happening. It's too much.

"Can I go back to dishes after?" I ask. Dishes. My safe place, where I can wear my dishwashing gloves and live vision-free for a while.

A droplet of dishwater that was caught in my coily hair races down my forehead, and I wipe it away and sigh, anticipating the answer.

"Sorry, champ," he says, although with his accent, it sounds more like "shamp." He leans against the doorjamb with his arms folded across his black apron and explains, "After Ross goes on break, I've got Ashlynn going home. I need you up there till you're off at three. Okay?"

It's going to *have* to be okay.

I can already feel my heart rate picking up speed, that racing adrenaline that makes me jittery like I've had six cups of coffee and a Red Bull. On really bad days, my mouth gets dry and I start sweating. Sometimes it happens for no reason. Sometimes it happens if I'm anxious about something that would make most people anxious, like an exam, or speaking up in class. Sometimes it happens because I'm with Talia. Today, it's happening because I have to do my job. Just the *thought* of going out there to the front counter freaks me out. It's pathetic. I've been working here for four years. I shouldn't be this afraid anymore. What kind of man am I? *Come on, Alex.* I steel myself, pinching the skin on the back of my hand, which is supposed to help with anxiety.

It doesn't.

I used to be able to wear cheap latex gloves up front. We used to *have* to wear them while scooping, as mandated by the health department. I'd put them on and go the rest of the day blissfully unaware of my—I don't even know what to call this—disorder? Affliction? Curse? I used to wear them home, stealing extra pairs when I could, desperate to keep my brain quiet for as long as possible. But after a few weeks of wearing the latex ones, their protection started to wear off. The visions started coming back about ten minutes after I put them on, and the discomfort of sweaty palms, and the strange looks I'd get in public, began to outweigh the respite they gave me. Eventually, I gave up on them. Now, all that works are those heavy-duty reinforced polyurethane dishwashing gloves that I'm leaving behind in the kitchen right now.

I take a deep breath and follow Scoop through the tiny hallway, which is crammed to the ceiling with unlabeled boxes of flavor powders, industrial cleaning products, ice cream toppings, napkins, and spoons.

This whole place is a fire hazard, a fall hazard, and an accessibility nightmare. Scoop sometimes sends me back here to put bottles and boxes away where they *actually* go, so we can have access to the handwashing sink on the wall behind the mountain, just before scheduled inspections. And it's always *me*, because I can squeeze my five-foot-seven, 140-pound ass into places some of the others can't. I shouldn't have to watch vision after vision of supplies I don't need, just to find some damn napkins. Not when I'm getting paid the same eleven dollars an hour as everyone else.

But I can't dwell on that or I'll get even more jittery and irritable. The quickest way to get through this day, like every day, is to take a deep breath, keep my head down, keep to myself, and keep my hands closed and close to me. I fold them against my shirt and slip between the boxes and the wall. Damn, I swear it gets narrower and narrower every time I walk through here. I keep my eyes on the back of Scoop's head and follow him out to the front counter, where the sunlight has already started cooking the employees. It smells faintly of sugar and dairy products.

The novelty of smelling ice cream all day wore off by the end of my first week. Now I barely smell anything. But I've heard that's normal. Aunt Mackie used to work in a movie theater, and she said eventually she stopped smelling popcorn when she walked in. After a while, it just began to smell faintly of butter substitute and hard work.

There's only one customer out here—a bearded man in his early thirties in shorts, a striped T-shirt, and expensive sunglasses. He's pulling a sample spoon out of his mouth and taking forever to decide on a flavor.

Ashlynn, who stands a foot taller than me and who always wears a too-tight brown ponytail that's creeping her hairline farther back than any twenty-year-old should have, glances over her shoulder at me with that flat-mouthed, marshmallowy face of hers. Ross, the malnourished Dracula-looking guy whose eyes always look like he hasn't slept in years but somehow always ends up at the scooping counter in the front, is feverishly tapping his foot, hands on hips, watching the man with the sunglasses, his eyes quietly urging the man to make a decision.

Scoop decides to bail him out.

"All right, Ross," he says, motioning toward the hallway with two fingers. "You're on break. Ashlynn, you're scooping."

Shit. That puts me at the register.

Calm down, Alex, I tell myself. *Just three more hours and you can go home and nap this stress away.*

Ross can't get his apron off fast enough. He turns from his post behind the counter, yanks his pink apron over his head, and has a cigarette and lighter out before he even reaches the hallway. Ashlynn nods and moves dutifully to the counter where Ross was standing. The customer, who's now watching Ross leave in the middle of the transaction, seems unfazed and points to a tub of green ice cream in the corner. Ashlynn never speaks unless she absolutely has to, so I'm sure she's relieved to be able to scoop ice cream and hand out samples with minimal conversation except "Welcome to Scoop's," "Which flavor?," "Cup or cone?," "What size?," and "Have a great day." That means I, on the other hand, am stuck at the register, touching everything—clicking buttons, counting cash, swiping cards, getting preordered ice cream cakes out of the freezer, distributing receipts, and handing out coupons and allergy info sheets. *And* I have to explain all the time that "yes, sir or ma'am, some of our flavors *do* have artificial colors and sweeteners, but they're all FDA-approved." It's the same answers day after day.

Our only gluten-free flavor is strawberry.

No, strawberry isn't vegan. Coffee and vanilla are our only vegan flavors.

Yes, the coffee is caffeinated.

Vanilla isn't GMO-free, but the Sweet Cream is.

No, the Sweet Cream isn't vegan. Only coffee and vanilla.

Shoot me.

I slip on a bubblegum-pink apron and pull my cobalt-blue visor down low on my forehead, canceling the visions for each, right after I see myself hanging both of them up at the end of a shift some time in the future. I sigh and adjust the visor so it rests comfortably. My hair is cut short—a fade on the sides and slightly longer coils on top. I was relieved I didn't have to carry an Afro pick and pocket-size styling gel anymore when we switched from baseball caps to visors last year, another expense that Scoop decided would be more effective at keeping us employees cool than blackout curtains. Apparently you lose 20 percent of your body heat through your head or something? I don't know.

In the corner of my eye, I see Ashlynn turn to leave down the hallway.

"We're out of spoons," she grumbles. "I'm going to find more in the back."

As soon as I'm left alone out here, the front door swings open, and I take a long, deep breath and log into the register, clicking my name and typing in my four-digit PIN.

I punch 1. Vision of me pressing the 0 on the register. *Stop.* I punch 0. Vision of me pressing the 0 again. *Stop.* I punch 0 again. Vision of me pressing the 4 on the register. *Stop.* I punch 4. Vision of the register's welcome screen. *Stop.*

"Hi, welcome to Scoop's," I say to whoever just walked in, as the register lights up with my name.

Welcome, Alex Rufus.

Shit, it's hot in here. It's three in the afternoon, and the sun is blinding through the west window, beating down on the whole area right behind the register where I am. Sweat is already beading on my forehead, but I put on my most convincing smile and look up at the customer. A woman about my height with short reddish-brown hair and bright green eyes walks up to the counter, looking like she stepped right out of a J.Crew catalog. The little girl holding her hand looks like she's about seven, but she's sucking her thumb with the enthusiasm of a jittery toddler. When they reach the counter, she buries her face in her mom's stomach and puts all her focus into her thumb.

"Hi," I say, trying to ignore the slippery suction noises

coming from the little girl's mouth. I'm sure this woman and her daughter are both cool, but I need them to get the hell out of here with those mouth sounds.

"What can I get you?" I ask. The woman is staring past my head at the board behind me as if it's changed in the last five years. Literally the only thing that's ever changed is our prices. She must be brand-new here.

"Canna get a child's size, and a single scoop fer me?"

Her accent is either Irish or Scottish—I can't really tell. She's reaching into her brown leather purse, fishing around for something to pay with, but I'm missing information.

"Which flavors, ma'am?" I ask.

"Oh!" she exclaims. "What's the pistachio flavor like?"

It tastes like pistachio, I wish I could say.

"It's nutty and a little less sweet than the others," I have to say.

God, it's so hot in here. I have to remove my glasses and wipe the sweat out of my eyes now, but it doesn't help much because my arms are already dewy. I end the vision of me putting the glasses back on my face. I use her indecisiveness to step away from the window and stand behind the ice cream counter instead. I rest my hands on the cold metal shelf behind the glass for some relief, until the room fades to black and I see an image of this place drenched in darkness except for moonlight. The window is still wide open, and the summer moon is outside in the sky, shining down on this place. It's peaceful after hours, and cool, and I long for that kind of quiet right now.

I miss the days when my gloves used to work.

I finally get through scooping one scoop of Caramel Peanut Butter Pretzel into a cup, and a scoop of cookies and cream into a cone for the girl, and get all three of us back to the register so they can pay and leave and take her thumb-sucking sounds with them. The mom hands me a twenty-dollar bill. Dammit. I have to count back two fives that I see are about to get stuffed into her purse, and two ones that are about to be dropped into the tip jar.

"Thanks." She smiles at me. "Mabel, say thank you to the nice young man."

Mabel looks up at me through her straight red bangs and blinks a few times in gratitude. I'll take it.

"My name's Ena," the woman says with another grin. "Mabel and I are new to Chicago. I own a consignment shop down the street. Maybe you've heard of it. It's called Mabelena's?"

I don't care. I *can't* care. I don't have the *energy* to care. My eyes are throbbing. The pressure in my sinuses is crushing. Ena and Mabel are kind, and I should probably be glad that they came in instead of some entitled asshole who's a hair trigger away from asking to speak to a manager. I suddenly feel guilty for hating this interaction so much. Ena has been nothing but friendly. She even cleaned up the floor when Mabel dropped her spoon. I should be grateful.

"I've heard of it," I finally say.

But I can't savor this moment forever. I concentrate and command my brain to end the vision. The sunlight zooms at me like I'm flying toward a light at the end of a long tunnel, and suddenly I'm back in the shop, behind the counter, and the J.Crew woman is staring at me expectantly as if she just asked me a question.

"I—I'm sorry," I say, without missing a beat. "Could you repeat that?"

"Oh, I asked if you go to school nearby. You sound so well-spoken."

Well-spoken? I'm talking about ice cream flavors here, not quoting MLK. But I know what she means. People tell me all the time that I'm "well-spoken," as opposed to however they were expecting me to sound.

"Thanks," I say.

She smiles at me and asks, "Canna try the Caramel Peanut Butter Pretzel?"

I pick up a plastic sample spoon and see a vision of it being thrown into the dirty spoon bin in just a few moments, and when I cancel the vision and the real world comes zooming back, I'm staring down at the ice cream flavors. I scoop out a tiny bit of the Caramel Peanut Butter Pretzel, not really caring that there's not a single piece of pretzel in the sample, and hold it out to her. She takes the spoon without touching my hand, thank goodness. Every vision I can prevent is an act of precious self-preservation.

"Oh, that's delicious!" she marvels. My head is spinning. My temples are throbbing. I'm dizzy.

ABOUT THE AUTHOR

Brittney Morris is the author of *SLAY* and *The Cost of Knowing*. She is also the founder and former president of the Boston University Creative Writing Club. She holds a BA in economics because back then she wanted to be a financial analyst. (She's now glad that didn't happen.) You can find her online at AuthorBrittneyMorris.com and on Twitter or Instagram @BrittneyMMorris.

RIVETED

BY *simon* teen ♥

BELIEVE IN YOUR SHELF

Visit RivetedLit.com & connect with us on social to:

DISCOVER NEW YA READS

READ BOOKS FOR FREE

DISCUSS YOUR FAVORITES

SHARE YOUR IDEAS

ENTER SWEEPSTAKES FOR THE CHANCE TO WIN BOOKS

Follow @SimonTeen on

to stay up to date with all things Riveted!